Deadly Unknowns
Death Agents Book Three

G. L. Didaleusky

ISBN: 978-1-62420-619-1

Credits

Cover Artist: Designs by Ms G
Editor: Sherry Derr-Wille

Dedication

Holly, the love of my life, who has put up with my time behind the computer.

Chapter One

The mysterious couple who had been observing the Federal Medical Investigators' team since they arrived in Pennsylvania five days ago walked up to Simon and Janet who sat at a booth in the hotel's lounge.

"Agent Woods and Bennett, we'd like to talk with you. My name is Tyler Welch, and this is Karen Rivers."

"Please have a seat," Simon said as he glanced across the table at Janet with a puzzled expression.

He was not sure why this couple wanted to talk with them at this time of the night when most people were getting ready for bed or watching TV in the comfort of their homes.

"Karen and I represent a private clandestine organization observing people with ESP and supernatural powers," Tyler said in a lower tone of voice, apparently not wanting anyone in the lounge to hear their conversation.

The closest people to them were two guys sitting at a small square table about eight feet away. The music from the wall speakers dampened conversations in the room, making it difficult to clearly hear what patrons were saying.

"We gather information on these people for the purpose of determining how these abilities came about. We're in the early stages of trying to genetically reproduce these abilities. Over the past five days we obtained DNA from you two and the rest of your FMI agents, including Danny Emerick who supposedly doesn't have any supernatural or ESP powers."

"I assume you obtained our DNA from the cups and glasses we drank from here in the restaurant?"

"We did," Tyler answered.

"If you're a genetic research company, why are you telling us about your organization? If you already obtained our DNA, what's the purpose of telling us what you had done?"

"We believe we can enhance your extrasensory perception abilities," Karen said. "We and our scientist are most intrigued of how Agent Bennett recently began hearing a forewarning voice in her head."

"You seem to know quite a bit about us."

"We heard about you and your agents' ESP abilities two days before your FMI team left Ocala. Your foreshadowing visions of deadly events happening within twenty-four hours, Agent Bennett's warning premonition feelings and voice, Agent Cliftwood's vision of a yellow glow around people with impending danger or death within twenty-four hours, and Agent Littlefield's super sense of smell. We didn't want to interfere with your investigation in Ocala or the investigation in Chambersburg. We came to Chambersburg a day before you and your team arrived. We started to observe you and your agents the first day you arrived. We saw you all enter the first cave site. No, we didn't see who placed the explosives at the cave entrance. We assumed the explosives were placed there prior to your and Detective Spurrier's arrival at the cave. Tyler and I arrived at the cave site about an hour before you all went inside. We didn't see anyone in the area of the cave."

Simon wasn't sure if he should believe these two strangers. Like everything else during any of their investigations, they needed proof, concrete evidence. "How can we be sure what you're telling us is the truth?"

Karen smirked. "Tyler and I figured you'd be skeptical. Right about now someone from our organization is contacting your FMI director, Brian Littlefield. Since you all will be leaving tomorrow morning and taking a few days off from your duties, we didn't want to wait until you and your agents returned to work."

These people obviously have been listening to our conversations, thought Simon. *Frank and Danny checked everyone's room and vehicle for electronic listening bugs. They must've been using remote listening devices directed at us when sitting at the restaurant, the lounge table, and when we were at the cave sites.*

"To know so much about us and our other agents, you must be using a remote listening device?"

Karen grinned. "Yes. This was one means of listening to your conversations. You're probably saying to yourself, 'you can't record any of our conversations unless you have a court subpoena, or we give you permission to record our conversation.' True scenario: if we were a government agency like the FBI, CIA, or Homeland Security. Since we're a private entity and not gathering information to distribute to the public or for a legal proceeding, our organization can't be brought up on invasion of privacy when everything we gather is from a public venue like a restaurant, including the area around the two caves and outside the Tillman's house. Besides, I don't think you want to let the world know about your unique abilities, abilities helping you solve mysterious medical deaths throughout the United States."

Simon knew Karen was right in what she said, especially regarding FMI's agent's extrasensory perception abilities. "You are right in what you said. I guess we're like you and your organization; we need anonymity to function at an efficient level."

Janet placed her drink down on the table, causing a clunking sound. Everyone glanced at her. Staring at Tyler, she said, "I have a question. You more than likely know where our home office is in Atlanta, so where is your facility? I'm sure it's a building you're doing your genetic research at."

Tyler chuckled. "You definitely get right to the point, don't you?"

"You seem to know a lot about us," Janet answered, "so I'm sure you already knew of my directness with people."

Tyler sat back, raising his eyebrows. "Touché, Agent Bennett. We know of your assertiveness." He then leaned forward, directing his eyes toward Janet, who sat across the table to his left. "To answer your first question, our facility is in Virginia Beach."

"Are you associated with the Edgar Casey Institute?"

"No, we're not."

Simon thought how appropriate to be in the same city as the leading ESP institute for the study of people with extrasensory perception abilities. Also, the same place where he wanted to take Janet to for rest and relaxation. Quite a coincidence.

"What exactly do you want from us? I heard your explanation regarding wanting to enhance ESP abilities through genetic research…but there has to be something more you want from us."

Tyler stared at Karen with a serious expression, then nodded, apparently wanting to her to answer Simon's question.

"You're very perceptive besides having foreshadowing visions," Karen answered. "Yes. There is something else we want from you and your agents."

"I thought so."

"Right now, I'm sure our director is asking your director about working together as a joint adventure. We can help you solve mysterious deaths, and you can help us determine where ESP abilities originate in the brain and how genetics likely plays a significant role. We probably wouldn't have pursued this relationship between our two entities if it hadn't been for Agent Bennett recently acquiring her inner voice warning her of imminent danger. Our scientists are anxious to understand how this happened."

"What you're saying is, you want to look into my brain?" Janet asked.

"Not physically of course. But through the eyes of CT, PET and other types of scanning devices."

Janet furled her eyebrows. Pursed her lips, then said, "Huh. I'd be a regular guinea pig for you to study." She turned her attention to Simon. "What do you think, Simon?"

Simon was intrigued by their proposal. He knew there had never been a scientific explanation of how people obtained their ESP abilities or supernatural powers. Maybe this organization was legitimate? According to Karen Rivers, they were on the brink of discovering and possibly replicating or enhancing these gifted people's abilities. "Even if what you're saying is true, our director would have to approve your proposal."

"By the way," Janet said, "what's the name of your organization?"

"Future Innovations Today or F.I.T. Exteriorly, we're a company dealing with technological research and development. The core to our organization is trying to understand how people with ESP and supernatural abilities came about. Like what we told you earlier."

Simon drank some of his rum and coke, then said, "In other words, a synergistic relationship."

"Yes. A good way to explain the relationship between us."

Simon's cell phone rang. He glanced down at the caller ID. It was Director Littlefield. "Hello."

"I assume someone from Future Innovations Today talked with you already?"

"Yes. Matter of fact, they're sitting with Agent Bennett and me right now in the hotel's lounge."

Simon's surroundings went completely away, replaced by the director sitting at his kitchen table with a mustached man in his mid-fifties. The five-second vision then disappeared.

"They told us their proposal. What do you want us to do?"

"We'll accept their offer. I already vetted their director, who's sitting across from me at my kitchen table, and their organization. He came to my house a couple of hours ago. The team can fly out tomorrow morning to Virginia Beach. I'll notify the pilots of your change in flight plans. I'll be flying out of Atlanta with their director tomorrow morning to Virginia Beach to inspect their facility. I'll see you and the agents there."

Simon put his phone away, then looked at Janet. "Director Littlefield accepted their offer. The FMI team is going to Virginia Beach tomorrow."

His and Janet's plan of being alone on a short vacation and walking along the warm and enchanting beach of a moonlit night had been altered by their new assignment, but not completely taken away. He winked at Janet. "I guess we'll have to make it a working vacation."

She grinned. "Sounds good to me."

"It'll be great working with you and your agents," Tyler said. "We'll see you all at our facility tomorrow."

He and Karen slid out from the booth and left the lounge.

Simon reached across the table and cuddled Janet's right hand with his. A sensuous warmth flowed over every inch of his body. "We'll make the best of it the next few days despite the change in our original plans."

Janet placed her other hand on top of Simon's. "We definitely don't have a mundane nine-to-five, Monday through Friday job, do we? You know what? I wouldn't want it any other way."

"I agree." He slowly brought his hands back and brought out his cell phone, then said, "We'll need to call the rest of the team and let them know what's happening. I'll have everyone meet us in my room in ten minutes."

"I'll call Jean and let her know," Janet said as she retrieved her phone from her blazer.

Frank, Danny and Jean were standing in the hallway outside Simon's door when he and Janet walked up to them. Five minutes had elapsed from the time they called the three of them from the lounge. Simon removed his cardkey. "I guess everyone is anxious to know what were about to tell you?"

He and Janet didn't mention anything about F.I.T. or what was going to be discussed, only about a change in plans for tomorrow.

Once everyone was in the room, Simon told them about Tyler Welch, Karen Rivers and Future Innovations Today. He then told them they'd be leaving tomorrow morning for Virginia Beach for evaluation and testing by F.I.T. scientists.

"What if we don't want to be evaluated or put through a battery of test?" Frank asked as he stood with his arms crossed, resting them against his chest.

Simon wasn't prepared for one of the agents refusing F.I.T.'s proposal. "I guess you can decline. I assume Director Littlefield didn't think any of the agents would refuse being examined and…"

"I'm just saying," Frank interrupted, "it would've been nice if all of us were involved with the decision."

Frank is correct in his statement, thought Simon. Although, it was Frank's brother, Director Brian Littlefield, who made the decision for the FMI agents to cooperate with Future Innovations Today. "You're right in what you said. Next time you talk with your brother, you might want to bring it up with him." Simon looked at Janet. "Was there anything I missed about the research company?"

"No. You discussed everything."

Simon stood up from the room's computer chair. "I want everyone to get a good night sleep. Like I mentioned earlier when coming to the hotel, our plane leaves at nine o'clock tomorrow morning from Hagerstown's airport. We'll leave the hotel around eight."

Everyone left the room except Janet, who sat at the end of the queen-size bed. Simon walked over to her. She stood. He gazed into her eyes, enticing eyes heightening his amorous emotions toward her. Her lips parted slightly in a gesture of "please press your lips against mine". Janet's soft, moistened lips pressed against Simon's eager lips. A surge of emotional electricity flowed through his body as he reached around her, drawing her closer to him. She reciprocated by caressing her arms around him.

A knock on the door sent a piercing chill through his body, causing him to release their communal embrace.

"You better answer the door," Janet said, slightly out of breath.

Simon shoulders slumped as he glanced at the nightstand clock. It was five minutes after eleven. "Damn. Poor timing." His amorous thoughts and emotions slowly dissipated. He reluctantly walked to the door and opened it.

A woman in her early thirties wearing a knee-length dark blue skirt and a white blouse stood in the hallway peering up at Simon with a smile. "Hi, Simon."

Simon's mouth gapped open. A cold emotional surge overwhelmed him. "What are you doing here?"

Janet now stood next to Simon. She gently laid her left hand on his back. A puzzled expression lit up her face as she stared at the mysterious woman standing in front of them.

The woman glanced at Janet without changing her elated expression. "I heard you were in Chambersburg," she said slightly slurring her words. "I thought we'd get a drink and talk about old times. Plus, I wanted to tell you…"

"Are you crazy or what?" Simon interrupted. "I have no interest in talking with you. My fiancée and I were about to retire."

He lied about Janet and his relationship but thought it would end his previous girlfriend's untimely presence.

"Oh, you have a woman in your life. She can come with us."

"Claudia. Please leave. Like I said, I have no interest in talking with you."

"Huh. I wanted to tell you something important. You have a daughter."

Simon's heart began to race as he held his breath, not sure how to respond to his ex-girlfriend's revelation. "What did you say?"

"You have a daughter. Her name is Alecia. She's three years old."

"I don't believe you. If it's true, why did you wait three years before telling me? None of this makes any sense."

"It doesn't matter. She's your child. I'm goin' to be filing for child support."

Simon wasn't going to accept anything Claudia said. He dated her for about a month. He then ended their relationship due to her overindulgence in alcohol. "I'll say it again, why did you wait three years to tell me about a child?"

"It is what it is." She swayed, probably because of too much alcohol in her system. "Since you don't want to have a drink with me, I'll see you in court." She turned to her left and walked away.

Simon stepped forward into the hallway and watched her stagger up the hallway toward the lobby. Five rooms up the hallway from his room, Karen Rivers walked into the corridor from her room as Claudia passed her by. She walked toward him.

"I heard what Claudia told you," Karen said standing in front of

Simon and Janet. "Can I come into your room and talk?"

"Sure. Come on in."

"Your ex-girlfriend never did say why she waited three years to tell you that you have a daughter," Janet said, placing her hand upon the small of his back. "I have a gut feeling there's more to her story then what she's telling you. It's my detective thinking and my woman's intuition."

Karen stood facing Simon and Janet in front of the turned off thirty-inch TV sitting on a long lowboy dresser. "I have to agree with what Janet said. Why would she want Janet to come with you to the lounge?"

Simon couldn't believe Karen was able to hear their conversation when her room was so far up the hallway from his room. Unless she was standing in the hallway or her door was open. The former conclusion wasn't true, since he saw Karen walk out of her room and into the hallway. Another possibility flashed across his mind. "For you to hear what Claudia said from your room, you must have exceptionally good hearing."

Karen smiled. "Better than normal people. I was in my early twenties when my hearing suddenly improved to the extent, I could hear two people whispering from across a crowded room. At times, I had to put ear plugs in my ears to block out noises around me: not loud noises but ordinary everyday noises most people tolerate without any difficulty or discomfort. Two years ago, I was approached by Future Innovations Today about their work with people with extraordinary abilities."

"You said a moment ago, you *had* to wear ear plugs to block noises," Janet said leaning her head slightly and peering at Karen's left ear. "It looks like you have plugs in your ears now.

"They're not ear plugs." She removed one from her ear and placed it in the palm of her hand. "The scientist at F.I.T. invented these reverse hearing aids. In other words, they lower the noise threshold, enabling me to function without the bombardment of a collage of sounds around me." She reached into her slacks' pocket and removed a small black gadget the size of a car's remote-control apparatus attached to her car's keyring. "I push this button to turn on or turn off my noise damping aid."

"When we were talking in the hotel lounge earlier, I remember you saying, 'This was one means of listening to your conversations.' Referring to a remote listening device. You are the other means of listening in on conversations."

"Very astute of you, Agent Bennett." Karen put the ear gadget back into her ear.

She then turned her attention to Simon. "The reason I wanted to talk with you was regarding the allegations your ex-girlfriend, Claudia, had made about you having a three-year-old daughter. Since now we're working together, Tyler and I can easily investigate this allegation. We'll get the three-year-old girl's DNA and match it with your DNA. We won't need a court order or permission from the mother, Claudia. The fact is, she won't even know we obtained her daughter's DNA."

It was a godsend Future Innovations Today happened to announce their synergistic partnership with FMI this evening. This was one coincidence Simon accepted with open arms. "Thank you. I'd appreciate you doing this for me. Won't this be a personal task, outside your normal duties as employees for your organization?"

"No, since these allegations could impede your well-being, affecting your daily operations as an agent for FMI and an associate of our company."

Simon felt relieved Karen and Tyler would investigate Claudia's allegation. If it turned out, he was Alecia's father, he'd take the responsibility of a father and take care of her. "Thanks again."

"We'll get back with you as soon as we get the needed information. It'll be a privilege working with you and your agents." Karen left the room.

The room was silent. No sounds from rooms adjacent to his or from the hallway. Janet stood a few feet away from Simon, looking up at him with a solemn expression. "I can't imagine what you're feeling now. One thing is for sure, it doesn't change my feelings toward you."

An emotional weight suddenly dissolved as he gazed into Janet's compassionate eyes. "I'm relieved you feel this way."

Janet stepped forward and hugged him. She then stepped away and said, "It'll be best I go to my room. There are a mixture of emotions running through us. We both need a good night's sleep after everything we went through today, including this evening."

"I agree."

He walked her to the door. He leaned down a kissed her. The amorous electricity created from her lips against his touched every nerve ending in his body. He then reached for the door handle, opening the door. "Goodnight."

Janet gently squeezed his hand, then said, "Goodnight, Simon."

She walked to her room across the hallway. After opening her door, she turned around and said in a soft tone of voice, "Goodnight."

Simon watched every step and action she took. He reciprocated with, "See you in the morning."

He closed his door, locking it behind him, as he walked back into his room, a room several minutes ago was filled with endearment and on the verge of intimacy between two people with amorous feelings toward each other. It was amazing how in a moment his mindset of the world around him was changed or at least interrupted by a woman in his past. He undressed, then laid in bed staring up at the white stucco ceiling, a ceiling lit up by the nightstand lamp to his right. He reached over and turned off the lamp. Darkness filled the room. The day's events ran through his mind: being introduced, then joining up with Future Innovations Today, and the disturbing, gut reaching accusation by an ex-girlfriend. The one thing standing out most of all was his embracing moment of holding and kissing Janet. The vision of Janet's embrace lit up his heart with warmth and pleasure. Silence encased the darkness.

A knock on the door startled him, increasing his heart rate, and breathing. Was the caller, Janet? Did she decide to be with him tonight? Or was the person on the other side of the door, Claudia? He turned the lamplight on, then rushed to the door. Simon peered through the door's peep hole. Something was blocking his view. He fumbled with the lock, as mixed emotions overwhelmed him.

He opened the door.

Chapter Two

A knocking sound awoke Simon as his eyes sprung open. The clock on the nightstand clock read 7:13 a.m. No one had come to his door after Janet left his room last night. He had been dreaming about someone knocking on his door. He never did see who was knocking on the door in his dream. He thought to himself, *A dream can seem like reality. At times reality can seem like a dream.* He shouted, "I'll be right there." After slipping on a pair of pants, he opened the door shirtless.

Janet stood in front of him and glanced at Simon's hairy chest. "Are you going to breakfast before we leave for the plane?"

"Yeah. Breakfast sounds good. Let me get dressed. I'll meet you in the restaurant in ten minutes."

Janet smirked. "I overslept, too. See you down there."

Simon hustled and finished getting dressed. He had already packed his clothes, several miscellaneous things, and most of his toiletries in his suitcase last night before going to bed. It was a habit he'd been doing over the past several years. This morning his idiosyncrasy paid off.

Janet sat at their usual table in the restaurant, along with all the other FMI agents. Tyler Welch and Karen Rivers also sat at the table. Simon quickly glanced around the room for Claudia. She was nowhere to be seen. He sighed, relieved he didn't have to again see or confront his crazy ex-girlfriend. "Good morning, everyone."

Everyone replied with a greeting. He sat next to Janet, the last empty seat at the table. "I see you already met Tyler and Karen."

"Yes, we have," Frank said, glancing around the round table.

"We're going to have to get a larger breakfast table if anyone else joins our group."

Everyone at the table chuckled except Simon, who smirked and shook his head. He then glanced around the table at a variety of breakfast meals in front of his agents and the two newest associates. "Sorry I'm a little late."

"Understandable with what you learned last night from an ex-girlfriend." Jean said sympathetically.

"I guess everyone heard what was said outside my door last night?"

"No," Danny said. "Only you, Janet and Karen heard what Claudia said to you. We all heard talking in the hallway but couldn't make out what was being said. Karen told us what happened. She and Tyler are going to investigate the allegation."

"She also told us about her exceptional hearing abilities," Frank added.

Simon peered at Tyler. "Do you have any supernatural abilities?"

"No." He smirked. "At least not at the present moment. Although, I do have a photographic memory."

"So, you can visualize sitting down at a table and seeing what you ate for dinner a month ago?" Danny asked.

"Yes. If it was a memorable meal, either good or bad. The scientists at F.I.T have studied the part of my brain responsible for a person's memory and recall."

"You're talking about the posterior parietal cortex of the parietal lobe of the brain," Frank said sitting up in his chair. "This is the part of the brain where visual stimuli are processed, and images are retained."

"Huh. Correct. It's true you have a talent for retaining a vast amount of trivial and interesting knowledge."

"Thanks. I'll take your comment as a compliment. I do eat my celery, salmon, omega-3 and eggs on a regular basis to boost my memory."

"Don't let his ego get any bigger than what it is," Jean stated. "We'll never be able to work with him."

"The scientist at the F.I.T. laboratories have enhanced my recall memory through a specialized procedure using electromagnetic techniques I don't completely understand."

The waitress walked up and placed a plate of two blueberry pancakes, three sausage links in front of him and the same order in front of Janet. "Will there be anything else?"

Simon frowned. "…I didn't…"

"I ordered for us," Janet interrupted. "I hope you don't mind?"

"No. Not at all. You must've read my mind. I was thinking about ordering sausage and pancakes when I sat down at the table." He looked up at the waitress, who was pouring coffee into his cup. "Thank you."

Janet picked up the syrup and poured it over her pancakes. "It wasn't hard to determine what you wanted for breakfast since you normally order pancakes and sausage every morning."

"I guess I'm a creature of habit."

"Aren't we all to some extent," Karen said.

Simon sipped his coffee, then said, "We have less than thirty minutes before we have to leave, except for Tyler and Karen."

~ * ~

Janet peered out the windshield of the Suburban from the front passenger seat at a sign. The sign read Hagerstown Regional Airport. Simon turned on an access road not permitted by the general airline passengers. Their ten-passenger jet stood on an isolated area adjacent to the tarmac, away from the main airline terminal. They boarded the plane. Janet sat next to Simon. She sat in the aisle seat, avoiding the window seat. "Like I said the last time we flew, I love the shortened time it takes to fly from one destination to another. It's the distance between the ground and the plane that bothers me. You must think I'm irrational and a wuss regarding flying."

"Not at all. Most people have at least one phobia, some minor and others petrifying. You already know I'm uneasy when I see a snake crossing my path."

The incident when they encountered a snake behind the church came to mind. "At least you have a chance to survive the bite. There isn't any chance for survival falling several thousand feet inside a plane and crashing into the ground."

"I can't dispute your analogy."

The plane moved, taxiing for a position on the runway. A moment later, the roar of the two jet engines and accelerated forward motion caused Janet to reach over with her sweaty palm and grasp onto Simon's dry hand. She squeezed her upper eyelids down over her eyes. He placed his other hand on top of their grasp hand, apparently reinforcing his concern regarding her phobia of flying. "Thank you, Simon."

After the plane leveled out, Janet opened her eyes. Jean, who sat across the aisle from her, said, "Doing okay?"

"Yes." Janet removed her hand from Simon's reassuring grip. "Can't believe I'm such a pussy willow when it comes to flying. Even after Frank telling me the odds of our plane crashing compared to other situations or events. You'd think I'd loosen up and lessen my fear."

"Fear is in the mind of the beholder," Frank said, who sat behind Jean and had a tangential view of Janet.

"Isn't the idiom 'beauty is in the eyes of the beholder' instead of 'fear' and 'mind'?" Jean questioned.

"I can say it this way, since I carry a poetic license in my wallet next to my driver's license."

Janet laughed. She loved these guys, trying to divert her mind away from her emotional state of fear. Of course, Simon's compassionate caring for her made her feel at ease. The emotional roller coaster Simon must be feeling from his ex-girlfriend's accusation had to be overwhelming. Although, he had an unwavering constitution capable of handling difficult situations. It was one of his traits she admired about him. A rumbling noise, then complete silence from the whooshing sound of the jet engines followed by a sudden forty-five-degree forward tilt of the plane caused Janet to squeeze the armrests, as nearly every muscle in her body tightened. "What in the hell is happening?"

"I think the jet engines stopped," Frank stated nervously.

"We lost power to the engines," announced the pilot over the PA system. "Fasten your seat belts. I'm going to try to restart the engines."

The word "try" created more anxiety in Janet's already trembling body as she felt her heart race, pounding against her chest wall. Her fear of the plane crashing to the Earth below was about to come true. She felt helpless. There were more things she wanted to do in life, and one of the things she wanted to do was to feel the intimacy of the man sitting next to her. She felt Simon's hand gently grasp her hand. Janet's eyes were closed, unable to see their plane passing through the cloud covering and the picturesque view of the Earth below them, a view getting closer and closer. Her thoughts focused on the past events of her life, each event lasting a few seconds before another one emerged in her mind's eye. Simon's tender embrace and kiss last night seemed to dampen, lesson her present frightening state of mind.

"Jean," Frank shouted. "Do we all have yellow glows?"

No answer. Jean sat by herself toward the front of the plane next to a window seat with the blind closed. She was wearing headphones, apparently unaware of their perilous situation.

"She must be wearing her headphones listening to music. Even if we all have yellow glows. There's nothing we can do. We're at the mercy of the pilots…and God."

An abrupt jerk and the whooshing sound of the jets' two engines filled the cabin as the plane's downward plunge began to rise. Everyone cheered, except Jean.

"You can open your eyes now," Simon said reaching over and placing his other hand on Janet's forearm.

Jean stood and faced everyone behind her. She frowned. "What happened? Are we turning around and going back to the airport?"

Frank stood, then began explaining to her what had happened.

Perspiration from Janet's forehead cascaded down onto her eyelids, nose, and cheeks as she opened her eyes. She turned her head and faced Simon, who had a broad smile. He didn't have a drop of sweat on his face. "I think the next time we have to go somewhere a distance away, I'll drive, take a bus or train."

"After what had happened, I may also take one of those options."

The co-pilot came out of the cockpit area of the plane and stopped in the aisle, facing everyone. "Is everyone okay back here?"

"We're all fine except for shattered nerves," Simon answered. "What happened to the plane?"

"We have no answer why or how it happened. The power to the engines suddenly stopped. Nothing like this has ever happened before. A total mystery."

"We deal with mysteries every day," Danny said. "Normally our feet are on solid ground when we solve them, not several thousand feet in the sky."

"I'm glad everyone's all right. We'll be landing at Virginia Beach in about ninety minutes. Of course, barring any other electrical or mechanical problems." He turned around and went back into the cockpit, closing the door behind him.

"I knew I should've driven my van to Virginia Beach instead of leaving it in Chambersburg until our next assignment."

"Maybe you should have it flown to Virginia Beach instead of having it flown to our next assignment," Janet suggested, "and after we're done there, we all can drive it to our next case. I love the challenge and excitement of being an FMI agent…but the death-defying excitement of a plane losing its power I can do without. If your van loses its power, we can park it along the side of the road and call road service. Unfortunately, there isn't air service when a plane's engines quit working and the clouds won't support the weight of a plane."

"I wonder if The Circle had anything to do with the plane losing its power?" Frank asked. "The co-pilot did say this type of thing has never happened before. It seems there's been a few ominous and death-defying events we've experienced since our investigation of The Circle in Ocala, Florida. I guess it's coincidence?"

Janet didn't believe in coincidence in most unexplained situations. "You know my feelings about coincidences, especially if there's a slight possibility this evil entity called The Circle was involved."

"I agree," Simon said, "but we still haven't found hard evidence to expose them and shut them down."

Janet removed a handkerchief from the inside pocket of her blazer and wiped the perspiration from her face. "All I know is the FMI team has faced the Reaper of Death before…too many times, as far as I'm concerned."

The remainder of the flight was uneventful as the jet's tires touched the concrete runway at the airport in Virginia Beach. The jet taxied to an airfreight port. A black Suburban awaited them as they stepped off the plane. Simon sat behind the driver seat and everyone else sat in their usual spots in the vehicle.

"You know it's interesting how we usually all sit in the same seats when we're in the Suburban," declared Frank. "It's like an unwritten doctrine where each of us sit. Simon sitting behind the steering wheel, Janet next to him in the front passenger seat, and Jean positioned between me and Danny in the back seat."

Jean buckled her seatbelt, then adjusted the strap length to fit around her body. "You know, Frank, being the trivial king of the world, you also come up with observations no other human being on earth would ever come up with."

"Maybe I'm not human but an alien dropped off by a passing starship?"

"I can believe you were dropped as a baby but not from a starship."

Everyone laughed, including Frank.

Janet reached out in front of her and removed a yellow square note over the GPS. The hotel's address had already been downloaded by the rental company per Director Littlefield's request. She turned on the navigation system. Simon put the Suburban in drive and drove away from the airport. Janet hoped they were heading for a hotel on the Atlantic beach where they could walk on the warm sandy shoreline with soothing waves periodically washing over their feet. The thought of a moonlit night cascading its glow across the ocean as she and Simon held hands and enjoyed the walk along cooling sands and a star-filled night.

After driving for about thirty minutes, a woman's voice from the GPS announced, "You have reached your destination on the right."

A ten-story hotel sat a few hundred yards from the Atlantic Ocean. The Director had indeed booked them into a hotel along the beach. Janet hoped she and Simon would have adjoining rooms. It would make life a wonderful thing.

"There are perks with this job," Danny said smiling.

Frank nodded. "It will be nice to have a couple or more relaxing days at a beachfront resort before we have to face another assignment. Even though we'll have to put up with Future Innovation Today's scientist probing our brains and minds for information regarding our ESP abilities."

Simon pulled underneath a roofed canopy in front of the hotel's entrance doorway. A valet came out of a small door to the left, he was pushing a luggage cart. After he loaded everyone's baggage, they all walked inside. Simon stepped up to the front counter and gave the registrar clerk his name. Any time the FMI team stayed at a hotel, Simon checked the rest of the agents under his name as responsible person for the group.

The clerk quickly typed on the desk computer's keyboard. "Yes, here it is, Dr. Woods, I have your reservations for six people."

"Six people? There's only five of us in our party. There must be a mistake. It must be a typographical error."

He peered at the monitor. "No. I have the reservation for six people and three rooms. The names registered are Simon Woods, Frank Littlefield, Danny Emerick, Jean Cliftwood, Janet Bennett, and Brian Littlefield. There are two queen-size beds in each room. I assume they'll be two people in each room."

Simon turned around. Forlorn faces stared back at him. "We'll have to double up. Choose your roommate."

Janet wanted to say to Simon, "I'll be your roommate," but she knew this arrangement wasn't going to happen. "Obviously, Jean and I will pair up in one of the rooms."

"Me and Danny will bunk together," Frank said.

Simon frowned. "Don't you want to share a room with your brother, Brian?"

"No thanks. I love my brother, but I'd rather have Danny as a roommate."

"In that case, I'll take Brian." He turned back around and faced the clerk. "I guess we're all set on the room pairings."

"It'll take a moment to make up the cardkeys for the rooms. I presume each of you want your own cardkey?"

"Yes," Simon answered for everyone.

A few minutes later, the clerk handed the cardkeys out. He then registered each of their names with the hotel's room number and corresponding cardkey. "Enjoy your stay. Our restaurant opens at seven a.m. and closes at ten p.m. The Golden Eagle Lounge opens at noon and closes at midnight. Our weight and exercise rooms are open twenty-four hours. Our hair salon opens at nine a.m. and closes at seven p.m. for both women and men."

The clerk didn't hesitate during his rhetorical spiel, which he'd probably said a few hundred times to new guests, thought Janet. She was disappointed each of them didn't have their own rooms. Even if the rooms had adjoining doors, it wouldn't make a difference since she and Simon would have roommates, eliminating night rendezvous in either of their rooms. Janet wasn't going to be discouraged by the turn of events. The power of stubbornness persevered inside of her. She and Simon would find a way to be intimately alone, even if they had to get a room in another hotel. A smile spread across her face,

Simon turned back around and stared at Janet. He frowned. "What are you smiling about?"

She felt a warm inner wave touch her face. *Am I blushing? I don't think I've ever blushed in my life.* "I'm glad we made it to the hotel in one piece."

Simon smirked. "I think we all feel that way."

Two men walked through the front entranceway door. One of them carried a suitcase. Frank turned to his left. "Hey, brother. Right on time. We already checked in. You'll be sharing a room with Simon."

Brian Littlefield stood about six feet two inches tall with short brown hair and a well-trimmed mustache. He wore a grey two-piece suit, a light-blue dress shirt without a tie and medium-brown laced dress shoes. His attire matched the color of his suitcase. Janet had never seen a picture of the director but had mentally visualized him being this stature and appearance. Of course, she had Frank's physical features to help her create this picture of his brother.

"Thanks, Frank. I'm glad you all are here in one piece. I heard what had happened to our jet after taking off from the airport in Hagerstown. The plane will be thoroughly examined before it takes off again. Anyway, this is Edward Larson, director of Future Innovations Today. He'll be taking all of us on a tour of their facility today after everyone gets settled in the rooms, including me."

"Shouldn't we have lunch before we go?" Frank asked.

Brian shook his head. "I see your appetite hasn't changed." He turned to Director Larson. "Why don't we all have lunch before going to your facility?"

"Sure. Probably be a good idea. We'll be burning a lot of calories walking around the building." He glanced at Frank with a grin.

Frank smiled back at the F.I.T. director. "You're a man of my own heart, Director Larson."

About twenty minutes later, the FMI team and Edward Larson sat at a table in the restaurant. The waitress had put two square tables together, allowing the seven of them to sit together.

After Janet ordered a hamburger and French fries, a feeling of danger overwhelmed her, followed by the word *evil* emanating from her inner voice.

Unbeknownst to her, while she was having a premonition feeling and inner voice warning, a man in his mid-twenties walked into the restaurant wearing a baseball cap with the Boston Red Sox's "B' logo. He sported a mustache and a medium-length beard. He sat down at a table near the front of the restaurant.

Janet glanced at the Director Larson, who sat across the table from her. Was her premonition and voice referring to the director? No.

She didn't think so. She would've experienced her ESP premonition when she first met the director in the lobby with Brian Littlefield. Janet turned her head toward the front of the restaurant. No one was standing. She then peered around the crowded room and didn't see anyone suspicious or staring at their table. She turned her attention back to the table conversation.

~ * ~

Alexander Mendelson, alias Caleb Johnson, sat down at a table across the room from the FMI team and Director Larson. Mendelson had grown a beard and mustache to disguise himself from the FMI agents. He felt confident none of the FMI agents would recognize him, especially with facial hair and a Red Sox's cap. Now, if he wore a Detroit Tiger's baseball cap, Agent Bennett might have focused her attention on him when she looked around the room after he sat down. Even with his disguise, he knew of her detective prowess and she might have figured out his identity, the guy who worked at the Ford dealership in Detroit before he went to Ocala and enrolled in the high school there as Caleb Johnson, the student who pulled the fire alarm minutes before a student died at 11:58 a.m. on the front steps of North Marion High School.

Mendelson glanced over toward the agents' table and snickered to himself. The FMI agents assumed he was employed by The Circle, but they couldn't find any evidence tying him with the covert world organization, or with the death of the security guard at the Ford Dealership in Detroit and the deaths of the people in Ocala. He removed a cell phone from a belt holster and pushed a speed dial icon. The phone rang twice.

"I hope you have good news," said the man at the other end of the call.

Alex knew Dr. Pearson would be disappointed about the FMI plane not crashing. "No. Plan A didn't happen."

"I tried to call you, but the call went to voice mail." Alex and Philip Pearson were indoctrinated by The Circle to never leave a voice mail or text message, which could lead to the prosecution of their illegal activities.

"I'm disappointed. I couldn't answer your call because I was doing an autopsy with a Wayne State University medical student. I assume plan B is in affect?"

"Yes. I have them all in my view."

Chapter Three

Simon reached out and turned the Suburban's ignition key, starting the engine. The rest of the FMI agents sat in their normal seats. Brian Littlefield rode with Director Larson. The F.I.T. building was about twenty minutes away.

"I didn't want to bring this up while we were in the restaurant." Janet said. "I had one of my premonition episodes, along with my inner voice saying, 'evil.' I thought maybe my premonition was referring to Director Larson. I doubted it was directed at him since I didn't experience it when we first met him in the lobby."

"You never get these premonitions for no reason," Simon said. "Your premonition was likely focused on someone in the restaurant. But who? I did scrutinize everyone in the room when we first walked in. Of course, what does evil look like?"

"If an evil entity was in the restaurant," Frank said, "they must've been wearing a disguise, hiding their horns, red eyes, and pointed tail."

"Are you ever serious?" Jean asked, tapping her elbow against his arm.

"Sure I am. An evil person can appear as an angel, an ordinary person, but underneath their façade, evil reigns."

"Very good description, Frank" Jean said, nodding. "Why didn't you say that in the first place?"

Frank shrugged his shoulders while raising his eyebrow and contorting his lips. "I take the Fifth. Otherwise, my answer might incriminate me."

Jean shook her head, "Huh. You're impossible sometimes."

"Are you guys done back there?" Simon asked.

Silence. No one responded to his question.

They obviously received the hint, thought Simon. "Like what we said at the lunch table a while ago, we'll try to take advantage of our stay in Virginia Beach and combine business and pleasure. We also must stay alert to our surroundings. Janet's premonition feeling and her inner voice was likely a warning to us, telling us we're probably still being watched. I'm not only referring to Tyler and Karen from F.I.T. I have a feeling The Circle is still watching nearly every move we make."

"I can vouch for this assumption," Danny said. "It seems to be a normal thing ever since someone blew my house up several days ago."

The Suburban pulled into the parking lot of Future Innovations Today's three-story building. Simon followed the director to the right side of the building to the employee parking area. He parked next to Director Larson's gray Range Rover. On the way to F.I.T. Simon periodically glanced at his sideview mirror for any vehicle following them. He also noticed Janet had been doing the same thing through her sideview mirror. Simon didn't see any suspicious vehicle.

They all walked through the side door of the facility, then stopped. They stood in a long hallway with doors on both sides. "The facility was built about five years ago. We have sixty employees, including bioengineering and medical scientists, research assistants, lab and electronic technicians to name some of the specialized groups working for us. We're funded by a group of people devoted to understanding ESP abilities in gifted individuals like most of you possess. We try to avoid publicity."

"We can appreciate anonymity," Brian Littlefield said.

Director Larson escorted them to the different departments, introducing the FMI agents to the personnel. He showed them the diagnostic machines. A Computerized Tomography scanner, Magnetic Resonance Imager, P.E.T scanner, 3-D scanner, and an experimental scanner that showed brain waves interacting with the different areas and levels of the brain in a three-dimensional image. "This new scanner replaces the conventional electroencephalogram, or EEG by its common name," stated Edward Larson when coming out of the room with the experimental scanner. "Our scientists use all these scanners and imagers to study and evaluate the brains of ESP individuals. Next, I'm going to take you to our genetics lab on the second floor."

Simon was impressed by the scanners and imagers. F.I.T.'s setup of diagnostic machines equaled if not exceeded what prominent research hospitals would have at their facilities. He turned to Janet, who walked beside him, as they made their way back toward the elevator in the center area of the hallway. "It's nice not having a case to solve."

"We definitely needed a break after what we all have gone through the past couple of weeks. I'm now sort of looking forward to know how my brain works and what in our brain separates us from people without ESP abilities."

They stepped off the elevator onto the second floor and stopped, forming a semi-circle around Director Larson and Littlefield. *This formation reminds me of when I was a resident making rounds with the attending physician*, thought Simon.

"This is my favorite area of our facility," Director Larson said. "for two reasons. First, I'm a geneticist. Second, we believe there's a gene marker somewhere in all your DNA. We still haven't found it."

"If you find this gene marker, what will you do with this knowledge?" Danny asked.

"Good question, Agent Emerick. It could open a vast amount of possibilities, such as genetically altering a normal DNA to one with ESP or supernatural abilities. We could possibly enhance an existing ability or add another aspect of their ESP abilities. This knowledge could enable us to recognize those individuals who hadn't manifested their abilities yet." He brought up his hand and coughed into his cupped hand. He then continued, "As you all know, most of you realized your abilities during your teenage years."

"Why is that?" Danny asked.

"We're hoping we'll be able to find out this fact." Larson turned and proceeded up the hallway to his left.

The first room on their right had an upper glassed wall running the length of the room, about fifty feet, and a wooden entrance door with the upper part glassed in leading into the room. Inside a white countertop with various laboratory machines ran the length of the back wall. In the center of the room stood four island counters; each of them had different types of apparatuses sitting on top of them. There were four people, three men and a woman, either standing or sitting in front of the counters. Each of the wore white lab coats. The woman appeared to be in her mid to late fifties, and the three men varied in age between their early thirties to late fifties. The room was brightly lit from fluorescent ceiling lights.

"The room has the odor of blood along with the pleasant smell of Irish Spring soap," Frank said.

Brian chuckled. "You could've kept this information to yourself. Since there isn't any relevance to the rest of us."

"Sorry. My mouth started moving before my brain could catch up to it."

Simon had been using this brand of soap since he was a teenager, even though he didn't use it during his shower this morning. He knew Janet liked its scent from her past comments to him, as he glanced down at her with a grin. *It's interesting how certain words or odors can conjure up memories, some pleasant and others not so pleasant. In this case...very pleasant.*

The woman in her early fifties lifted her head up from what she was doing. "I use Irish Spring bodywash with my shower in the morning. So does my husband."

A man in his late fifties raised his hand. "I'm the husband."

"A husband-and-wife team working together," Frank said. "I guess neither of you can call home and say, 'Sorry, honey, I have to work late tonight.'"

Everyone in the room laughed.

"Agent Littlefield is the team jokester," Jean stated.

Director Larson raised his arm, pointing it toward the woman employee. "This is Hilda Stephens and her husband, Rod Stephens. Both are geneticists. To their right is Peter Fleming, a genetic technologist." He smiled and nodded. "To his right is Richard Bunting, a genetic technologist." He briefly waved. Larson looked at Director Littlefield. "This is our genetic team. The manner of speaking, we are seeking the key to unlock the DNA door to a person's ESP abilities, which most of your FMI agents possess."

"You explained to me at my house of how you plan to come up with possible answers to an ESP person's abilities. Can you explain what you told me to my agents.?"

"Sure. We're gathering information from all the diagnostic scanners, looking for a common anomaly, a variation in individuals with ESP abilities. It may be so subtle the trained eye may not notice it. On the third floor we have a supercomputer capable of analyzing all our data and hopefully coming up with an answer."

"I'd love to see your computer," Danny said eagerly.

"Me, too," added Frank.

"I'd love to show you...but it's a restricted area. Off limits to most of the employees here at F.I.T. It would be like flying on a commercial airline. You wouldn't be allowed to step into the cockpit while it was on the ground or in the air. Our cockpit is on the third floor."

"That's understandable," Danny replied, bowing his head in disappointment. "Although, it sure would've been nice to see what your computer looked like. Plus, how your computer worked."

"You know, since FMI is now sharing resources with us, including personnel, I can justify allowing you and your team to view our supercomputer."

FMI's computer geeks displayed broad smiles. Simon didn't care one way or the other if he saw the computer, since he had limited knowledge of computers. He reached over and touched Janet's forearm. "Do you and Jean want to see their computer system?"

"Not really," Janet answered.

"I'd rather start reading a good medical thriller or take a dog for a walk than inspect a computer," Jean said. "I've heard Frank and Danny talk about their computers and had no idea what they were talking about."

"You all can stay with us," Hilda Stephens suggested. "I'll show you how we obtain DNA and how we do a genotype analysis. Matter of fact, we've been working on each of your DNA the past couple of days." She turned to her director. "If that's okay with you?"

"Great idea. We'll be back in about thirty minutes." The three of them left the room and headed for the elevator to take them to the third floor.

Hilda reached up and rubbed the back of her neck. "Can I get anyone something to drink? We have bottled water and pop."

"You can tell we're near the northern states when you said pop instead of soda," Janet said. "I don't want anything, thank you."

"Me neither," replied Jean.

"None for me, but thanks for asking. So, how far have you gotten on our genotype?"

"I know you and Jean know what genotype means," Janet said, "but I don't have a clue in what it means."

"Sorry," Hilda said. "We take a person's DNA, then map every branch coming off the DNA's helix. The helix is shaped like a corkscrew, a spring with tentacles projecting out from it. If you get my picture? These tentacles contain genes, the building block to all living creatures. It's what makes us as humans unique and similar from one another. Our physical appearance, such as the color of our hair, eyes, skin tone, and many other traits. The one trait we're looking for is the ESP trait, if there even is one. Mapping the DNA helix is a long and tedious procedure."

"Karen Rivers mentioned to me the main reason your company was anxious to examine us was because of my recent inner warning voice."

"Yes. We obtained your DNA prior to you adding your inner voice joining your premonition feeling. We will get another sample of DNA from you tomorrow. We'll then compare the two and see if we can isolate the area in your genotype that had changed, giving us the exact location of your ESP abilities. At least, it's what we're expecting will happen. We're hoping our newly invented micro-projection DNA analyzer will isolate this gene."

"I've never heard of such an analyzer," Simon injected.

"You wouldn't. My husband recently invented it."

The name Future Innovations Today definitely depicts their company, thought Simon. He wondered if there were any other surprises awaiting him and the other agents regarding this research company. They all talked for the next thirty minutes discussing F.I.T.'s advancements in genetic research and the medical cases solved by the FMI team. Simon liked Hilda and Rod; they were personable and seemed genuine. Simon normally had a neutral position before judging people he met, but these two, especially Hilda, made him feel at ease and were easy to talk with. Simon's peripheral vision caught people walking down the hallway outside the genetic lab. He turned his head toward the hallway and saw Director Larson, Frank and Danny. His two agents were talking to one another with broad smiles on their faces.

They walked into the room. "What an unbelievable computer system they have," Danny stated.

"It's beyond anything we've ever seen," Frank added. "I'm sorry. I can't tell you what we saw. If we did, we'd have to…"

"Kill you," interrupted Jean.

"Jean. Don't take the wind out of my sail."

Simon cleared his throat. "If you guys were impressed, I'd say F.I.T. must have a state-of-the-art system for analyzing data."

"They sure do, boss…I mean, Simon."

The director smirked. "The tour of our facility is done. As Director Littlefield and I discussed earlier, we'll start our tests on the four of you tomorrow morning about eight o'clock."

"If it's okay with you, Agent Bennett," Hilda said, "I'd like to get a sample of your DNA now, so we can start our genotyping on it so we can eventually compare it with your previous DNA genotype."

"Sure. No problem."

The FMI team left together after Janet gave a sample of her blood to Richard Bunting, the lab tech. Director Littlefield stayed with Larson to go over the agreement and few other things between the two clandestine organizations.

Simon left Future Innovation Today's parking lot and headed back to the hotel.

Janet glanced down at her watch, then announced, "The good news is we have the next eighteen hours to ourselves, no obligations to our FMI duties or to Future Innovations Today. Let's enjoy our time to the fullest extent."

"Amen," Frank replied.

"Normally with your statement there's a bad news part," Danny said.

"You're right. But today we won't allow anything negative or bad to happen to any of us," Janet vowed.

Simon stopped for a red light. "Although, we still have to be vigilant and keep our eyes and ears, and as for Frank, his nose, alert for any trouble."

The light changed, but he hesitated, making sure no one was running a red light. Past harrowing experiences were an asset, now and in the future, as far as Simon was concerned. He proceeded to the hotel. Simon tried to block out negativity thoughts by thinking of being with Janet alone. A sensuous warmth covered his body.

Simon parked the Suburban in the hotel's parking lot away from any large trees.

Frank said, "How'd you guys like to play miniature golf? I saw a course a few blocks from here." Danny and Jean agreed. "What about you guys in the front seats? Are you up for a challenge?"

Simon glanced at Janet. "We're going to pass on your offer. Thanks for asking."

"So, what are you two going to do?" Frank asked.

Simon couldn't tell him the entire truth. "We're going to walk along the beach and get our feet wet in the Atlantic Ocean."

"Maybe we can…"

Jean bumped her elbow in Frank's side, as she looked up at him with a scowling expression, which stopped him from continuing. "You and Janet have a great day."

When Simon returned to his room, he put on a pair of shorts, followed by a pullover shirt. Then he slipped on a pair of white socks and tennis shoes. He left his holster and Glock in the room. He left the room, walked across the hallway to Jean and Janet's room. He knocked on the door. He inhaled deeply, as his heart rate increased. His legs felt slightly rubbery, anticipating the woman he had strong amorous feelings for was about to open the door. The door opened.

Jean stood staring up at him with a grin. "Janet will be right with you."

A few seconds passed, then Janet appeared walking out of the bathroom wearing white shorts, a button-down light-blue blouse and a pair of white tennis shoes completing her casual attire. She wasn't carrying her gun.

"Hi, Simon. I'm all set for our walk."

Jean stepped aside, allowing Janet to pass. "You and Simon have fun. We'll talk with you later."

They walked up the hallway toward the lobby. Simon's cell phone rang. He reluctantly removed it from his belt holster. He glanced at the caller ID. "It's Tyler Welch from F.I.T."

Poor timing. He didn't want anything to interfere with his and Janet's time together. He wanted to turn his phone off but knew he couldn't in case it was Director Littlefield or one of the agents needing assistance. "Hey, Tyler. What did you find out?" Simon sat down in a lobby chair, as did Janet.

"We returned a buccal sample from the three-year-old girl."

"How were you able to swap her without drawing suspicion from Claudia?"

"While the mother was distracted by Karen, I stuck a cotton swap inside the girl's mouth and obtained a buccal smear."

"Amazing the girl didn't scream."

"No. She was quite cooperative. In less than five seconds we had her DNA. We also discovered Claudia was thirty thousand dollars in debt, behind in car payments and apartment rent."

"So, she needs money." Simon pressed his shoulders against the chair. "That's what this is all about, taking me to court to get child support money."

"There's more to this story. She had been supported by a guy for the past three years who thought Alecia was her daughter. He had obtained a paternity test three months ago and found out he wasn't the father. The guy left, leaving her without any financial support. Once we get the three-year-old's DNA and match your DNA with hers, you'll know if you're the father of this child. I'd say it'll be fifty-fifty odds since you were with Claudia around the time of her getting pregnant. Of course, along with probably a few other males."

"I appreciate what you and Karen have done for me."

"We'll take Alecia's DNA to our lab when we land in Virginia Beach about ninety minutes from now."

"So, you're already flying back."

"Yes. Our jet left the airport a few minutes ago. We'll call you as soon as we get the results of the paternity test."

"Thanks again." Simon put his phone away, then gazed into Janet's eyes. He then told her what Tyler had said.

"I had a feeling this woman wasn't telling you the whole truth. She was trying to play on your emotions, so you'd accept Alecia as your daughter and support her financially."

Simon stood, as did Janet. "A devious act for money from a desperate woman. Let's go and enjoy our walk along the ocean's beach. It's probably been five years since I walked on a beach."

"Living in Florida my whole life, the last time I spent time on the warm sands of the Atlantic shoreline was when I stayed at a resort hotel in Ormond Beach for a sheriff's department conference a couple of months ago."

"Ormond Beach?"

"Oh, yeah. It's about an hour and a half drive due east on State Road Forty from Ocala."

They walked out the back door of their hotel, passing a swimming pool to the left. Simon looked to his left. There were about twenty people between the ages of seven to eighty, either lying on solarium-type chairs or swimming. "The pool looks enticing."

"If you rather go swimming, I'll go back to my room and change into a bathing suit."

"Oh, no. I was saying how inviting it looked, not that I wanted to go swimming."

They stepped down onto wooden steps of the large deck surrounding the hotel's pool. The warm ocean breeze blew against him enhancing the odor of fresh salty air. The sun was behind them as they made their way to the beach. There were people underneath beach umbrellas either lying on the sand or on lounge chairs. Several people were wading or swimming in the ocean near the shore or about thirty yards out.

Janet stopped. "We need to remove our tennis shoes. You have to feel the warm, soft sand on the bottom of our feet and between our toes."

"You're the expert in beach walking."

"I wouldn't call myself an expert. I've probably only walked on beaches about twelve hundred times since I was a kid."

"Yeah. Right. Compared to my maybe twelve times since I was little."

They both laughed, then began removing their shoes and socks, stuffing the socks inside their tennis shoes. They then carried their shoes, Janet in her right hand and Simon in his left hand.

~ * ~

Alexander Mendelson wearing sunglasses, a Boston Red Sox's cap, light blue T-shirt, and shorts stood on the pool deck, peering at Simon and Janet as they walked toward the ocean's shoreline. He had the appearance of a typical tourist. A smirk spread across his face.

Chapter Four

Janet felt Simon's hand grasp onto her left hand. She welcomed the tender touch from a man she dearly cared for. "Doesn't the sand feel great?"

"No doubt."

They walked for about twenty minutes, talking about their younger years as teenagers and the stupid kid stuff they did. They then turned around and walked back toward the hotel.

"Let's get our feet wet." He pulled her with him to the shoreline and stepped into the water. The water covered their ankles before a wave rolled in, raising the water to mid-calf. "Woah. That's cold water."

Janet released their grip, bent down, and splashed the ocean water onto his upper legs. He grimaced, then reached down and splashed water onto her. They repeated the maneuver a few times before she yelled, "Truce, truce."

Simon laughed. "Okay. I agree."

Janet noticed several people walking along the shoreline smiling at them. She smiled back, then looked down in front of her. Her white blouse and shorts had large wet spots. Janet peered at her cohort in the water fight. He was equally wet. "Definitely refreshing. Don't you think?"

"A cold beer sitting in an air-conditioned room would be refreshing. Although, I have to say this was a quick way to cool down on a hot summer day. Why don't we go back to the hotel and change into dry clothes?"

"Sounds like a good idea to me."

They joined hands and strolled back toward the hotel. She glanced to her left at a couple around their age sitting on the sand next to each other. The man was rubbing suntan lotion on the woman's back. Both had beaming smiles, apparently enjoying each other's company. Janet's mind wandered to Simon, imagining his soft hand slowly and gently rubbing lotion on her bare back. As she and Simon began walking up the wooden stairs to the pool deck, a frigid chill overwhelmed her, causing her to squeeze Simon's hand, then her inner voice said, "*Evil.*"

"I'm having one of my premonition feelings. My inner voice warned me. There's something evil on the pool deck." A moment later, they released their hand grip on each other and stepped onto the deck. Janet glanced around the deck, not sure what person or persons were evil. No one stood out or looked familiar. There were couples sunbathing by the pool, people frolicking in the pool, others sitting in lounge chairs reading from books, tablets or staring down at iPhones. Which person or persons was her ESP directing its forewarning premonition toward? A man in his mid to late twenties wearing a baseball cap in the far-right corner of the deck glanced toward them, then went back to his iPhone.

Simon also glanced around the deck. "I don't see any suspicious people or familiar faces. This is the second time your premonition and voice detected someone or something bad or evil."

"Unless someone suddenly stands up and points a weapon at us, there's no way to know where evil exists."

"I retained a mental note of most of the people on this deck. If you get this premonition again, maybe I'll be able to recognize the person or people responsible for your warning feeling and inner voice."

"You think like me, Simon. Because I also attained a mental vision of the people on the deck."

They walked into the hotel's air-conditioned hallway. "The air feels almost cold after walking outside in the hot sun." He stopped and stared in front of him with a blank expression.

Janet knew what was happening with Simon. He was having a premonition vision. Several seconds passed, he blinked a couple of times, then looked down at her. "Did you have one of your visions?"

"Yes. I saw Frank, Danny and Jean playing miniature golf, then getting into the Suburban…then an explosion."

She glanced at her watch. "They've been gone about forty minutes."

"I'll call Frank and warn him." Simon pushed the speed dial to Frank's cell phone. Several seconds passed. "He's not answering. I'll call Danny."

"I'll call Jean." Janet called her number. The phone rang five times, then a recording came on to leave a message. She glanced over at Simon, who shook his head, indicating Danny didn't pick up. Were they already dead? Was that the reason they didn't answer their phones?

"We don't have a car," he said with a panic voice and expression.

"We'll get one." They ran down the hallway toward the front desk. The clerk stood behind the counter checking a man and woman into the hotel. "We have an emergency and need to get hold of the miniature golf establishment a few blocks from here. Do you have their number?"

"Yes. I have it, agent." The clerk reached to his left, picked up a plastic covered sheet from the top of the counter and peered down at it. "We have the listings of the spots of interest in the immediate area of the hotel. Here it is." He gave Janet the phone number.

Janet dialed the number from her cell phone. Busy signal. "The phone is busy." She looked up at the clerk. "We need a vehicle right now."

The clerk's mouth gaped open, as his eyebrows raised showing the upper whites of his eyes. "I-I…"

Director Littlefield walked through the entranceway door. Janet turned toward him. "Thank God, you're here. We need your car."

"I don't have a vehicle. I was dropped off. What's going…"

"The agents are in danger," Simon interrupted. "They're not answering their phones. Plus, I can't get a hold of the miniature golf course."

"You can use my car," said the middle-aged man who had been checking into the hotel. "It's right out front. Here's my keys."

"You're a godsend. Thank you."

Janet grabbed his keys. Simon, Brian and Janet ran out of the lobby to the car under the entranceway canopy.

Simon sped away from the hotel. "I saw the miniature golf place about three blocks from here on the right." He turned right onto the four-lane street.

Janet told Brian what Simon saw in his vision. "Do you think it's The Circle?" Brian asked.

"Odds are, it's most likely them. Right now, we need to warn your brother and the others. I'll call the miniature golf course, again."

She dialed the number. A busy signal.

A few minutes later, the miniature golf sign came into view about fifty yards to their right. "There it is," Simon said, as he slowed the car down to make the turn into the parking lot.

A loud explosion shook their car, as a cloud of smoke catapulted to the sky to their right. "We're…we're too late," Janet said, holding back all the built-up anxiety she was experiencing as they hurried to the miniature golf establishment to save the FMI agents from a tragic incident. About fifty yards in front of them, she saw Frank, Danny and Jean get out of the black Suburban.

"Thank God. They're not dead."

In front of the three agents, about forty yards away, remnants of a propane tank stood as the top half had been blown off. Four vehicles in front of the tank were severely damaged by the blast. "If anyone is in those vehicles, they're surely dead or severely injured."

Simon pulled up next to the agents. Everyone exited the car. "Is everyone okay?" Brian asked.

"We're all fine." Frank answered. "On the other hand, we might not have been if I parked near the propane tank. There was a large tree near the tank, so I decided to park over here. I remembered what happened to our other vehicle at the hotel in Chambersburg. I guess I've become superstitious."

"Being superstitious was a life saver in this situation," Brian said, reaching over and tapping his brother's shoulder in a gesture of caring.

Frank frowned. "Why are you guys here?"

"I had a vision of the three of you being blown up sitting in the car at the miniature golf course parking lot. We came here to warn you. We thought maybe an explosive device was planted in the Suburban."

"It still could be," Danny interjected. "Maybe we should check the car?"

Frank turned and looked at the Suburban. "Good idea, since I was distracted by the propane tank blowing up before I turned the ignition key. Although, when we sat inside the Suburban, I didn't smell anything unusual such as an explosive or any other foreign odor."

People had now gathered in the parking lot examining the damage done by the explosion. The sound of emergency vehicles could be heard in the distance, along with the crescendo of voices from people expressing their shock of the devastation done by the propane tank.

Frank and Danny began examining the Suburban for any explosive devices. Danny cautiously peered underneath the vehicle while Frank sat in the front seat of the car and checked underneath the dashboard.

"I found it," Danny yelled. He laid on his back, the upper half of his body was underneath the rear of the vehicle. "It has a motion detector detonator with a timer set at twenty seconds attached to the explosive. If we had moved the vehicle an inch, in twenty seconds it would've detonated and blown us all up and burned us to death since the device is attached to the gas tank."

"Get out from under the car," Janet demanded. "We'll call the local sheriff's bomb squad to remove it."

"Oh, oh. No time for the bomb squad."

"What do you mean no bomb squad?" Brian questioned.

"The motion of my hand near the device must've set it off. Run!"

Everyone ran away from the Suburban, yelling to people around them to also run. Janet couldn't believe this was happening. Things were going so good for the FMI team today. How many people were going to die now? Twenty seconds passed. *No explosion,* thought Janet. She stopped running, turned around and saw Danny standing behind the car, holding an object in his left hand, and waving with his right hand.

"It's okay," he shouted.

The rest of the FMI agents stopped and turned around. Everyone stared at Danny. "Why didn't the bomb go off?" Simon asked as he walked up to Janet.

"Maybe it wasn't real or by the grace of God, it was a dud."

They all walked toward Danny. "I defused the bomb," he said when the agents were several feet away.

"How did you know how to neutralize an explosive device?" Janet asked.

"There were three wires, like in the movies. Which color to cut? Since I didn't have wire cutters or a knife, I could only pull out one of the wires, either white, black or green, from the explosive." He reached down and showed an unattached green wire.

"What made you pull the green wire?"

"You're not going to believe this…the green wire moved without me touching it."

"What do you mean by moved?"

"As I laid there staring at the wires, the green wire wiggled like a worm crawling over the ground. When the timer showed two seconds, I pulled out the green wire, giving you all as much time to get away before the bomb exploded. Then unbelievable. No explosion. I defused the bomb and saved the day as in the movies."

"Except this was no movie script," Simon said. "If the wire moving was your mind playing tricks on you during a moment of extreme stress, so be it. It saved your life."

"Besides," Frank said, "if the Suburban had blown up, I don't think any car rental company would've ever rented us a vehicle again. I'm kidding, of course. You're a real hero, my friend."

"I'm no hero. Thanks anyway. I'm sure any of you would've stayed and done the same thing."

"Are you crazy?" Frank interjected. "I would've scooted from under the Suburban and run like hell."

Jean slapped her hand against Frank's arm. "This is a serious situation."

Two sheriff's cars pulled up behind the FMI agents, followed by the fire department's EMT first responders and the paramedic's vehicle. Director Littlefield explained to the deputies what happened. They decided to move the explosive device to an open area, away from any structures.

The deputies called the bomb squad to dispose the bomb. The remaining cars in the parking lot would be inspected by bomb squad personnel, making sure no other explosive devices were planted in other cars. Before Danny put the defused device down, Frank snapped several closeup pictures of it from his cell phone. He also inconspicuously sniffed the device for any familiar or foreign odors, including the type of explosive.

Frank walked back to the FMI team. "The bomb is made of C-4 explosive material. Enough likely to severely damage every car in the entire parking lot and kill any person in the immediate area."

Two sheriff detectives walked up to the FMI team.

About two and half hours later, nearing seven o'clock in the evening, the cars in the parking lot were checked out. All of them were void of explosives. The sheriff detectives talked with each of the FMI agents. The FMI team left the parking lot and headed back to the hotel.

Simon drove the borrowed car with Brian in the front passenger seat and Janet in the back seat. Brian brushed down the hair on the back of his head with his hand. "If this was The Circle who planted the explosive device, what was their purpose? We're not trying to solve medical deaths here in Virginia Beach. It doesn't make any sense to me."

"Whoever the perp or perps are," Janet said, "The Circle or some other person or entity want us dead."

"True," added Simon. "It's another déjà vu incident of an explosive device being placed on our car. For whatever reason, someone wants to silence us."

Janet stared at Simon's eyes and face reflection in the rearview mirror above the dashboard. He glanced back at her and winked. She smiled back at him, acknowledging his amorous action. A feeling of disappointment crossed her mind. They likely wouldn't have an intimate moment together. Was there a conspiracy preventing them from enjoying each other's company? *It sure seems like it,* she thought.

Simon parked the car in the hotel's parking lot across from the front entranceway. Frank pulled up next to him and parked the Suburban. They slid out of their vehicles and walked into the lobby. Simon walked up to the front desk. A young male clerk was typing something on the computer keyboard. "Can you call the man who loaned me his car?"

"He and his wife are in the restaurant having dinner."

"Thank you."

"Did everything turn out okay?"

"Yes. Everyone is safe and sound. Thanks for asking."

Frank rubbed his stomach. "My stomach is talking back at me, saying I need food to fill the empty space."

"Sounds like a good idea," Brian agreed. "Why don't we all go for dinner?"

Everyone agreed. The six of them walked into the restaurant.

Janet peered around the room. There was the couple who loaned out their car sitting at a far booth against the far-right corner of the room against the wall. "There's the couple that loaned us their car."

"I see them," Simon replied. "I'll be right back."

A table with six chairs was to Janet's left. She walked over to the table with everyone and sat down. She saw Simon hand the couple their car keys, then shake the man's hand. He walked back to their table and sat next to her. Jean sat on the other side of her. No one had made the attempt before Simon came to the table to sit in the other chair next to Janet. It was an unwritten rule to leave two empty chairs next to each other for Janet and Simon.

"I thanked the man and his wife for the use of their car. It turned out he's a homicide detective for the New York police department. I told him everyone was safe. He didn't ask me what the emergency was about. I'm glad he didn't since I would've had to lie to him or at least told a half-truth."

"It was a miracle no one was injured or killed by the propane explosion," Jean said, picking up her mixed drink glass.

"A miraculous coincidence since it stopped me from starting the car and leaving the parking lot. You know if the propane tank hadn't exploded, I would've probably met the three of you at the front entrance of the parking lot. Likely all six of us would've been killed, and anyone else near us."

"I guess it shows someone is watching over us," Jean said, "either heavenly or a moral entity here on Earth."

Janet normally didn't believe in coincidence but in this situation, it might have been the case, because there wasn't any logical reason to have blown up the propane tank, then planted a bomb underneath the Suburban if the perp only wanted the FMI agents killed. Due to their ESP abilities, the team had avoided another disastrous event that could've taken their lives. "If it wasn't for Danny, we wouldn't be here discussing divine intervention."

"Amen," Frank said, raising his glass. "Let's toast the man of the hour, Danny."

Everyone raised their glass or bottle in a toasting gesture.

After the toast, Brian set his glass down. "The sheriff's bomb squad said they'll take the defused explosive device, and have it analyzed by the FBI forensic lab division. Maybe they'll be able to determine who had made the bomb."

Simon nodded. "We can hope they'll be able to identify the perpetrators. From our previous experiences with explosive devices, I'm a little skeptical they'll find an answer." He sipped a drink then set his glass down on the table. "I've been thinking about what Danny told us about the green wire moving. What if he wasn't imagining the wire moved? What if the wire really moved, prompting him to pull it away from the explosive?"

"It would be impossible," Jean replied.

"Not if Danny possessed ESP powers, a form of telekinesis."

"You mean, I moved the wire with my mind?"

"Yes. That's what I'm saying. Your analytical mind searched your brain's memory cells for a logical answer to your dilemma. Once you found it, you directed a telekinetic force from your brain to move the green wire, confirming your choice of which wire to pull."

Danny reached up and touched both sides of his head with his fingertips. "Sounds incredible. Are you saying I now have ESP abilities, like the rest of you?"

"Yes. Quite possible."

Frank, who sat next to Danny, reached over with his hand and tapped his forearm. "If the ESP force is with you, my friend, you're now truly a wizard."

Brian leaned forward toward Danny, who sat directly across from him. "We'll have you tested tomorrow at Future Innovation Today like the rest of the FMI agents."

Everyone ate dinner, conversing various subjects from politics to treating indigestion. Janet finished her second mixed drink of rum and coke. It was nearly eight-thirty. The day sure didn't turn out the way she'd planned it, although she and Simon did have their walk on the beach. Brian paid the bill. They all meandered back toward their respective rooms. Janet gazed up at Simon as they neared their rooms. "It should be a new experience tomorrow for all of us. Not sure if I'm looking forward to it or dreading it."

"I know what you're saying. Have a good night's sleep."

"You, too."

"Don't the rest of us count?" Frank said as he stood by his room door with his cardkey in his hand."

Simon chuckled. "All right. You all have a good night's sleep. See you in the morning." His cell phone rang. He peered at the caller ID. "It's Tyler Welch."

"He might have the DNA results on your alleged daughter," Janet said.

All the FMI agents stopped and stood near their room doors, waiting to hear what Welch was about to tell Simon.

Chapter Five

Simon glanced around him and saw the FMI team staring at him. "Hi, Tyler. Do you have the results of the DNA?"

"Yes. Since the lab already had your DNA results, it didn't take long to analyze the girl's and compare it with yours. You're not the father."

A warm wave passed over his body as he pushed his shoulders back and raised his head while a mental state of jubilation touched every cell in his body. He stared down at Janet. "The DNA doesn't match. I'm not the father of Alecia."

"I knew she was only wanting money from you," Janet said. "This now proves it."

"I talked with Director Larson about your results," Tyler said. "He gave me the okay to investigate and try to locate if you have any children or siblings. As you probably know, our supercomputer on the third floor of F.I.T. can identify DNA results from millions of people throughout the world. I'll be giving them yours and the three-year-old girl's DNA results tomorrow morning. They'll do a search and try to match the results with other DNA in the computer data base."

"I don't know what to say, other than thank you. I guess it's possible I may have a sibling since I know nothing about my biological parents."

"We're all one team, now, helping each other. Talk to you tomorrow. Goodnight."

"Goodnight."

Simon told everyone what Tyler said to him.

"Being affiliated with F.I.T. sure has been an asset for you," Danny said, standing next to Frank. Frank opened their door and they walked inside, closing the door behind them.

"See you at breakfast in the morning," Janet said as she turned and walked to her room. Jean had already gone inside, leaving the door open for her.

Brian also left the door open after he went inside their room. Simon glanced at Janet as she closed her door. A smile lit up her face as she stared back at him. He closed his door with a sigh of contentment for having a wonderful woman about to be part of his life and knowing he wasn't the father of a three-year-old child.

Simon laid in bed as sleep was about to grab him and cradle him into an abyss of silence and darkness.

A seven o'clock alarm awakened Simon from a sound and peaceful night's sleep. He glanced over at Brian's bed on the other side of the nightstand. The bed was made. Simon reached over and turned off the alarm. The morning light sneaked around the edges of the drawn window curtains. Simon sat up in bed and looked around a dimly lit room. Brian was absent. The room door opened. His semi-awake mind saw Janet walk into the room. The room light went on, momentarily causing him to squint. Once his eyes adjusted to the artificial light, Brian walked across the room, not Janet. "Oh. It's you."

"Sorry I disappointed you," Brian said as he held a paper cup of coffee.

"No. I didn't mean…"

"You don't have to explain," he interrupted. "I sometimes have that effect on people."

Simon chuckled. *Humor must be a Littlefield trait,* thought Simon. He slid out of bed, showered, then put his clothes on within twenty-five minutes. His cell phone rang. It was Janet. "Good morning."

"Morning. Are you going to breakfast?"

"Absolutely. Brian left a few minutes ago."

"So did Jean. I'll come over to your room."

"Sure. I'll be here."

A few seconds later, a light tap on the door pierced the silence inside Simon's room. He opened the door and Janet quickly walked in, closing the door behind him. She reached out and drew Simon against her. Their lips touched, causing each of them to draw their bodies closer. Simon's entire body seemed to fuse together with Janet's sensuous soft curves as every nerve ending on his skin became electrified. His heart raced with excitement. He heard familiar voices in the hallway. It was Frank and Danny walking by the door. Each of them held their breath, not making a sound. The voices became fainter.

Janet released her caressing arms and moved back a step. A grin appeared. "I feel like a teenager stealing a kiss from a boy as my parents walk down the hallway toward my bedroom."

Simon rubbed his lips together. "Keep stealing kisses from me, as far as I'm concerned."

"I enjoyed it very much too. We better go down to the restaurant."

"You're right. We don't want rumors about us."

"I believe we're beyond the rumor stage of our relationship. I'm sure the rest of the agents know we've become inseparable. Jean definitely does."

Simon figured Janet had mentioned her amorous feelings toward him to Jean, or Jean suspected a blossoming relationship between them had fully bloomed. "I guess we haven't been very inconspicuous."

They walked into the restaurant. Half the tables were occupied by hotel guests. Across the room the FMI agents sat at their usual table. Two chairs next to each other were waiting for them.

"Hi, you two," Frank said with a grin.

"I'm glad everyone's here. We'll need a breakfast to fuel us for a long day of diagnostic testing. Especially Frank."

"You know me like a book, boss."

The FMI team had eaten their breakfast, conversing on various subjects, and avoiding mentioning their ESP abilities so people at nearby tables wouldn't hear about their extraordinary capabilities. It was eight thirty, everyone had eaten their breakfast and drank their coffee or juice when Brian said, "It's time to leave."

Simon peered across the room at a man with a beard and mustache. He hadn't noticed him during most of their breakfast. There was something about the man that looked familiar. He was at the pool yesterday, but it wasn't what drew Simon to his appearance. The bearded man appeared solemn, as if he lost his best friend. The man glanced at Simon, or at least toward their table. He quickly looked down at his cell phone. Simon turned to Janet, who was talking with Jean. Several seconds later, he said, "Sorry to interrupt you. Does the man across the room sitting alone look familiar?"

Janet peered across the room. "What man?"

Simon turned and didn't see the man. "He must've gotten up and left. He was at the pool yesterday. There was something familiar about him, like I've seen him somewhere other than in Virginia Beach."

~ * ~

Simon parked the Suburban in the F.I.T. employees parking lot. Brian called Director Larson a few minutes before they parked. An employee was standing outside by the side entrance to the facility. He led everyone to the employee's lounge. Larson greeted them along with four other employees.

"Since we only have one of each of the diagnostic machines," Larson said, "we've planned out an agenda of events for all of you. Director Littlefield called me yesterday evening regarding Danny Emerick's possible ESP event. We've put him on our agenda. We have five procedures to be done on each of you this morning. The CT, MRI, PET, EEG scanners and a complete blood profile and Danny Emerick's initial DNA sequencing. We already did another DNA genome sequencing on Agent Bennett yesterday."

"I'm the only agent here without a background in science or medicine," Janet said, "so, what is exactly a genome sequencing? I know of DNA regarding identifying a perp or a victim in a crime."

"Sorry. I thought you'd know what it consists of. Anyway, Genome sequencing is the most direct method of detecting mutations, such as single nucleotide polymorphisms and copy number variations. Oops. In plain English, it detects areas of your DNA containing abnormal genes, genes detecting hereditary diseases. In you and the other agents, we're looking for genes responsible for your ESP abilities. I hope I explained it to you okay?"

"Almost perfectly. Thank you."

Each agent went with a F.I.T. employee to their respective testing sites. Simon walked into the CT scanner room. The pure white scanner consisted of a long narrow table and a circular structure at the front of the table. Digital red numbers glowed on a panel embedded on the right side of the circular structure. "You know, this thing looks like a portal into another dimension," Simon declared.

"You must like watching science fiction movies," the technician said. "I agree it does look like a portal to another world, time or place. I can guarantee, you'll stay right here in this room. Have you ever had a CT scan done?"

"No. But I've ordered many of them on patients."

"Then you know we'll be adding a contrast material into your vein?"

"Yes. I know the procedure and side effects after injecting the contrast material."

"Good."

The technician injected the contrast through a vein in his left arm. He placed a cushioned restraint on each side of his head, preventing him from moving his head during the scan. The tech then reached to his right and pushed a button on the machine. The table slowly moved forward. When Simon's head was completely inside the circular arch, the table stopped. "Stay still, don't move your head even with your head in the cushioned restraint."

Simon wondered if anything would go wrong during the scan. Would it stop working in the middle of the scan due to some mysterious malfunction? A serene silence enveloped him.

The technician went into a room with a large glass window, giving him a view of the scanner and the patient lying on the table. The circular arch moved slowly forward then backward several times. Three screens in front of him projected Simon's brain. The screens showed numerous levels of his brain. He leaned forward and said into a microphone, "We're all done. The table will move you out from under the portal. Welcome home, time traveler."

Simon laughed. The table began moving. A moment later, the table stopped, bringing Simon out from underneath the circular opening. The technician now stood next to him and removed the cushioned head restraint. Simon inhaled a deep sigh, then said, "That was a very smooth and uneventful trip."

"I'm glad you enjoyed it. You'll next go to the MRI scanner."

The man who brought him to the CT scanner room walked from behind the glass partitioned room and escorted Simon to the next scanner. Two hours later, Simon had completed the MRI and PET scans. He walked out of the PET scan room. The next test was the EEG scan, then blood work. Coming up the hallway toward him was Janet escorted by a F.I.T. employee. A surge of sensuous warmth engulfed him. "Hey. How's it going?"

"Good. Other than lying on cold surfaces, having my arm poked with a needle followed by a feeling of tiny needles sticking all over my body and hot flashes lasting a few minutes, I'm doing swell. You'd think with all the newest technology available to mankind, they'd figure out how to eliminate these inconveniences."

Simon chuckled. "You're absolutely correct. I couldn't have said it any better. Have you seen or talked with any of the other agents?"

"I briefly talked with Frank and Jean. They mentioned it was a new experience they'd rather never have to do again."

Cell phones rang. Since Simon and Janet didn't have theirs because they had to leave them with Director Larson due to interference with some the scanners if they rang during the scan, the two employees picked up and listened to whoever was at the other end of the call.

They put their phones away. "We're taking you back to the lounge."

Simon frowned. "Do you know why since we still have other test to do?"

"No. I don't," said the male employee with Simon. The female employee with Janet shrugged her shoulders.

They all started walking up the hallway. Simon could only speculate why they were deterred to the employee lounge. Something went wrong with one of the scanners, with one of the agents, or something completely innocuous. A few minutes later, they walked into the lounge. Simon saw the other agents standing together talking, except for Danny, who wasn't in the room. Director Larson and Littlefield stood several feet away from the team talking. No one had solemn expressions. Matter of fact, they all seemed to be in good spirits with most of them smiling. *Why isn't Danny here?* Simon thought.

"Danny isn't here," Janet said to Simon.

"Maybe he's in the middle of being tested?"

Director Larson turned and faced them. "Welcome back. We..."

"Where's Danny Emerick?" Janet asked.

"You do get right to the point, don't you, Agent Bennett?"

"I'm a concerned agent, making sure he's okay."

"He's all right and should be here in a few minutes. Help yourself to coffee, juice or a soda over there." He pointed to a coffee makers and juice dispenser sitting on a counter against the far wall and soda machine against the wall to the right of the counter.

Simon and Janet poured themselves a glass of orange juice, then sat down at a table. He sipped some of the juice, then said, "I don't know about you, but I needed a little break."

"I agree. Feels good to relax."

Danny walked into the room with a Future Innovation Today employee. "Hi, everyone."

"Since everyone is here now," Director Larson said, "the reason I called you all here was to give you a break from the testing, plus talk to you about information we obtained. We know three of you had a harrowing incident yesterday at the miniature golf course, which I'm told was not unusual for your FMI team. Anyway, Frank gave us pictures of the explosive device from his cell phone. I had our guys on the third-floor check to see if they could identify the device and see if this type of device had been used before. The good news is they discovered it had been used in a car bombing two years ago in Detroit, Michigan. Two detectives were killed. They were investigating the theft of vehicles at car dealership and the death…"

"Of a night security guard," Janet interrupted, completing Larson's statement. "It was a Ford dealership."

The director furrowed his forehead. "Did someone already tell you about our findings?"

"No. A few weeks ago, FMI, I mean Agent Woods and I investigated a two-year-old suspicious death case of the security guard, Walter Osborn. We suspected his death was at the hands of The Circle but couldn't prove it. I don't remember any mention of two detectives dying during the investigation." She turned to Simon. "Did you read anything in Osborn's file regarding the death of the two detectives?"

"No. You'd think Detective Morse of the Detroit Police Department would've told us about the detectives being killed, especially by a car bombing."

Simon thought about Wayne County Medical Examiner, Phillip Pearson. Why didn't he mention the two detectives being killed? Had someone removed the car bombing incident from the case file on the dead security guard? *These questions need to be answered*, thought Simon.

"Sounds like the same people are responsible for the placement of the two explosive devices," Brian said, glancing at each of the FMI agents. "From what we know about The Circle, they have people placed in all levels of government, likely law enforcement, and down to a high school student."

"And a flower shop owner," Jean said.

"Yes. You're right, a flower shop owner."

Frank chuckled. "Who's now pushing up daisies."

Director Larson frowned, apparently not sure why Frank chuckled along with groans and snickers from the other FMI agents. "Obviously, insiders' knowledge."

"Yes," Janet confirmed. "Didn't mean to interrupt your

statement. You said the good news is…is there a second part to your statement regarding bad news?"

"Yes, but you answered it when you said The Circle is probably responsible for planting the explosive devices. We couldn't determine who was responsible. So, we helped each other in this scenario. We have a choice of finishing up the remaining test now or leave and have lunch at a nearby restaurant then come back here after eating lunch. It's up to you all. What will it be?"

"We know what Frank will vote for," Jean said. "I'll vote for lunch now.

The rest of the FMI team all said go to lunch. Afterwards, they would come back and finish the testing. Frank drove with Jean in the front passenger's seat. Janet sat in the middle of the backseat with Danny and Simon on either side. Brian rode with Director Larson in his SUV.

Simon, sitting behind the driver seat, reached for his seatbelt and brought it across his body, inserting the flanged metal end into the receptacle to his right. Simon's hand touched Janet's as she clicked her seat belt into the receptacle next to him. He clasped his hand around her hand for several seconds, enjoying the amorous sensation running throughout his body.

Frank parked the Suburban next to Director Larson's SUV in the parking lot of Sheppard's Restaurant. The lot was more than three-quarters filled. "Food must be good here since there's only a few parking spaces left."

The waitress brought three four-person square tables together to accommodate the seven of them, enabling easier conversation eye to eye with plenty of space in front of them to eat. They all ordered lunch and drinks. No alcoholic beverages. Jean said, "From what I heard, if you drink alcohol before noon, you may be considered an alcoholic."

"There's an exception to this assumption," Danny said. "People will have a medicinal drink called a Bloody Mary in the morning after waking up to relieve symptoms of a hangover."

Director Larson's cell phone rang interrupting Jean and Danny's conversation. The director listened for about a minute, then said to the caller, "Thank you. I'll pass this information on to Agent Woods."

Simon glanced at Janet, who had a look of puzzlement. Was it about the results of one of the tests done this morning? Did they find a brain tumor? Or was it something completely different? These questions flashed across his mind.

Director Larson peered at Simon, who sat across the table from him, and said, "We're sure we found a DNA match. You have a brother."

Chapter Six

"I can't believe it. I have a brother. Do you know where he lives?" Simon asked.

"That's what's so strange. The last home address we found was a vacant lot in Atlanta, Georgia. The reason we had his DNA on file was because he had applied for a job with the State of Georgia Correctional Institution as a psychologist. For some reason he never accepted the job. All the information on the job application seemed legitimate. His name on the application was Kenneth Workman. He's not married. No children. Graduated from Georgia State with a doctorate in clinical psychology. About three years ago, all credit card and bank activity stopped. No IRS filing for the past three years."

"It could mean he's either dead or obtained another identity," Janet stated.

Simon didn't want to believe he's dead. "Maybe he's in the FBI or CIA witness protection program?"

"There's no evidence he's in the witness protection program."

"What about his parents? They would be my parents."

"He was adopted as an infant about a year before you were adopted. Both of you were born outside a hospital, and each of you were left on the doorstep of a couple's house. This explains why there's no hospital record of your births. We're still searching for any further information on your brother," Director Larson said. "As soon as we find something, we'll let you know."

"I can't say how much I appreciate your help."

"We're as anxious to find him as you are. He may also have ESP abilities."

Janet inconspicuously reached under the table and gently squeezed Simon's lower thigh. He responded to her compassionate gesture by pressing down on his toes and raising his leg a few inches. Her tender touch seemed to lessen his built-up anxiety of learning about his brother. They ordered lunch. While eating, more questions flowed across his mind, why had his mother or father left them for someone else to raise? What were they hiding? These questions may never be answered if his biological parents continue keeping their identity hidden. When he was in his early twenties, he tried to find out who his birth mother was but immediately encountered a brick wall with no leads to an answer. Overall, he had a normal childhood with loving adoptive parents.

After eating they went back to F.I.T. and continued their testing. Simon sat on a cushioned exam chair in a room with a light blue ceiling, walls and floor. According to the technician doing the testing, the light blue color created calmness in the mind, relieving any anxiety in the patient being tested. Electrodes the size of a dime were positioned on Simon's scalp and forehead, secured with tiny sticky pads. No wires attached to the electrodes as in a standard electroencephalogram. Each electrode sent a signal to a circular apparatus attached to the top of the chair like a halo. The halo spun slowly around his head. In front of Simon, about three feet away, a twenty-inch monitor was attached to a tripod.

"I'm going to show you a series of soundless videos every thirty seconds on the monitor," stated the technician. "We want to see how your brainwaves reacts to the different video snippets. First, I'll take an EEG for thirty seconds without any video."

"Okay. I'm ready." Simon had never heard of an EEG being done this way. The technology of wireless EEGs, as far as he knew, didn't exist at research hospitals or institutions, except for here at the F.I.T. facility. The technician told Simon this newly invented technology gave them a three-dimensional view of brain waves when stimulated by different visual scenes on the monitor. The electrical activity of the beta and alpha waves would be traced to the exact location of the brain being stimulated, and how each wave responded to certain visual scenes on the monitor. They were not concerned about theta, gamma, or delta waves since they were related more to sleep and deep relaxation.

Simon stared at a thirty-second tranquil scene of ocean waves rhythmically splashing on a rocky shoreline. A violent scene of medieval men slashing and stabbing each other in a battle. An endearing scene of babies smiling up at someone leaning over them. A thrilling excitement riding in a twisting and turning roller coaster. Finally, the solemn sadness of animals and people dying in the embrace of their love ones. Most of the different emotions a person would go through in their lives were depicted in the videos.

The halo device above Simon's head stopped rotating, then slowly rose, allowing him to lean forward and get up from the exam chair. "We're all done, Agent Woods."

Simon stood. "Quite an experience. See anything unusual?"

"The doctors view the EEG scanner results of your brain waves on a CD. I only administer the test."

Even if the tech saw something unusual on his computer screen, he couldn't tell me what he saw. "Thank you. Have a good day."

Simon followed the F.I.T. escort to the last test of the day: blood work. Thirty minutes later, Simon walked out of the blood chemistry lab with a cotton ball and strip of tape over the flexor area of his left elbow, indicating blood had been drawn.

"I'll take you back to the lunchroom," said the escort.

One thing was for sure about all these tests I've gone through today, thought Simon, *if there was a blood vessel problem such as an aneurysm, hardening or narrowing of an artery, or a brain tumor it would show up on one or more of these brain scans.* "Had any of the scans ever shown a brain tumor or vessel abnormality the participant had no knowledge or symptoms of before the test?"

"Yes. We've seen a few and fortunately saved them from a devastating tragedy."

When they walked into the lunchroom, Frank and Danny were sitting at a table talking. No one else was in the room. Simon's escort left. "Hey guys. I assume you're done with testing."

"Yep," Frank answered. "The experience was worth a billion dollars, but I wouldn't give ten dollars to do it again."

"You changed the saying."

"Cost of living went up."

Simon chuckled. He never knew what would come out of Frank's mouth. Even without his ESP ability of super smell or his computer expertise, he was an asset to FMI with his refreshing, offbeat humor. About thirty minutes later, Janet and Jean walked into the lunchroom with smiles across their faces. "Why are the two of you smiling?"

"For two reasons," Janet answered. "First, we completed these tests. Second, it's only four o'clock and we have a warm, sunny day to enjoy the next several hours at a beach resort."

"Director Larson may want to go over the test results with us today."

"Not today," Larson said as he and Director Littlefield walked toward them after entering the lunchroom unnoticed by the agents. "We'll go over all your test results tomorrow morning around nine o'clock."

"Enjoy the rest of the day off," Brian said. "You deserve it."

Simon and Janet walked out of the lunchroom together. Frank, Danny and Jean walked ahead of them. Brian stayed with Edward Larson and would be driven back to the hotel by a staff member. Simon wanted to spend quality time with Janet without any agents in the immediate vicinity. He thought about telling the other agents he and Janet planned on going to the Edgar Casey Institute. Not a good idea. Frank and Danny would probably want to go there, and maybe Jean. He could be up front and tell everyone they wanted to spend time alone. When everyone sat inside the Suburban, Simon said, "Janet and I…"

"The three of us," Frank interrupted almost simultaneously with Simon's words. "Sorry, Simon. Go ahead."

"No. You go first."

"Me, Danny and Jean decided to go to the Edgar Casey Institute and check it out. It supposed to have all kinds of neat things regarding

ESP and the history of the clairvoyant Edgar Casey. You two are welcome to come along with us."

Perfect timing. "Janet and I are going to stick around the hotel and probably go to the swimming pool and relax."

"Okay. We'll probably be gone for a couple of hours. When we get back, we all can go for dinner around seven."

"Dinner sounds good," Janet said, confirming Frank's proposal and reinforcing Simon's plans for the two of them.

Frank dropped Simon and Janet off at the front entrance to the hotel, then left with Danny and Jean.

Simon gazed into Janet's eyes as they stood outside at the front entrance door. "It's you and I now for the next two hours. What do you want to do?"

"Be with you…alone."

Simon's heart rate and breathing increased as they walked inside and headed down the hallway. "Your room or mine?"

"My room. We don't know when Director Littlefield will be coming back to the hotel."

~ * ~

"You're right. I guess I'm not thinking straight."

Janet smirked. *Your mind was focused on one thing…me.* Her breathing increased as thoughts of Simon holding her in his arms, their bodies pressed against each other, and their lips touching excited every sensuous part of her body. Her room was several feet away as she removed the cardkey from her blazer pocket. She reached out with the cardkey and inserted it into the door lock slot. Click. She quickly pushed down on the door handle and opened the door. They walked inside and closed the door. Janet grabbed his hand led him to the foot of the bed. She pulled him toward her then stopped before their bodies and lips touched. A feeling of doom overwhelmed her, followed by her inner voice: *Danger.* "Something is wrong."

"What did I do wrong?"

"No. It's not you. I had one of my premonition feelings. My inner voice said, 'danger.' There has to be something in the room that could harm or kill us." She began looking around the room for anything out of place. "Look for some minute detail we'd normally overlook." Her amorous excitement now changed to a frightened like excitement fueled with suspicion.

"Unfortunately, I wouldn't know if something wasn't where it shouldn't be. Other than something obvious like a bomb." Simon bent down and looked under a lamp shade between the two queen-size beds.

Janet began gently pulling out dresser drawers, peering inside for something dangerous or lethal. She checked every drawer in the long dresser with a flat screen TV sitting on top of it. All the drawers contained their clothes and accessories, nothing suspicious. She leaned forward and peered behind the TV. "I found something." Attached to the back of the TV was a grey, rectangular plastic device the size of a flip-top cell phone. Was it an explosive device? Even as small as the device was, if it contained an explosive material the damage could be devastating, as pieces of the TV would act like shrapnel and impale anyone in their immediate vicinity. "Not sure what it is. Could be a listening bug, an explosive or something else."

"What should we do?"

"I don't believe it's an explosive mechanism. The device isn't like the one under the Suburban at the miniature golf course. This one is much larger and has an LED timer. We need Danny and Frank here. They have scanning instruments capable of telling us what it is and is not. I think we should call them."

"You're the expert in these situations. I'll give Danny a call." Simon removed his cell phone and called Danny. "Sorry to tell you this, but we need you guys to come back to the hotel. Janet and I found a strange device attached to the back of Janet and Jean's TV. Not sure what it is." A pause. "We'll see you in a bit." He put his phone away. "They'll be here in about ten minutes."

"I think we should check your room for the device."

"Should we tell the hotel's management?"

"Not yet. I don't want to call anyone or do anything until we know what we're dealing with."

"Your inner voice did say danger."

"True. Although, I don't think we're in immediate danger. It's a gut feeling."

Was she making the right decision in not notifying the sheriff's department and bomb squad? The device could be innocuous. Many times, she'd relied on her gut feeling during an investigation. Most of the times, it turned out correct. She understood the potential gravity of Simon's comment regarding her inner voice warning her about danger. They left her room and walked across the hallway to Simon's room. She didn't have an ominous feeling or hear her inner voice as he opened the door.

Simon walked over to the side of the TV, stopped, leaned forward, and peered behind the flat screen. "It's here. Same as the one behind your TV."

"I'm assuming now we'll find one of these things attached behind Frank and Danny's TV."

"More than likely." He stood back a step or two with a puzzled expression. "I wonder if what we're looking at is an explosive device and they're set to go off at the same time when we're all in our rooms tonight?"

"That would make sense. Otherwise, after the first explosion we'd likely run out of our rooms and unknowingly avoid being blown up. Of course, this is assuming we're dealing with an explosive. It could still be a listening device. Although, none I've ever seen during my years as a sheriff detective."

Janet heard the room door open behind her. She turned around and saw Brian Littlefield walk into the room. A smile lit up his face. He was probably thinking the two of us we're about to do something romantically, or had already done it, thought Janet. "Hi, Brian."

"Hey, how's things going?"

"Things were going good until Simon and I found planted devices behind mine and Jean's TV," she turned and pointed to the TV on the long dresser, "and now this TV. We're thinking Frank and Danny's TV probably has one too."

"Do you know what it is?"

"No. Danny and Frank with Jean should be here any moment. Between the two guys they should be able to determine what it is."

Frank and Danny's voices emanated from the hallway through the opened room door. "They're here," Simon said stepping to his right of Janet and Brian, apparently wanting to get a clear view of the doorway.

Janet leaned to her right of Brian and saw them looking into her room. "We're over here," she shouted. The three of them turned around, then walked into Simon and Brian's room.

"I thought you said the device was in your room?" Frank questioned Janet.

"It is...but we also found one of the devices in here, behind this TV. There's probably one of these things behind your TV too."

Frank leaned over the TV, lowered his head above the apparatus and inhaled deeply through his nose. "Odor of Old Spice and coconut." He leaned back, pausing momentarily. "These are the two scents I smelled upstairs at the florist shop in Ocala. It's the same smells inside the pickup truck of the dead guy hit by a vehicle crossing a street."

Janet didn't believe in coincidence, especially in this scenario. "The odds of having two people with the exact scents isn't coincidental. I'd say we're dealing with the same guy or another person using the same products. Maybe the dead guy in Ocala wasn't the one using these two things...but someone else. Did you pick up any other distinct odors, such as explosives or a poisonous gas or chemical?"

"No, I didn't."

While they were talking, Danny went into a drawer in the dresser and removed a handheld rectangular-shaped electronic gadget, then peered behind the TV directing the gadget at the mysterious device. "It's an electronic device. No evidence of transmitting signals, ruling out a listening bug. I'm going to remove it to get a better look at it."

"Do you think this would be wise?" Janet asked taking a step back. "Or safe?"

"I'm pretty sure." There was a hint of skepticism in Danny's voice.

Frank disconnected the TV from the wall plugs for the electric power and cable. He then with Brian turned the TV a hundred and eighty degrees, exposing the back of the TV. Since the back of the television was plastic, they concluded the device had some type of adhesive substance allowing it to stick to a plastic surface. Danny held a screwdriver type of tool with a thin, flat end and placed it behind the mysterious device. He then slowly pushed the tool, separating the cell phone-shaped mechanism from the TV. He now held it in his hand with his eyes closed. "My God, I'm seeing the inside of this thing."

"What do you see?" Janet asked.

"Hum. Interesting. It contains a clear powdery substance, a tiny round battery at one end, and an electronic circuit chip. There are two small nozzles about an inch long, half an inch in diameter positioned on both sides of the device. The chip's current is pulsating like a clock. Whatever the powdery substance is, I believe it's going to be released at a designated time."

"Like tonight when all of us are sleeping in our beds." Janet's mind flashed back to her partner at the sheriff's office in Ocala. "There was another event regarding a white powdery substance, Detective Matters. He was exposed to the substance blown into his face by an employee of The Circle. I wonder if it's the same substance?"

"It might very well be," Simon answered. "We'll need to have it analyzed. I know the perfect place."

"Future Innovations Today," suggested Brian Littlefield.

"Exactly. We'll need to remove the device from Janet and Jean's TV."

"I'll check our TV," Danny said. He left the room, then returned in less than a minute. "We also have one behind our TV."

Danny and Frank went into Janet and Jean's room and removed the device. They then went to their room and removed the device from the third TV. Within fifteen minutes, they had all three devices. Danny placed the devices into one airtight plastic container. While the two of them were gone, Brian called Director Larson and informed him of what they had found. He agreed to analyze the powder. Brian volunteered to take the mysterious powder to the lab at F.I.T.

When all the agents were in Simon and Brian's room, Janet turned to Jean and said, "I thought of something, why didn't you see yellow halos around all of us when we were in Simon and Brian's room if the powder substance is deadly?"

"It may not be deadly," Brian suggested.

"I don't have a good answer," Jean answered. "Unless like what Director Littlefield said, it's not a lethal substance. Once we discovered the powdery substance, our deadly fate was stopped and the threat of us dying from inhaling the mysterious powder eliminated the perp's devious purpose."

Simon said, "Whatever the powder turns out to be, Janet's inner voice caused us to investigate her inner warning voice stating the presence of danger. Plus, she was right about her gut feeling: the powdery substance didn't pose an immediate danger to them."

"Yes. Thank goodness they both were." A chilling thought flashed across her mind. "If The Circle is trying to kill us, we must be getting too close to their evil operations."

"I agree," Brian said as he rubbed his nose, then sneezed.

"Bless you," Jean said.

"Thank you. The pollen count must be awfully high today. I've been sneezing on and off all day."

"We need to look at the hotel's surveillance," Frank said, "and see who had planted these devices on our TVs."

"Good idea," Janet agreed.

"I'll be headed to the lab, now," Brian said. He turned to Frank. "Call me if you find the person responsible for planting these devices"

"You'll be the first." He handed his brother the key to the Suburban.

"Do you want company?" Jean asked.

"That'll be very nice, Thank you."

They all left the room together. Brian and Jean walked up the hallway and the remaining four agents went into Danny and Frank's room. The two computer wizards turned their computers on.

Janet stood next to Simon as they stared down at the monitors. She thought about Simon's embrace near the foot of her bed. A warm, sensuous sensation wrapped around her like a blanket. There had to be a conspiracy from some unknown entity preventing them from being intimately alone.

"I figure we had about a nine-hour window of our rooms unoccupied," Danny said, "from around seven-thirty this morning to five o'clock this afternoon when the two of you came back to Janet and Jean's room."

"You're right about your assumption," agreed Janet.

He seemed to emphasize 'Janet and Jean' in his statement. She and Simon had been inseparable since their investigation in Ocala. They hadn't been exactly inconspicuous in their relationship.

Once Frank and Danny hacked into the hotel's security system surveillance videos, they divided the time, one getting the first five hours and the other the next four and a half hours. They both sped up the video, focusing on anyone entering their rooms. About ten minutes elapsed. "I have something," Frank said, "I think it's our perp. The time is ten minutes after eleven this morning."

A man wearing a white hoody shirt with his head bent down walked down the hallway. It was impossible to see his face. The man was carrying a plastic bag. He stopped in front of Frank and Danny's room door. The video then went blank, as the monitor displayed a white screen. "What the hell," Frank said as he moved his fingers rapidly over the keyboard.

"I'll check the lobby video and see where this person came from," Danny said.

A moment later, the screen showed the person entering the hotel through the front entrance door. Again, the person's identity was covered by the hoody. "I'll check the parking lot and see what car he came from."

Several seconds later, the video of the hotel's parking lot came into view on the monitor. The video went blank for about five minutes before coming back on. The hooded person wasn't seen in the parking lot surveillance video.

Danny and Frank checked all the hotel's videos for the person wearing a white hoody. The person wasn't in any of the videos. It was as if he appeared at the front door of the hotel and the hallway leading to Frank and Danny's room, then was erased. "Whoever deleted the videos," Janet said, "why didn't they delete the perp all together? Why only leave a snippet of them?"

"Not sure," Danny answered. "I'm assuming the person would know these videos would be viewed by homicide detectives after someone found our bodies dead in our rooms."

Janet nodded. "Maybe to show they were in control, saying catch me if you can."

Frank called his brother, putting him on speaker, and told him what they found on the hotel's surveillance videos.

"Damn. I was hoping we'd have the identity of the perp. Anyway, Jean and I dropped off the powder at the lab. The technicians said they'd have the results of the powder tomorrow morning. We're heading back to the hotel. See you in a bit."

"It's almost six-thirty," Frank said glancing down at his watch. "Anybody ready for supper?"

"Supper sounds good to me," Janet said. *Although, I'd rather be lying next to Simon on a secluded island beach somewhere.*

"Yeah. Sounds good." Simon agreed.

"Sure. Okay." Danny added.

The restaurant was crowded. Janet saw many familiar faces. One of those patrons was a man with a mustache and full beard sitting alone at a table to her right. Several people in the room looked up at them as they walked into the restaurant. The four of them sat at a table in the middle of the room.

~ * ~

Alexander Mandelson sat at his table with a grin. He dialed his cell phone, waited a moment, then said to the person at the other end of his call, "Everything will be taken care of tonight. They'll all have a peaceful sleep."

Chapter Seven

Simon had peered around the room when they walked into the restaurant and saw many familiar faces in the room, guests of the hotel like they've been for the past two days. The FMI agents sat at a rectangle six-chair table with Janet sitting to his right. They all ordered Friday's special, a fried shrimp and fish platter. While waiting for their order, each of them sipped on their mixed alcohol drinks. Simon glanced down at his rum and Coke. "It's a shame we weren't able to enjoy any significant leisure time, today."

"True," Frank said, "but then again, if you hadn't found those mysterious devices behind the TVs, it might've been our final day on Earth."

"I'll drink to that," Danny said raising his glass. Everyone raised their glasses in a general toast.

Simon winked at Janet. She reciprocated with a quick eyebrow raising and smile. Their embrace at the foot of the bed still lingered in his mind. It seemed to Simon the mythical creature Cupid was teasing them, preventing him and Janet from fulfilling their amorous intentions toward each other. He knew there would be another opportunity for them to be together, alone.

Their drinks were about half drunk when the waitress brought them their meals. Brian and Jean walked into the restaurant as the waitress placed the last meal on the table. They sat down in the last two empty chairs, then ordered the Friday special. After eating, Brian paid the bill on their organization's credit card. "It's still quite early. I could go for another drink at the hotel's lounge. Anyone interested?"

"Sure," Jean answered.

Frank and Danny nodded in agreement.

"Sounds good to me," Simon agreed.

"I'm up for another drink," Janet said. "Not much we can do until tomorrow morning when we get the results of the powder analysis."

Simon glanced around the restaurant as they walked toward the entrance doorway. Most of the people who were present when they walked into the restaurant were gone and replaced with new faces. The man with the beard and mustache was also gone. It still bothered Simon the man looked familiar but couldn't pinpoint where he'd seen the guy before. Maybe the guy only looked like somebody he'd seen before.

Music was playing in the lounge when they entered and sat down at a table. Right after they ordered their drinks, Simon's cell phone rang. He glanced at the caller ID. No name and a phone number he didn't recognize. "Hello."

"Is this Doctor Simon Woods?"

"Yes. I'm Simon Woods."

"This is Special Agent Collins of the FBI. We're asking you not to pursue the whereabouts of your brother, Kenneth Workman."

"Why not? How can I be sure you're who you say you are?"

"Come to the pool at your hotel. I'll be wearing a blue Hawaiian shirt and white shorts and sneakers. We can talk more in private. There are some other things I need to talk about. Don't want to talk over the phone about it or in a room with many people capable of hearing our conversation."

"I'll be right there. I'm going to bring Agent Bennett with me."

A short pause. "That'll be fine."

Simon put his cell phone away, then said, "An FBI agent wants to talk with me about my brother by the pool outside." He turned to Janet. "Can you come with me?"

"Absolutely. I'll come with you. I wonder why he didn't walk up to our table and present himself to us?" Janet asked.

Simon told her and everyone else at the table what the FBI agent said, then stood.

"The agent may be undercover." Janet said as she also stood.

The area around the pool was lit up. A young couple was in the pool. At the far end of the pool deck at a small round table with four chairs sat a man in his thirties wearing a blue Hawaiian shirt. Simon and Janet walked up to him and sat down.

The man brought out a black leather billfold and shoved it across the glass table to Simon. Simon opened it. An official-looking FBI identification with the name Special Agent Collins below the logo. He slid the billfold back to the agent. "You probably wondering why I'm not wearing an agent's typical dark suit, white shirt, black tie and shoes."

"It did cross my mind," Simon answered.

"First of all, I'd be quite conspicuous at a beach resort hotel. Second, we're sure you're being targeted by someone who wants to harm your team. The Circle comes to mind."

"So, you know about The Circle and its demonic plans?"

"We know they're a legitimate world organization with many subsidiaries. We suspected they were involved with the eleven-thirty-eight deaths in Ocala and several other incidences. We've never had any concrete evidence to prove their illegal activities."

"You said not to pursue my brother. How'd you know he's my brother?"

"We didn't know he was your brother until about a week ago when Claudia Stone tried to find Kenneth Workman to tell him he was the father of the three-year-old girl Alecia. When she was unable to locate your brother, Claudia pursued you and found out where you worked. She then traced you to Chambersburg, Pennsylvania. To go back three years ago, she had been with a few men around the time she got pregnant. Claudia convinced a guy three years ago she was carrying his child. About a month ago, the guy found out he wasn't Alecia's biological father. He left Claudia and the three-year-old. She then tried to extort money and support from the other guys, but to no avail. When she couldn't find Workman, you were the next suitor on her list of so to speak, sperm donors. We then obtained information Future Innovations Today was looking into the whereabouts of Kenneth Workman through the Internet. F.I.T.'s inquiry caused us to do a computer search of their supercomputer. We found Kenneth Workman's DNA didn't match Alecia's DNA. What F.I.T. did find out…you were Workman's brother."

"This answers a couple of questions running through my mind. But what does my brother have to do with the FBI? Why has he dropped off the radar with no record of him for the past three years?"

The agent glanced around the pool deck, shifted in his chair, then leaned forward, staring at Simon. "Your brother is an FBI agent. He's presently working undercover on a case for the past six months."

"I thought he was a clinical psychologist?"

"He is…that is was. He joined the FBI about three years ago. The only record of him on the Internet was prior to three years ago. We deleted any information about him ever being an FBI agent. Knowing he'd be an undercover agent in different scenarios, it was decided to delete any information about him from the Internet after joining the bureau. We wanted to protect his family and friends from any repercussions from the people and organizations he'd be investigating."

Simon rubbed the back of his neck. "Why did the FBI want eliminate his name? Is this standard procedure for the FBI?"

"No, it's not standard procedure. Your brother is an exception. He has a special gift. An ability to tell if a person is lying or telling the truth. Similar but more accurate than a lie detector machine. It's probably why he became a clinical psychologist. When he applied for a position as a clinical psychologist for a state prison, a normal FBI check was done. His report showed allegations of possible federal HIPPA violations but never could be proven. His file was flagged sending it to an agent in the FBI's records department, who thoroughly reviewed the information in your brother's file. An agent was sent to talk with him. During Workman's interview his ESP ability was discovered. We immediately recruited him."

Director Larson wondering if my brother had ESP abilities was answered by Special Agent Collins. "I have a question, does my brother know about me?"

"No, he doesn't know about you. Unfortunately, we can't inform him yet because of his undercover role. Knowing he has a brother might hinder his thinking and state of mind, jeopardizing his tenuous position."

Janet sat back in her wicker chair. "I'm sure your agency knows about me, Simon and our other agents at FMI?"

"Yes. Each of you have unique ESP abilities. A select few of our FBI agents know about your agents' abilities or Agent Workman's special ability."

"A-need-to-know type of scenario."

"Correct. Since we're all Federal employees with high level clearance, were able to discuss classified information."

Simon thought about his brother's ESP ability, an ability FMI could've used during their previous investigations. Such as knowing if Adam Fletcher, the leader of Eternal Order of Zeus in Pennsylvania, was affiliated with The Circle. "I want to thank you for sharing the information about my brother. Can you let me know when I can meet my brother or at least talk to him on the phone or Skype?"

"Sure will, Agent Woods. You can inform the rest of your team what was discussed here. I'm sure they'll want to know why I contacted you. I'll keep in touch with you."

"Thanks." Simon stood and shook his hand, as did Janet.

They walked back to the lounge. The song about destiny was playing on the electronic music box. He briefly placed his hand on Janet's back and said, "This song could be our song to each other."

"Could be. We'll have to wait and see."

Everyone at their table peered at them when they walked up to the table, then sat. "I can't say much in here. After we're through drinking, we'll go back to my and Brian's room where I'll go over what the FBI agent told us. All I can say to you right now, it was positively informative information."

They finished their drinks, then left the lounge. Simon opened the room door and went inside followed by everyone. He told them what FBI Agent Collins said at the poolside.

"I never knew the FBI knew about The Circle," Brian said standing in front of the room's TV, "or about the FBI scrutinizing The

Circle for illegal activities."

"The FBI doesn't have concrete evidence to refer them to the Attorney General's Office," Janet said. "They're in the same situation we were in during our case in Ocala. Nothing to charge them on for prosecution." She stood next to Simon and put her hands on her hips. "I have a feeling they'll slip up somewhere, some minute detail will present itself to us, leading us to enough evidence to shut them down and put people in federal prison."

Brian smiled. "I like your attitude. You have detective blood running through your veins. I knew you were the right person for our team." He sighed. "It's getting late. Tomorrow we go back to Future Innovations Today to discuss all your testing results with Director Larson. Also, we should have the results on the mysterious powder."

Simon briefly rubbed shoulders with Janet, who gazed up at him and grinned. Another day without being alone with the woman he had strong amorous feelings toward. Tomorrow was another day. Would they be able to be alone? He would sure try to finagle a way, if possible, as he watched Janet, and everyone else, walk out of the room.

~ * ~

Future Innovations Today building came into view as the FMI team's Suburban approached the front gate. The sun was still below the treetops on a cloudless morning. A security guard passed them through the gate. Frank parked the vehicle at the side of the building. "Good morning," said an employee waiting for them at the side door. "I'll be taking you to our conference room. Director Larson and other staff will be there to go over your test results."

They walked inside. Brian asked, "Do you know if you received the results of the powdery substance?"

"I don't know. I work in the human resource department."

A couple of minutes later, Simon saw a small rectangular sign protruding out from above a door. The sign read CONFERENCE ROOM. "Soon we'll find out if we have normal-appearing brains."

"Normal is in the eyes of the beholder," Frank said.

"If we were all normal, they wouldn't have asked us to be tested," Jean said.

"Got me there, little one."

They all walked into the conference room, except the escort who left. Simon saw Director Larson, Hilda and Rod Stephens, the geneticist and another man and woman he hadn't seen before. A large seventy-two-inch monitor was attached to a wall a few feet from the end of a long wooden conference room table with at least twenty chairs. Everyone was standing and talking to one another.

"Good morning everyone," Director Larson said. "I'm sure you're all anxious to hear what we found regarding your test yesterday. Plus, the results of the white powdery substance. Everyone please, take a seat." He motioned his arms as if conducting an orchestra.

"I guess my no-nonsense, let's-get-to-the-point demeanor has rubbed off on to the director," Janet said in a low tone of voice to Simon, as they walked toward the far end of the table.

Simon replied, "Seems like it."

He and Janet sat next to each other. Hilda and Rod Stephens sat directly across the table from them with Director Larson sitting next to them in the last chair. Brian Littlefield sat across from Larson. Everyone else sat to their left at the table.

"First of all, we don't have the results of the white powdery substance yet. We should have the results any time now. We'll now go over your test results. I'll have Gary Turner and Penelope Russo go over the results."

Gary had a small remote-control keyboard in front of him and pushed a key. The monitor immediately turned white. He then typed something on the keyboard. Immediately the screen displayed multiple views of CT and PET scans with the names of the FMI agents underneath the scans. He picked up a small cylindrical device and turned it on. A laser light projected out onto the screen with a red arrow at the end of the narrow beam. Gary moved the arrow to Janet's CT scan. "This is Agent Bennett's brain. This area of her brain is the right parietal. It shows a small area of increased density." He moved the arrow to the other agent's CT scan. "If you noticed there also is this increased density about the size of a green pea on all the scans. The PET scan also picked up this suspicious area on all the scans. We concluded this must be the area your ESP abilities originate from."

"Are you saying it's a tumor?" Simon asked.

"No. It's not a tumor or some type of implant. Possibly a hyperactive synaptic area. Not a hundred percent sure what it means. A possible way to know what we're looking at is to do a biopsy of the site."

"Nobody is going to take a piece of my brain," Frank said. "Unless I'm dead."

"Oh, no. I'm not saying will do a biopsy. Besides, there's no guarantee we'd get an answer. We'll probably reassess the area in the near future." The screen went black. "Penelope is now going to discuss the EEG scan."

"Good morning. The next scan I'm going to show you is a new technology developed here at our facility."

She typed something on a keyboard in front of her. The screen displayed a three-dimensional brain with red and blue wavy lines overlying the brain. Underneath the brain a rectangular panel displayed oscillating red and blue waves.

"What we're seeing here is Agent Bennett's alpha and beta brain waves. The red waves are her alpha waves, and the blue lines are her beta waves."

She moved her fingers across the keyboard. The screen displayed the image of ocean waves, medieval men in a battle, the endearing scene of babies smiling, a roller coaster ride, and the solemn scene of death. Above each scene Janet's oscillating brain waves. "What we see here is when her brain waves pass over the suspicious area in the right parietal area of the brain, there's a slight spike in the beta wave. I've never seen this phenomenon before. This spike is the same in all the FMI agents. Of course, we're not sure what it means or if it has to do with your ESP. In other words, there's no scientific explanation for the anomaly

Simon slid slightly forward in his chair and peered at Ms. Russo.

"What about other people you've tested with ESP abilities, like Karen Rivers? Does she have this anomaly in her EEG scan? Also, does she have the pea-size density in her right parietal area of her brain?"

"To answer your first question, yes. The spike shows up near the base of the brain. As far as any suspicious density in the brain, Gary can answer this question."

"There is a density or area of hyperactivity in Ms. River's brain, but it's adjacent to the Medulla Oblongata...an area of the brain of the cochlear and vestibular nuclei, where hearing is deciphered. What's interesting, we have studied numerous CT and Pet brain scans on people claiming they have ESP abilities, but we found out they didn't, only an overactive imagination."

"How many people have you discovered with these abnormal findings, such as our FMI team and Ms. Rivers?"

"That's it so far. We started this program a few months ago. Our initial purpose at F.I.T. is genetic research and the study of the brain with people claiming they have ESP abilities. We know there are other people in the world with ESP abilities. How many? At this point in our research, there's no guessable number."

Director Larson cleared his throat. "Next I'll have Hilda and Rod talk about your DNA analysis."

Hilda typed on the keyboard. The screen on the wall showed the names of all the FMI agents with their DNA graph. "As you can see, all of you have a different DNA pattern. Everyone has their own unique pattern except for identical twins. What we're in the process of doing is a DNA genome sequencing which will lay out any genetic abnormality, plus see if there is anything common with all of you, some gene you all share. We're not completely done yet with your sequencing."

Rod added, "One of the things we're focusing on is seeing if Agent Bennett's sequencing changed after acquiring an inner voice warning accompanying her premonition feeling. As we stated yesterday, we'll be doing a second whole genome sequencing on Agent Bennett to compare it with her first one, since she recently developed another ESP ability. It normally takes between four to eight weeks to complete whole genome sequencing, but we have been able to shorten it to less than two weeks. Since we obtained DNA samples from all of you over the past week, we should have some of your results in less than a week."

Director Larson's cell phone rang. The room went completely quiet as he listened to the caller. Simon saw the director's face change from a stern expression to one of concern as he furrowed his eyebrows and forehead. "I'll connect you to the conference room screen so you can tell everyone here what the white powdery substance turned out to be."

The screen lit up, showing a man in his late forties with a white lab coat. "Hi, everyone. I'm Steve Fox. I performed a Total Ion Chromatogram on the white powdery substance. I placed the compound into a vial of liquid, then placed it into this chromatogram machine." He stepped aside, allowing everyone to view the lab machine. "The chromatogram identifies the elements in the compound. The result was quite unusual…something I've never seen before."

Chapter Eight

"The compound is normally only harmful if it enters directly into the bloodstream from a cut or sharp pointed object such as a needle or an arrow. But not if ingested or inhaled. This stuff is deadly if inhaled. I've never seen it in this form, a powder. The compound paralyzes all your muscles, especially your chest muscles, preventing you from taking a breath. More than likely you all would've died peacefully in your sleep."

"Are you saying it was curare, a muscle-paralyzing compound?" Simon asked.

"Yes. Although this form of curare is different, having an unusual attached radical, making it an airborne compound with deadly consequences. It makes a perfect killing compound."

"We'll need to contact the FBI and let them know what you found," Brian suggested.

"I'll be calling them after we're done here," Larson said. "You and I will need to talk with an agent. I'm sure they'll have many questions to ask us beside picking up the remaining three devices with the curare-type compound, along with the one we tested."

"Maybe the FBI will be able to trace who made this lethal compound," Simon added. "They have the means and manpower to do a thorough investigation. Even with Frank and Danny's exceptional computer expertise, they're no match to the FBI's vast amount of electronic, computer and telecommunication resources. Plus, their FBI lab is the best in the world in analyzing forensic evidence." Simon was amazed the bureau, with all their sophisticated means of identifying and gathering information on criminal individuals and enterprises, couldn't find enough evidence to bring down The Circle. The evil, clandestine organization, presenting itself as a reputable world enterprise, must have impenetrable computer firewalls. "I still believe The Circle is behind some of the potential deadly events we've personally encountered the past few weeks. Recently including the planted car bomb and the devices containing curare."

"We'll have to catch them during a criminal act," Janet said, "before the judicial system intervenes."

"From what we've seen so far," Frank said, "some of the people connected with The Circle that could've testified against them unexpectedly died in a car crash, were shot or supposedly committed suicide."

Director Larson stood and faced everyone at the table. "I want to thank everyone from FMI for participating in our study here at Future Innovations Today. Director Littlefield will be notified when the DNA genome sequencing is completed." He turned his attention to Brian. "We can go to my office to make the phone call to the FBI office."

Brian stood and looked down at the FMI team. "You all need to return to the hotel. I'm sure FBI agents will want to talk with you and the hotel's personnel. Sorry, this hasn't been a relaxing two days for all of you."

~ * ~

Within two hours, two FBI agents arrived at the hotel with three forensic personnel. Special Agent Collins was one of the investigating agents. He wore a black suit, white shirt, and black tied-down shoes. He walked up to Simon and Janet standing in the lobby.

"Good afternoon, agent," Janet said. "I almost didn't recognize you with your work clothes on."

"You have keen eye for facial recognition."

"It's part of my job description."

They both chuckled.

I didn't find it very funny, thought Simon. "I assume you know what rooms the TVs with the lethal compound were attached to."

"Yes. Director Littlefield told me when we talked on the phone earlier this morning. We'll take charge of the investigation now."

The FBI obtained the hotel's video surveillance CDs, fingerprinted the three TVs, talked with hotel housekeeping people, the front desk clerks, and the FMI team. It was almost four o'clock when the FBI completed their initial investigation. Janet and Special Agent Collins stood in the hallway outside her room talking about investigative procedures. Periodically one or both would laugh. Simon walked toward them from up the hallway.

Simon frowned wondering why they were laughing as a sinking feeling in the pit of his stomach overwhelmed him. His breathing increased. He couldn't remember the last time the feeling of jealousy had aroused him. Sure, Collins was good looking, maintained himself with assuredness and had a kind demeanor. Any woman would be attracted to a man with these characteristics. He breathed in deeply, trying to relax his anxiety as he walked up to them. Janet's back was toward him. "Hey, guys."

Janet turned around. A smile lit up her face. "Hi, Simon. We were just talking about you."

"No wonder my ears were ringing." He chuckled with a forced smile.

"Janet was telling me how the two of you worked so good together solving medical mysteries. I'd love to have a partnership like the two of you have."

Simon felt foolish for feeling jealous. "Yes. We do have a good working relationship."

A male FBI forensic agent in his late twenties walked out of Frank and Danny's room. "I'm all done checking the three rooms."

"Okay." Agent Collins turned his attention back to Janet. "I'll let you know if we find anything. Thanks for your cooperation."

"I hope you find out who did this," Simon said reaching out and shaking hands with Collins. Janet also shook his hand.

Agent Collins nodded. "We'll do our best." He then proceeded up the hallway toward the front lobby.

Simon's cell phone rang. He glanced at the caller ID. It was Brian Littlefield. "Hi, Brian. The FBI is done with their investigation."

"Couldn't be better timing. I received a call from our office in Atlanta. CDC needs our assistance on solving several mysterious deaths in Pine Bluff, Arkansas. You and your team need to fly there today."

Simon stared at Janet. She looked up at him with sparkling piercing eyes, causing a surge of amorous warmth to encompass his body. They wouldn't have the opportunity of being intimately together in Virginia Beach. "It's Director Littlefield. We have another case."

Her loving expression changed to one of disappointment.

"What are we investigating? I'm putting you on speaker so Agent Bennett can hear what you have to say."

"Sure. As I was telling Simon, our Atlanta office called me about mysterious deaths in Pine Bluff, Arkansas. Their health department called for our assistance in the deaths of five people at different locations in the county dying within seventy-two hours without any medical cause. Blood tests, toxicology and autopsies were normal. They all died within two days of each other. None of the victims were related or worked together. I'll have all the details in a report for each of our agents when you get on the plane."

"What time do we have to leave?" Simon asked.

"Four o'clock this afternoon. You can tell Danny that his van will be waiting at the airport for him when you guys land in Pine Bluff. I'll have two vehicles for you and the others."

"Thanks. I'll let everyone know. Talk to you later." Simon put his cell phone away, then said, "I was hoping we…"

"I was too, Simon," Janet interrupted, apparently knowing what he was about to say to her. She reached out and gently squeezed his hand. "We better go tell the others about our new assignment."

~ * ~

The plane lifted off the runway at four-thirty. After the plane leveled off, Simon brought everyone to the round conference table toward the front of the plane and handed each of them the file on the next case in Pine Bluff. Simon and the agents began reading the file named Deadly Unknowns.

Summary of Medical Examiner's report. Undetermined medical death of five people in Pine Bluff, Arkansas dying after manifesting deafness, followed by muteness, followed by blindness, then death within seventy-two hours. The last two medical events occurred about twenty hours of each other. No medical explanation. All labs/autopsies are normal....

The remainder of the report described each of the victim's blood test, toxicology, tissue analysis, autopsy findings, medical history. Each victim died at different times, on different days within a one-week span. The last victim died two days ago.

"I know this might sound callous or unprofessional," Frank said, "but don't these deaths depict the proverb—see no evil, hear no evil and speak no evil?"

Simon looked up from the report. "You're correct in what you said about the proverb. These deaths may be sending a message to someone. Another possibility, the deaths are an act of nature without human intervention. If I were a betting person, I'd put my money on a demonic entity and not on an act of nature. No matter which scenario we're looking at, we'll need to determine the cause of the victims' demise, including the why."

"I'm up for solving another medical mystery," Jean said closing her folder.

"I'll second that," Danny said. "I know I'm the rookie agent. But my adrenaline is primed for another case. Especially when my van will be at the airport in Pine Bluff."

The setting sun hung above the western horizon as FMI's ten-passenger jet plane descended toward Pine Bluff Regional Airport-Grider Field.

~ * ~

Janet closed her eyes and squeezed Simon's hand as the plane banked to the right, then descended toward the ground. Her breathing increased as her heart pounded against her chest. She manifested the same physical signs when the jet had taken off in Virginia earlier. "You'd think I'd be getting less tense regarding taking off and landing."

"It may take a while. In the meantime, I don't mind holding your hand."

Janet snickered to herself. *He wouldn't mind holding my hand any time.*

The sound of the rubber tires striking the concrete runway caused her to sigh, relieving the fear-of-flying syndrome she had no control over. Not having control over her emotions and fears bothered her. For now, there wasn't anything she could do to eliminate its hold on her.

Around seven o'clock, their jet taxied to an area where three vehicles were parked next to a hanger. A black Suburban and Taurus, and of course, Danny's white van. Danny reacted like a child receiving a new bicycle for Christmas or his birthday.

Frank gently tapped the back of Danny's shoulder. "I guess you missed your van. Eh, partner?"

"You better believe it. I miss all my electronic gadgets and computers."

Janet was grateful Danny had his drone during their Deadly Seizures Case in Chambersburg. It unquestionably came into play to help them solve the mysterious seizure deaths. His inventive prowess and computer expertise would surely be needed in this new case facing the FMI team.

Before they stepped off the plane, Brian assigned the Taurus to Frank and Jean. He and Janet would drive the Suburban, and of course, Danny would drive his van. They all stood together on the tarmac near the three lined-up vehicles. "The hotel we'll be staying at has been put into the vehicles' GPS," Simon announced. "Janet and I will be meeting with the lead detective in the case before going to the hotel. We'll meet everyone there. Like in Virginia Beach, we'll be sharing rooms. Except for me. I'll have my own room."

A rush of tingling warmth spread over Janet's entire body. The thought of being intimately alone with Simon excited her as if it was their wedding night. She glanced up at him and saw a Cheshire grin. He obviously was thinking what she was thinking.

Simon stared at Frank. "For those who may be hungry, there's a Denny's Restaurant adjacent to the hotel."

A smile spread across Frank's face. "We'll scout out the restaurant after we check into our hotel room."

Simon chuckled. "Thanks, Frank. I knew I could rely on you for making sure the restaurant was compliant to our standards."

"Any time, boss."

Simon drove the Suburban into the Pine Bluff Police Department's parking lot and parked in the visitor's space. Simon and Janet exited their vehicle, then walked into the police station to the front desk counter. Simon displayed his FMI badge to an officer behind the counter. "We're here to see Detective Rhodes."

"Yes, sir." He turned to his left. "Officer Reynolds will take you to him."

They walked toward the back of the building, then turned left into a large room with several desks. Three people wearing sports coats sat alone at their desks. "Detective Rhodes, the agents from F.M.I. are here to see you."

The detective, who appeared to be in his late forties, turned around in his chair. He smiled as he stood. "I didn't expect you for another thirty minutes."

"We came right to the police station from our plane," Janet said. "The rest of the agents are at the hotel." *Oh no, I did it again. Jumping ahead of Simon.*

"I'm Agent Woods. This is Agent Bennett." Simon reached out a shook hands with the detective, as did Janet. "We're here to assist in your investigation of these deaths."

"We're glad you're here. Please have a seat." He directed them to two cushioned chairs on each side of his desk. "I'll go over what information we have on these deaths. Which I'm sure you already know are determined as Death Undetermined from the autopsy report of medical examiner's office. There wasn't any trace of trauma or poisoning in any of the victims. A true Sherlock Holmes mystery."

Janet briefly snickered. "Since I'm a previous major crime detective and Agent Woods is a doctor, I'd say we'd fit the persona of Holmes and Watson."

The detective chuckled. "My. My. I'm in the company of a famous crime-solving duo." He opened a file lying on his desk in front of him. A serious expression spread across his face. "I interviewed the victim's families. None of the victims knew each other, nor did they belong to a common organization such as the Moose or Eagles, nor did they attend the same church. Our investigation is at a complete standstill. Did you get the autopsy report yet?"

"Yes. We reviewed it on the plane from Virginia Beach. Like your police report, no pertinent information. The autopsy and blood work didn't reveal a cause of their deaths."

"Hopefully, you and your agents can find a cause for these five deaths. If you need any assistance, please give me a call. I'll give you my cell phone number." He gave his number to Janet. She and Simon put the detective's number into their phones. "Also, here's the name, address and phone number of the deceased victims, along with their families." The detective handed Janet two sheets of paper inside a manila folder.

"Thanks, Detective Rhodes. We'll keep in touch."

"I'll walk out with you. It's been a long day. I'm ready to go home."

Janet and Simon waved to the detective as his car passed by them in the parking lot. "Sounds like we have a lot of investigation to do on these five deaths," Janet declared. "As usual, no clues to direct us to an answer to these deaths."

"That's what I love about this job. Trying to find a needle in a haystack."

Janet grinned. "If the haystack was the size of a loaf of bread, I wouldn't mind looking for the needle."

They both chuckled.

Simon pulled out of the police parking lot and headed for the hotel. Janet looked forward to being with Simon. What was she going to tell Jean? *"I'll be back in a few hours, there something I have to do."* Jean would obviously know where she's going and who she'd be with. Does it really matter at this point? She and Simon were adults with no commitments with another person.

"Can you call Frank and let him know we're on our way to the hotel. They'll probably be at the restaurant. Tell him to wait for us. We'll need to go over tomorrow's schedule."

Janet called and spoke with Frank. "We should be there in about ten minutes. Talk to you then." Simon was correct, Frank, Jean and Danny had recently sat down at the restaurant and ordered dinner.

She and Simon walked into the restaurant. The front section of the restaurant was nearly filled with patrons. One empty table was left. No sight of the FMI team. The waitress said, "Are you two with Frank?"

"Yes. We are." Simon answered.

"They're in the back room to your right."

"Thank you," Janet said.

They walked toward the back room. She glanced at the people sitting at each table or booth and didn't see a familiar face. Ever since she joined the FMI team, she had become more aware of people in public places, devious people wanting to do harm to her and the FMI agents. When they walked into the other section of the restaurant, Janet saw the FMI team sitting at a table to their far right about twenty feet away. The only other people in the room were a middle-aged man and woman sitting at a booth near the archway between the two rooms.

Frank waved his arms in front of him, acknowledging their presence.

Janet and Simon sat at the table next to each other. The waitress walked up to the table and wrote down their orders. After she left, Simon said, "Detective Rhodes, the lead detective, didn't have any leads to the cause of the deaths or who was possibly responsible for their deaths."

"Like we said on the plane," Frank said, "this is our normal presentation of mysterious, undetermined medical deaths."

"You're right," Simon said as he poured coffee into Janet's empty coffee cup. He then poured coffee into his cup. "The agenda for tomorrow will be this: Frank and Jean will interview two of the victims' immediate families. Janet and I will interview the next two victims' families. Whoever is done first will interview the fifth victim's family. We'll then do the same at the victim's place of employment. Pretty much our normal protocol for investigating mysterious deaths. We need to find a common thread connecting these deaths. As for Danny, I want you to check the victims' social media sites for anything that might connect these victims' deaths."

After finishing dinner, they all walked back to the hotel. Simon asked everyone if they wanted to go to the hotel lounge for a nightcap before retiring to bed. Everyone declined except Janet. Simon stopped at the front desk to check in and get his room's cardkey. They then walked into the lounge and sat at a table. Simon ordered drinks for them. "This will be your third case with FMI."

"Hard to believe. Seems like I've been doing this for quite a while, not almost two weeks."

"To be exact, you started working with us twelve days and..." Simon glanced at his watch, "...eleven and a half hours ago. I rounded off the minutes and seconds. You've been an FMI agent for seven days and about seven hours."

"You sure seem to keep track of me."

"Just part of my job, ma'am...just part of my job."

Janet laughed along with Simon. She couldn't have asked for a better partner, and one she cared about deeply. Within ten minutes they finished their drinks.

Simon inconspicuously sighed. "Would you like to come back to my room?"

"Yes."

Her heart raced, as it seemed to pound against her chest wall. She was anxious to be in the arms of a man she dearly cared for. As they walked down the hallway, her breathing increased as her body ached passionately for Simon's body to be pressing against hers.

Simon removed his cardkey from his pocket, stopped in front of his hotel room and slid the cardkey into the door lock.

The TV was on, as were the room lights. Someone was in the room.

Chapter Nine

Janet removed her Glock as her sheriff's training and forte kicked in, putting her on high alert for an intruder, someone who might have lethal intentions toward Simon and her. The TV was on to muffle the sound of a gunshot. *What other reason would the TV be on?* she thought. The bathroom door quickly opened to their left. Janet raised her Glock, pointing it toward the intruder. "Director Littlefield. It's you." She immediately lowered her gun.

"By your gesture, you were expecting someone else."

"We didn't know you were coming to Pine Bluff," Simon said as he put his cardkey into his blazer pocket.

"I decided to come and assist in the investigation for a day or two. Since we're a new division of CDC, I thought it would be good to be part of an investigation."

"Glad to have you here."

Janet didn't think it was a good idea for their director to be here. Especially when he'd be sharing the room with Simon. Cupid was playing a dirty trick on Simon and her for the second time. "It's getting late. I'll see you guys tomorrow morning at breakfast." She glanced at Simon and noticed disappointment mapped across his face.

"Yeah. See you at breakfast around eight."

Janet left, heading across the hallway to her and Jean's room. The TV was on when she opened the door. Jean was sitting up in bed. "Oh. You're awake."

"I'd didn't think you'd be back yet. Is everything all right?"

I'm sure Jean's comment was directed at Simon and me. Should

I tell Jean that Simon and I were about to engage in a romantic moment, sharing each other's passionate feelings toward each other? No. Why bring up disappointed feelings?

"Everything is fine. Director Littlefield is here. He's sharing a room with Simon. The Director is going to be with us for the next couple of days."

"Oh. Too bad...well, I guess we'll have to do everything by the book. Which of course, we do anyway." Jean grinned. "At least most of the time."

Janet put night clothes on, then laid on her back in bed. Her mind dwelled on what could have happened if Director Littlefield hadn't shown up. A warm sensation encompassed her body with amorous thoughts as she drifted off to sleep in a darkened and quiet room.

~ * ~

The sound of the shower running awakened her from a sound sleep. The morning sun's rays filtered around the curtains and into the room. The clock on the nightstand between the two beds read 7:12 a.m.

It was 7:50 when she and Jean left their room. The men had likely already left for the restaurant due to the fact that, a few minutes ago, Janet heard two doors close within a minute or two of each other. She missed Simon knocking on her door before going to breakfast. The backroom of the restaurant was at about fifty percent capacity. They had put two square tables side by side, forming a rectangle to allow the six of them to sit together and talk easily to each other. She and Jean greeted everyone with a good morning before sitting down. Janet sat next to Simon. A full cup of coffee sat on the table in front of her. Janet inconspicuously brushed the side of her right knee against the side of Simon's left knee.

Simon grinned. He glanced around the table then said, "Since our whole team is here now, Director Littlefield will be tagging along with us, observing our investigation. He'll first be with Frank and Jean this morning, then he'll be with Janet and me this afternoon."

"What about me?" Danny interrupted.

"I appreciate your contribution to this team," Brian answered. "You're a vital asset. But my computer knowledge and capabilities are minimal. There's no way I'd learn anything other than you're a computer wizard. Which of course, I already know you are. Frank knows my computer inadequacies since he's close to your knowhow of computers. You continue doing what you do best. I'd be a distraction, hindering your progress."

Danny sat back in his chair, slightly stuck out his chest as he raised his chin in a proud gesture. "Thanks. I'll do my best."

Janet stared at Danny sitting across from her. His newly acquired telekinetic capabilities were added assets to his computer wizardry.

"Simon. What can you tell us about the symptoms and signs of the five victims?" Jean asked as she set down her cup of coffee on the table.

"I don't have anything to add to the police report. To reiterate what was in the report: there was an exact sequence of medical manifestations each of the victim's presented with. First there was sudden hearing loss. A day or two later they lost their voice, unable to talk other than making grunting sounds. About one or two days later the victims lost their vision. Between six and seven days from their initial symptom, they died of an undetermined cause. There isn't anything in the medical archives of medicine describing these three prodromal events before dying."

"There are people born deaf and blind, called congenital deaf/blindness," Frank said matter-of-factly. "It can also be acquired from an infection of the brain, trauma, or stroke. One of these persons was Helen Keller. Her deafness and blindness occurred when she was about eighteen months old due likely to an infection from a bacterium called *Neisseria meningitidis* or meningococcal meningitis, which caused swelling of the linings covering the brain and spinal cord."

Simon chuckled. "You still amaze me with your diversity of knowledge."

"Like all our other cases, I do research on where we're going, including the terrain, environment and medical circumstances regarding the deaths we'll be investigating. Danny and I did the research together last night in our room. What you said about people suddenly going deaf, mute, and blind followed by unexplained death has never been recorded. Like we've said on our other medical cases, we're facing a true medical mystery."

Simon put another teaspoon of sugar into his coffee. "The doctors in the hospital did spinal taps on all our victims and didn't find any infectious organism. The spinal fluid was clear and normal. In other words, no signs of meningitis. Also, the brain autopsy reports on the victims didn't show any signs of infection, blood clots, brain hemorrhages or tumors. Like you said, we're facing another true medical mystery."

Everyone ate their breakfast, then departed the hotel except for Danny, who went back to his hotel room to search the Internet for any pertinent information on the five victims. Janet buckled herself into the front passenger's seat belt. She glanced at Simon who started their vehicle. "One of these times we'll have the opportunity of being alone."

"I'm starting to wonder if fate doesn't want us to be together, other than solving cases together. I've always believed a person can create his own fate in life. We'll have our time."

"I know we will." Janet reached out and put the first victim's home address into the Suburban's GPS. A moment later, when they stopped at the parking lot's entrance leading to the street, the GPS's female voice announced, "Turn left onto Parker Street."

Janet peered down at the fact sheet for each of the victims. "The first victim was a thirty-two-year-old named Barbara Casper. We'll be talking with her husband, Ronald."

About fifteen minutes later, Simon pulled their vehicle into the driveway of a colonial-style home. A blue SUV was parked in front of him. They exited the Suburban and walked up to the front door. Janet rang the doorbell. This was one of her toughest duties of being a detective or an FMI agent, talking to a family member of a deceased victim.

The front door opened. An unshaven, short stocky man in his mid-thirties stood before them. "Can I help you?"

Janet and Brian brought out their FMI ID and displayed it to Mr. Casper. "I'm Agent Bennett and this is Agent Woods. We're a division of CDC investigating your wife's death. Can we talk with you?"

"Sure. Please come in."

He stepped aside, allowing Janet and Brian entrance into the house. They went to the living room and sat.

Janet sat on the couch with Simon. She looked in front of her at Ronald Casper, who sat in a cushioned armchair. "From our records, your wife didn't have any medical conditions or problems. Am I right?"

"Yes. She never complained of anything. Then…she lost her hearing. I drove her to the emergency room. They ran all kinds of tests, including brain scans. They didn't find anything wrong. The next day, my wife couldn't speak. It was as if someone during the night removed her voice box. Her vocal cords appeared normal according to the doctors. They had no idea what was causing her deafness or why she couldn't talk. Two days later, they discharged her from the hospital. On the way to our car in front of the hospital she went blind. We immediately turned around and headed back into the hospital. They readmitted her to the hospital." He glanced down at the living room floor as tears streaked down his cheeks, along with a deep sigh. "She…she died the next day."

"I'm so sorry for your loss," Janet said, as she held back a tear in her right eye.

"We never had children." A short pause. "Now I wish we had."

"Had you or your wife travelled to another country in the past few months?" Simon asked.

"No. Neither of us like flying. My wife is afraid of heights. And I have severe motion sickness."

Janet could appreciate what he said about flying even though she doesn't have either of these two conditions. "Had she been sick or fallen prior to her first symptom of hearing loss?"

"No. She was in excellent health."

"Did you or your wife know any of these people?" Simon read off the names of the other victims.

"No. I don't recognize any of the names. The police detective asked me the same question when I talked with him the other day."

"Had your wife taken any medications prior to her deafness?"

"No. Like I said, she was in excellent health. We don't use street drugs…if you were about to ask me. The police detective already asked me that question."

Janet knew there had to be something tangible, such as an implant, a chemical compound, an organism, a virus that caused these five people to go deaf, mute, blind, then unexplained death. There had to be a common link between these victims like the last two cases she and the FMI team solved. She proceeded to ask Mr. Casper where they shopped for groceries, what they did for entertainment and if they belonged to any organizations such as the Eagles, Moose, Elks or any other fraternal groups. She wrote down his answers into a small notebook. Not knowing what the other victims' spouses or relatives would answer, they'd need to wait until all the interviews were completed before a conclusion could be made if there's a common thread connecting the victims. "I understand your wife worked for a company called Cloverleaf Manufacturing." Simon stated.

"Yes. She worked eight years for them. The company makes gauges for different machinery."

Simon thanked Mr. Casper. They left his house, then sat inside in their vehicle. "No surprises here. Who's are next victim's family?"

Janet peered at the sheet with the list of victims. "The next person is a forty-five-year-old male, Timothy Martin." She placed his address in the GPS. "We'll be talking to his wife, Jessica. She works from home on her computer for a medical supply company."

Janet thought about her ex-partner Bill Matters' wife, who worked at home from her computer. Bill came close to losing his life from a woman from The Circle blowing a white powdery substance into his face, causing him to go into a coma, then miraculously he awoke a couple of days later. The substance might have been curare. Since the compound likely metabolized into an untraceable inert substance before doctors checked Matters' bronchial tubes, they'd never know for sure.

Janet and Simon spent about forty minutes interviewing Jessica

Martin. None of her answers about her husband, other than the three medical conditions leading to death, matched any of the first victim's history.

When they were outside going to their vehicle, Simon said, "As the saying goes, 'no smoking guns here.' There's no common thread between the first two victims pointing to a cause or entity that may be responsible for their deaths."

"Maybe Frank and Jean's interviews were more productive than ours? I'll give them a call."

Frank's phone rang three times before he picked up. "Hi, Frank. It's Janet. How's the interviews going?"

"A moment ago, we started the second interview. Nothing significant so far. How's it going with you guys?"

"We finished two interviews. Nothing stands out. We'll need to compare notes and see if there's something tying all these victims together. Simon and I will interview the fifth victim's family. We'll meet back at the hotel and discuss our information. We'll also discuss the five victim's place of employment, which we'll investigate tomorrow morning."

"Okay. See you at the hotel."

Janet put her phone away, then put in the home address of the fifth victim in the GPS. "The fifth and last victim is Larry Mandle. He's an unmarried twenty-eight-year-old finish carpenter, living with his parents. Maybe the last victim will give us a clue in these mysterious deaths?"

"Wouldn't that be nice."

They interviewed the grieving parents of the fifth victim. Again, a healthy young man with no medical conditions. He smoked marijuana occasionally, but was not a habitual user. His deafness, muteness, blindness, then death wasn't any different than the other victims. She and Simon drove back to the hotel. Janet called Frank and told him to tell everyone to meet in his room in about fifteen minutes.

Simon knocked on Frank and Danny's hotel room door. Jean answered the door. "We have a guest," Jean stated as they walked into the room.

Standing and talking to Frank was Karen Rivers. Brian was standing behind Danny, who sat in a chair in front of his laptop computer which sat on a desktop.

"Hi, Ms. Rivers," Janet said as she walked up to the F.I.T. employee. "I assume you're not here in Pine Bluff on vacation?"

She snickered. "No. It's not on my top ten vacation places to visit. I'll be helping you guys investigate the five unexplained deaths."

"Great," Simon said. "We can definitely use your help."

We can? Janet frowned as she glanced at Simon's jubilant expression toward Karen Rivers. *Sure. She's cute.* Janet doubted she was Simon's type. *My God. I'm becoming jealous.*

Brian turned and faced them. "I talked with Edward Larson from F.I.T. this morning before leaving with Frank and Jean. We thought it would be good to have Ms. Rivers assist us on this investigation. She has investigative experience and of course, her extraordinary hearing may be useful during our investigation."

Janet didn't get an ominous feeling or hear her forewarning inner voice before Jean answered the door a moment ago, therefore, she would probably be an asset and not a hindrance to their FMI team.

Ms. Rivers turned to Janet and said, "Like I was telling Director Littlefield and the other agents before you and Agent Woods arrived, the DNA sequencing should be done in two to three days. Hopefully, the scientist will find the gene responsible for all our ESP abilities. Especially your DNA sequencing, Janet, since they'll be able to compare your DNA sequencing before and after you added an ESP ability."

"You seem to have a lot of knowledge of this subject."

"I have a degree in biochemistry from the University of Virginia. I heard about F.I.T. in Virginia Beach and their research on extrasensory perception. To make a long story short, they obtained my DNA. I then accepted a position in their biochemistry research lab when I learned there was an opening. After I was working there about a month, I volunteered to obtain information on your FMI agents when we learned the agents might have ESP abilities. You know the rest about us after we met in Chambersburg."

Janet chuckled to herself. She didn't expect a detailed summation from Karen. Ms. Rivers had a similar trait like Simon's. They both had a tendency of rambling when only a short answer was needed. "Like what Simon said, 'we can definitely use your help.' "

"Thanks, Agent Bennett."

"Call me, Janet."

"Thanks, Janet."

Brian reached up and rubbed his chin between his thumb and index finger, then said, "Miss Rivers, we'll have you work with Agents Bennett and Woods. I've seen enough of FMI's technique in interviewing from Agent Littlefield and Cliftwood this morning. There's no need for me to follow Simon and Janet around. I'll stay with Danny, even though I said earlier this morning, I might get in his way. It's the prerogative I have being the director of FMI."

Janet didn't think they needed another investigator tagging along with them. Karen might get in the way of their investigation. The phrase, *two is company, three's a crowd,* flashed across her mind. The resurgence of jealousy flared up again. She had to get a hold of herself and not let emotions take over her thinking. It will only cause trouble. "We'll be glad to…"

"Please be quiet," Karen Rivers demanded. "I hear a vehicle alarm going off. That's weird. A male voice is shouting, 'Stay away from the vehicle.' "

"It's my van security alarm," Danny said, as he stood up from his chair. An expression of concern joined his alarming voice. "Someone might be trying to break into my van." He ran out of the room and down the hallway.

"Maybe someone placed a bomb underneath his van?" Janet questioned. She hurried into the hallway. Danny was halfway up the hallway. She shouted, "Danny. Danny. Stop." She sped toward him.

He stopped and turned around. Janet was about thirty feet away from him. "Someone may have attempted to place an explosive device on your van. Be careful. Let me go with you."

She might get her premonition feeling and her inner warning voice regarding a dangerous or deadly outcome if he opened his van. They walked up the hallway, through the lobby to the parking lot.

"My van is over there," he said, pointing to the back row of the hotel's front parking lot, about fifty yards away. The alarm's warning voice repeated the same line every several seconds. There were only a couple of empty parking spaces. Danny pointed his remote control attached to his van's keys and pressed the alarm icon, turning off the alarm system.

Would Janet's ESP premonition and inner warning voice be activated as they approached Danny's van?

Chapter Ten

Janet's breathing increased as they stepped closer to the van. She scanned the area, looking for people or individuals. No one was seen or heard. Only the sound of vehicles coming from the street adjacent to the hotel filled the air. Scattered white clouds set the background of a nearly blue sky. The sun shone down its warm rays directly over their head. She heard footsteps behind her and Danny. She stopped and quickly turned around, as did Danny. Frank and Simon hurried toward them. Frank was carrying an apparatus the size of a transistor radio. "What are you two doing here?" Janet asked.

"I thought maybe an electronic detection device would check for an explosive or listening device." Frank held up the gadget in front of him.

"Good idea." She glanced at Simon. "Why did you come? You could be putting yourself in harm's way if a bomb is planted on Danny's van."

He frowned. "Because I wanted to be here."

Simon was her boss, as was Director Littlefield. "I didn't want anyone else to get hurt, that's all."

Frank handed the device to Danny. "I'll be able to smell anything unusual around or inside the van."

Karen Rivers walked up with Director Littlefield as the FMI team stood about thirty feet away from Danny's van. "I thought you could use my hearing in case there's a mechanical apparatus with moving parts inside or underneath the van."

Brian said, "I'm here to observe from a safe distance."

How could Janet dispute the ESP abilities of everyone present? "I guess we'll cover most of the van's possible hidden and potential lethal factors with all of our ESP abilities."

"This is what I call teamwork," proclaimed the director.

Everyone approached the van, except Brian who stood about thirty feet away. Janet stopped about a foot away from the front door of the van. No premonition feeling. No inner warning voice. "I don't feel or hear anything. We'll need to check the outside."

Danny turned on the electronic detector and slowly scanned the exterior of the van. Frank laid on his back, peered underneath the front of the van while sniffing, then moved meticulously around the van. Karen asked everyone not to talk, as she placed her ear a couple of inches from the van and listened intently for any mechanism with moving parts. She moved slowly around the van. Danny's device didn't interfere with Karen's hearing. Simon stood with Brian as they observed the FMI team and their newest loaned member search the van for a possible explosive or some other menacing gadget. Thirteen minutes elapsed. Nothing lethal or suspicious was found or detected. Simon and Brian walked up to the van. "Check inside the van," Simon said, "and see if anything was missing or tampered with."

Danny thoroughly checked inside the van. "Everything is fine. Not sure why my alarm went off. Maybe someone bumped into the van, or in fact, someone was attempting to break in but after my alarm sounded, they ran away."

"Whatever the cause, your van is safe. We need to discuss what we found and didn't find with our interviews of the victims' families. Why don't we all go to the restaurant and have lunch before we continue our investigation?" He glanced at Frank and grinned.

"Sounds good to me," Frank agreed.

Janet glanced at Karen, then Simon. Janet thought about when she sat in a booth at Northgate Diner and was asked by Simon to assist in the Whispers Before Death case in Ocala. She sighed. *Will Karen be asked to join the FMI team after solving the deaths in Pine Bluff? Time will tell.*

They all sat at a table in the restaurant next to the hotel. Janet sat next to Simon. Everyone sat at their normal position at the table except Karen, who sat between Danny and Frank. The conversation at the lunch table focused on their interviews this morning, and what information Danny found during his Internet search of the five victims, including all the social media sites. After about forty minutes of discussion, between bites of their lunch, it was concluded there wasn't a common denominator connecting the five victims. None of the victims knew each other. None of them frequented the same establishment such as a church, social group, or club either on the Internet or physically.

"As far as I can see," Simon concluded, "if we're going to solve these mysterious deaths, we'll need a little luck and a lot more investigative work. The answer may be at the victims' places of work. Since there hadn't been another person experiencing the triad of signs before dying in the past three days, whatever or whoever caused their demise may have stopped or gone on to another location. This case isn't any different from any of our other investigations of undetermined medical deaths. We're either seeing a deliberate evil act by someone, Mother Nature surfacing a deadly entity or we're seeing the hand of divine intervention. Our job is to determine which one it is."

"Amen." Frank orated. "Let's hope it's the first or second. We don't have direct communication to the last cause."

Everyone chuckled, including Karen Rivers, who momentarily placed her hand on top of Frank's forearm, then said, "You're a funny guy. I like humor in a person."

Frank glanced down at Karen's hand, then into her deep blue eyes. Janet saw a slight blush blossom across his face. *I think Frank might be smitten by this woman.* She had never seen Frank blush before.

"Hi, everyone," Detective Rhodes said as he approached the restaurant table.

"What a surprise," Simon replied. "I'm glad you're here. I want you to meet the rest of the FMI team. Simon went around the table and introduced each of the agents. When he came to Karen Rivers, he introduced her as a consultant to the investigation.

"Oh my God," Jean blurted out as she stared up at the detective, causing everyone to peer at her with bewilderment.

"What's wrong?" Brian asked, who sat next to her at the table.

Jean answered, "The detective has a yellow…"

Brian shook his head in a negative gesture, interrupting Jean's answer. He then whispered, "no."

The detective stood directly behind Karen Rivers. Ms. Rivers turned her head to the left, closing her eyes. Janet saw her reach into her jacket pocket and remove her remote-control apparatus attached to her car's keyring. Karen turned off her ear dampening device. Ms. Rivers was obviously hearing something, something outside, in the other room or something near here, thought Janet.

Karen stood and faced the detective. "You look awful pale, is what Agent Cliftwood is trying to say. Are you feeling all right?"

"Fine. Other than a little indigestion."

"Do you mind if I take your pulse? I have medical training as an EMT."

"Sure. Go ahead."

"Please sit down."

The detective sat down on Karen's chair.

Karen placed her fingers over the anterior aspect of his left wrist. "You pulse is irregular. You might be in Atrial Fibrillation or have a heart block."

Simon stood, came around the table and felt the detective's left radial pulse. Concern rose from Simon's face. "Ms. Rivers is right in her assessment. Plus, you feel cool and clammy. With your complaint of indigestion, you may be on the verge of having a serious heart problem…such as a heart attack. We should call EMS right now."

"I think I'm having indigestion from the hamburger and fries I had before coming here. Although, I did feel my heart skipping a beat a few minutes before coming into the restaurant. I'd have to say, your agents are very observant."

Janet would've liked to tell the detective about their ESP abilities. She knew the fewer people knew about FMI's abilities, the better they'd be able to investigate unsolved medical deaths. Otherwise, the news media would be following the team around from state to state, city to city. It would be a distraction in their investigations.

Within ten minutes, EMS and paramedics arrived and put the detective on a gurney. They started an I.V., put him on oxygen through a nasal cannula, then did an EKG. The paramedic peered at the EKG printout, then handed it to Simon and said, "Looks like a Third-Degree AV Block."

Simon peered at the printout. "You're absolutely right. We need to get him to the hospital."

"What does Third-Degree something Block mean?" Detective Rhodes asked.

"It means the electrical impulse from the top of the heart is having difficulty reaching the bottom of your heart, preventing it from beating efficiently. You'll need a pacemaker for your heart, helping the cardiac muscle to beat at a normal rate."

"I almost went to the office instead of coming here. I guess it's my lucky day?"

The paramedics pushed the gurney through the restaurant and into the ambulance. A moment later, the ambulance's flashing emergency lights lit up along with the screeching siren warning drivers to move out of the way. They sped toward the hospital.

Janet sighed as she and the agents, including Karen Rivers, peered through the restaurant window at the paramedic's emergency vehicle leave the restaurant's parking lot. "You know if the detective hadn't stopped by to talk with us, he probably would've died."

"You're right," Simon interjected. "His heart would have stopped or gone into a rhythm that wouldn't have been able to sustain life." He looked at Jean. "I assume the detective still had his yellow glow when the paramedics wheeled him out of the restaurant?"

"Yes. It doesn't mean he'll die. It'll all depend if the doctors at the hospital can insert the pacemaker before his heart stops or goes into a life-threatening rhythm."

They all sat down at their table.

Janet turned to Jean. "You said a moment ago, the detective could die before he gets to the hospital?"

"It's possible."

"I hope he'll make it." Janet drank the rest of her iced tea, then set the empty glass down on the table. She turned to Simon. "What about the victims' places of employment?"

"Tomorrow we'll split the five job sites like we did today with the families of the victims. Except, Janet, Karen and I will investigate two." He looked at Frank. "You and Jean will investigate the remaining three job sites."

Frank furrowed his eyebrows. "Why is that?"

"Because I am your boss."

Frank bowed his head, glancing away with an embarrassing expression. "I didn't mean…"

"Don't worry about it," Simon interrupted. "The real reason is one place of employment the three of us will be investigating tomorrow is forty miles away."

Frank sighed, raised his head, and sat back in his chair. "Oh. That makes sense, boss."

Brian Littlefield's cell phone rang. Everyone at the table stopped talking as they all glanced at the director. "Hello." A pause. "Yes, I'm director of the Federal Medical Investigators." He listened to the caller for about a minute. "Yes. I'll send a couple of my agents to you. Thanks for calling." Brian put his phone away, then looked at Simon. "A body from a car accident came to the morgue early this morning. The man went suddenly blind while driving his car and crashed into a tree, killing him."

"How did they know he went blind?" Simon asked. "Was someone in the car with him?"

"Yes, his wife. The wife said the day before he lost his hearing, then this morning he couldn't talk. He was driving himself along with his wife to the hospital when he lost his sight. The man wasn't wearing a seatbelt. Luckily, his wife was wearing one. She wasn't injured."

"How did the medical examiner's office know to call you?" Simon asked.

"I had called the Jefferson County Medical Examiner & Coroner's office when we were in Virginia Beach, after I received the news about the five deaths here in Pine Bluff. I asked them to notify me if any new similar deaths came into their morgue. The medical examiner is going to perform an autopsy in about an hour. Since this person didn't die like the other five victims, whatever caused the others' deaths may be inside this man's body. I want you to go to the autopsy, since you'll understand the findings, if any, during the autopsy."

"Who wants to go with me to the autopsy?" He looked at the agents for an apparent response.

"I'd rather stay here," Frank answered.

"Me too," added Danny. "The thought of looking down at a dead body as someone opens up their insides is not an item on my bucket list of things to do or see before I die."

"I've seen my share of autopsies," Jean said.

"I'll go with you," Janet answered as she inconspicuously under the table bumped the side of her shoe against Simon's."

"Can I go with you guys?" Karen asked. "I've always wanted to see an autopsy."

Simon looked at Brian across the table. "It's up to Director Littlefield."

"Sure. You can go with them."

Janet was hoping Karen would want to stay with Frank and get acquainted with him after her flirtatious mannerism toward him. Maybe Karen did want to play up to Simon, or she was flirtatious with all men. Janet had to keep a close eye on her.

~ * ~

Simon parked the Suburban in the parking lot of Jefferson County Medical Examiner & Coroner's office building. A security guard met them inside the front entrance lobby. "I'm Agent Woods of FMI, and these are my associates. We're here to see Dr. Bunting."

"He called earlier and told me about your agency. Follow me. I'll take you all to the morgue."

As they turned right to another hallway, the odor of formaldehyde permeated the air.

"Smells like formaldehyde," Karen said.

"It is," Simon agreed. "I thought you never been to an autopsy?"

"I haven't. In college our biochemistry labs were down the hallway from a pathology room containing cadavers for the medical students. The odor is very distinct."

The guard stopped, turned to his left and knocked on a door. Above the door a sign read, AUTOPSY ROOM. A few seconds later, a man in his early thirties, wearing a blue paper gown with paper shoe coverings, opened the door. "These are the agents from FMI."

"Thanks, Ralph."

The security guard left.

"Please come in. My name is Sean Birch. I'm Dr. Bunting's pathologist assistant."

Simon introduced himself, Janet, and Karen to Sean Birch. They all walked across the gray tiled floor to a deceased male body lying supine on a long metal exam table. A rubber, rectangular block was underneath the upper aspect of the body, pushing the corpse's chest wall upward. A blue towel covered the head while another one covered the genital area. There were two other metal exam tables, neither were occupied. Metal wall shelves with glass front doors ran along a wall in front of them. To their left at the far end of the room were six cooler drawers where corpses were kept before and after autopsies.

"Can you tell us something about Robert Sears?" Simon inquired.

"Yes," answered Sean. "The deceased was a retired sixty-six-year-old man without any major medical conditions. He wasn't taking any prescribed medications."

A door to the left opened and in walked a man in his mid-fifties garbed with a blue paper gown, surgical cap, and shoe coverings. "Good afternoon, everyone." He exaggerated a deep breath, then said, "Welcome to my world." He stopped a few feet from the head of the autopsy table.

Simon chuckled to himself. Most of the pathologist and medical examiners he'd met had a sense of humor or were good natured. He guessed they would have to be since their patients were dead. They couldn't talk, tell them where they hurt, or what symptoms they were experiencing before dying. Forensic science had to be their voice. "Thank you for allowing us to observe your autopsy."

"My pleasure. It's great to have an audience during one of my autopsies. Normally it's only Sean and me…and of course our guest on the table. I understand you're a medical doctor, Dr. Woods."

"Word gets around fast."

"Not really. Director Littlefield told me about your credentials."

He glanced at Janet then Karen.

"This is Agent Bennett." Simon directed his attention to her, who stood to his right. "Agent Bennett is former sheriff detective." He then turned toward Karen to his left. "Ag…that is Ms. Rivers. She is a consultant, a biochemist, assisting us in our investigation."

"Please to meet everyone. I assume y'all have seen an autopsy?"

"This will be my first autopsy," Karen answered.

"Hum. If you feel faint or like you're going to throw up there's a sink over there." He pointed to Karen's right at a stainless-steel sink against a wall. "You can close your eyes or turn away from the table."

"I don't think that'll happen, Dr. Bunting. I have a strong stomach. Not too many things bother me."

"Okay then. The reason I wanted y'all here was to give me feedback during the autopsy. Something you found in your investigation of the other victims may be pertinent to this death. As you already know, Robert Sears died in a car crash, apparently from head trauma. Although, I never assume the cause of death until I complete my autopsy. I've had many surprises. Like the previous five deaths with the same presentation of going suddenly deaf, mute, and blind. Of course, the final stage of undetermined death. Like I told your director yesterday, I've never seen or had any other medical examiner seen a person present with these symptomologies before death. A true medical mystery. Hopefully, we'll find something in Mr. Sears that wasn't present in the other five corpses."

"Did you do the other five victims' autopsies?" Simon asked, as he glanced down at autopsy table and the sixth victim.

"I did. Was there anything in your investigation I should check for?"

"We're not done with our investigation. So far, we don't have any clues pointing to a cause of their deaths."

Dr. Bunting walked to the right side of the table. Simon, Janet, and Karen stood on the left side of the table about one to two feet away from the corpse. Sean stood to the left of the medical examiner. A small metal table containing autopsy instruments stood between them. A small microphone was attached to the top of the pathologist's paper gown. He picked up surgical gloves from the metal table and put them on, then put on a plastic shield to protect his face. Sean handed him a scalpel. "Ms. Rivers, it sounds like I'm talking to myself; I'll be dictating my autopsy into a voice-activated dictation system. The program is set up for only recognizing my voice. I'll be using specific words, START, STOP, CONTINUE, then COMPLETED during my dictation referring to begin, pause, restart and finish the autopsy report. I'm sure Dr. Woods and Agent Bennett already know this."

They both nodded.

"Before I begin the autopsy, we already did a complete x-ray of the body. Surprisingly, there weren't any broken bones, including the bones in the neck and skull. There was bruising of the forehead when Mr. Sears struck the inflated airbag."

"It could mean internal injury from the car crash caused his death?" Simon commented.

"That could be one possibility."

He turned his attention toward the corpse. "START. This is case 1442. The deceased name is Robert Sears. I'll be making a 'Y' incision now. STOP."

Dr. Bunting placed the blade on the upper right chest area, cutting through the skin at a forty-five-degree angle to the upper mid-abdomen, exposing the right lung behind the ribs. He made the same incision from the upper left chest area, which was followed by an incision down the mid-abdomen to the lower pubic area, exposing the abdominal organs. With the help of Sean, they removed the whole ribcage. He removed both lungs, which were grossly normal. He then removed the larynx, esophagus, neck ligaments and arteries. He opened the larynx and esophagus. Dr. Bunting dictated what he did. "CONTINUE. Normal-appearing lungs. Tissue inside larynx and esophagus appear normal. STOP."

The medical examiner removed all the abdominal organs and weighed each one, then proceeded to describe the contents in the stomach. That was followed by him describing the appearance of the liver, pancreas, spleen, intestines, prostate gland. All of them were entirely normal.

During the autopsy, Simon glanced at Karen for any negative reaction. None. She seemed to have a strong constitution, unphased by the autopsy.

"As you know, Dr. Woods, the tissue analysis from the organs and the blood analysis results will take a few days. Hopefully, something will show up pointing to the cause of Mr. Sears going deaf, mute and blind since he didn't die suddenly like the other five deaths. Of course, I still have the brain to examine." He turned his attention toward Karen. "What do you think about the autopsy?"

"I find it fascinating and informative." She crossed her arms, resting them against her breast. "What I'm looking forward to is the brain exam. The brain seems to be the focal point of the victims' three symptoms before dying."

"Very good," Dr. Bunting said with a grin. "You're astute in your thinking. I thought the same thing when I began examining the first victim's brain. My thinking changed after completing the fifth brain, when there wasn't any evidence pointing to the cause of their deaths. Disappointing to say the least. Mr. Sears's brain may be different since he likely died of trauma to the brain. We'll soon find out."

He placed his scalpel about an inch above the right ear, pressing it against the scalp and began cutting through the thick skin of the scalp. He went completely around the skull, three hundred and sixty degrees.

Sean picked up a cylindrical metal instrument about a foot long with a circular blade at one end. He turned it on with a toggle switch at the opposite end. A high-pitched sound pierced the air, causing Simon, Janet and Karen to cringe. Sean placed the vibrated blade above the right ear, positioning the blade into the incision made by Dr. Bunting. He pressed down with the vibrating blade against the skull bone and began cutting through the bone. He went completing around the skull, along the forehead hairline and ending above the right ear. He then turned the saw off and placed it on the metal table. Sean reached down placing his gloved hands on both sides of the scalp and lifted the boney skull cap off the top of the head, exposing the brain,

"Oh my God," Karen said as her jaw dropped a few inches in apparent astonishment.

"Are you okay?" Simon asked. He was getting ready to catch her in case she began to pass out.

"Yes. I read about pathologist removing the top of the skull to get access to the brain, but as the saying goes, 'a picture is worth a thousand words.' This is a good example."

Dr. Bunting said, "CONTINUE. Using number fifteen scalpel blade, I made a three-hundred-and-sixty-degree incision around the scalp parallel to the forehead hairline. Using a Stryker saw, removed the skull cap, exposing the brain. STOP." He leaned forward and peered around the top of the brain. "CONTINUE. The upper hemispheres of the brain appear normal. STOP." He looked up at his audience. "I don't see any hemorrhaging, tumors, bruising of the brain. I'll remove the brain to get a better look at the total brain." Dr. Bunting, using a scalpel, he detached the brain from the spinal cord, major arteries, veins and nerves. He placed the brain on the metal table next to him and meticulously examined every inch of the brain. "CONTINUE. The right and left hemispheres of the brain externally appear grossly normal. STOP."

"So far, no evidence of trauma to the brain from the car accident." Simon stated.

"Not yet Dr. Woods. When I excise the hemispheres, we'll get a better look at the different structures inside of the brain." He looked at

Sean. "Hand me…"

Before he finished his command, Sean handed him a different shaped scalpel blade attached to a metal handle.

"Thanks."

Simon peered at Sean and nodded. "A good assistant knows your next move during surgical procedures."

Sean smiled and nodded, acknowledging Simon's statement.

Dr. Bunting made his incision, dividing the brain in half. He frowned as he stared down at the divided brain. "What in God's name is that?"

Chapter Eleven

Dr. Bunting leaned forward peering down at the brain. "I've never seen anything like this before."

Simon, Janet, and Karen walked around the exam table to the other side. Simon stared down at the brain. A tiny, black, worm-like entity about half an inch in length and a quarter of an inch in diameter slowly meandered between the crevices near the brain stem. "What are we looking at?"

"Not sure. I've seen maggots, blowfly larvae, but nothing like what we're seeing here inside this brain." He picked up a silver-colored forceps from the tray and gently pinched the wiggling creature, placing it into a clear plastic specimen container.

"Do you think this is what caused all these deaths?" Janet asked.

Dr. Bunting peered at the creature inside the container. "Don't have an answer to your question until after its analyzed. Whatever it is, how did it get into the brain?"

"Maybe through the blood stream when it was a tiny larva?" Simon suggested.

"Maybe? If that's true, some of its crawly friends should still be in Mr. Sears's blood." He turned to Sean. "Prepare a blood smear. Let's see if there are more of these things in his blood."

The medical examiner continued to dissect the brain, dictating his negative findings. A few minutes later, he had completed dissecting several sections of the brain. He didn't find any more of the strange creatures.

"The slide is ready," Sean announced. Dr. Bunting walked across the room to a microscope sitting on a white counter with several other different apparatuses.

Simon touched Janet's forearm. "We may be getting the answer to the cause of these deaths."

"Wouldn't that be great news," Karen exclaimed, jumping ahead of Janet's response to Simon's positive statement.

"If this mysterious thing turns out to be the cause of our victim's deaths," Janet said touching Simon's hand. "the next question would be, was it introduced to the six people intentionally, accidentally by someone, or was it an unfortunate act of Mother Nature?"

"The blood smear is clear of any culprits," Dr. Bunting said disappointedly. "It'll be a day or two before all the tissue and blood analyses reports are completed on Mr. Sears. Unfortunately, the tissue and blood report on the other victims were normal with no evidence of this thing harboring somewhere in their bodies. Of course, I wasn't specifically looking for it either." He dictated the blood smear results, then said, "COMPLETED." He turned to his audience. "This completes my autopsy of Robert Sears."

"I'll be anxious to know what this thing is," Simon said, "and if it was the cause of Mr. Sears's death. Please give me or Director Littlefield a call when you get the results."

"Sure will."

~ * ~

The three of them now sat inside the Suburban. Janet said, "I'm glad we were there during the autopsy. When we receive the pathology results, we'll be able to visualize in our mind what the crawly thing actually looked like."

Karen leaned forward from the backseat toward the opening between the front seats. "I observed you guys and the other FMI agents in Chambersburg investigating the cavers' deaths. I thought how exciting and rewarding your job was. Now being part of your team, not an outsider looking, is great. If you know what I mean?"

"I'm sure Janet can appreciate what you're saying, since she was in your position a few weeks ago."

Janet peered at Simon with a frown. She obviously didn't welcome his comment. "My situation was different, being a sheriff detective and used to investigating major crimes."

Karen sat back and buckled her seatbelt, not responding to Janet's comment.

Simon felt a situational chill inside the car between the two female occupants. He probably shouldn't have compared Janet with Karen. Women could be territorial when it came to caring about a male friend, especially when another female, a competitor, appeared to be encroaching on her love interest, namely him. "It's near five o'clock. Janet, can you call Director Littlefield and let him know we're leaving the morgue? Ask him if he'll let everyone know to meet in our room for a discussion on our findings with the medical examiner."

"Sure. I'll be glad to call for you." She emphasized the *you*.

After making the call to their director, and telling him everything discovered at the autopsy, she put her phone away. She then said to Simon, "He's also excited about the pathologist having a possible diagnosis of the previous undetermined death assessment of the six victims."

"After discussing our findings with the other agents," Karen said directing her question toward Simon, "what are we going to do the rest of the evening?"

Simon had to be careful in answering Karen's question, since he didn't know what motive she might have for asking it. "Agent Bennett and I have some things to go over. You can do what you want, like relax. Nothing more is planned until tomorrow morning when we interview the victims' places of employment."

He glanced at Janet, who displayed a grin. She obviously was pleased with his answer to Karen.

"Oh. I see. No more excitement for the day."

Simon thought about what he and Janet could do for excitement. Of course, he kept his thoughts to himself.

He parked the Suburban in the hotel's parking lot. They exited the vehicle, then walked toward the entranceway.

~ * ~

A dark-blue sedan had pulled into the parking lot several seconds behind them, parking several spaces down from their vehicle. A full-bearded man sat behind the steering wheel and watched the trio go into the hotel. Alex Mandelson speed dialed a number. The name on the phone was P. Pearson. After the second ring, Alex said, "They're back to the hotel after visiting Jefferson Medical Examiner's Office. The examiner did an autopsy on Robert Sears. He died in a car crash. Sears went blind while driving his car and struck a tree, killing him. Not sure if they found anything during the autopsy."

"I'll find out. FMI still doesn't know what killed the other five people, just like they won't know why Sears went deaf, mute, and blind. Of course, he would've died tomorrow if he hadn't killed himself in the car accident. Continue watching them."

~ * ~

Simon removed his cardkey from his pants' pocket to open his hotel room door. The door was ajar. He heard a mixture of voices inside the room. The three of them walked into the room.

Frank sniffed. "Formaldehyde."

Simon chuckled. "Can't get anything by you. I'm glad we didn't stop for pizza, otherwise you would've asked if we brought back some for you."

"You know me well, boss."

Simon proceeded and told everyone in the room what the medical examiner found inside the brain of the sixth victim, Robert Sears.

"Holy crap," Frank exclaimed. "Worms in the brain. This sounds like a B-movie horror flick."

"They found one worm-like creature. Won't know exactly what

it is until it's analyzed by the forensic lab people. We'll probably know by tomorrow."

"How did the thing get into the victim's brain?" Jean asked.

"Dr. Bunting, the medical examiner, believes it may have come from the blood stream. The blood or tissue taken from our victim may hold the answer. All the autopsy specimens are sent to the forensic lab department for analysis."

Danny stood, then asked, "So, the other victims didn't have this thing inside them?"

"No. I suspect the pathologist will have the forensic lab personnel examine more tissue samples from the other five victims' various organs, like the liver, spleen, kidneys, and heart."

"The game is afoot," Frank proclaimed.

"What does that supposed to mean?" Karen questioned.

"Don't ask him," Jean said. "We'll be here a while, as he explains its meaning."

"I'll give a brief explanation. It basically means 'something exciting has started or is happening.' The phrase first appeared in the play *King Henry IV* written by William Shakespeare in 1597. Sherlock Holmes also used the infamous phase."

"You're an extraordinary person," Karen said with admiration, staring into his eyes.

Simon peered at Janet, who gazed back at him with a sparkle in her eyes, along with a smile. Was she reacting to Karen's flirtatious comment toward Frank, deferring any suspicious interest the biochemist may have toward him?

"It's almost five-thirty," Brian said. "Why don't we all go for dinner? I'm buying."

Frank didn't respond to the mention of food, instead continued staring at Karen. *He is obviously smitten,* thought Simon as he glanced at Frank then Karen.

"I have to stop by my room," Karen said. "I'll catch up with you all."

'I'll wait for you," Frank suggested. "We can walk over to the restaurant together."

Simon looked at Frank with envy because he wished Janet had a room for herself, instead of having to share it with Jean. The restaurant was filled with patrons as the waitress escorted the party of seven to the far end of the restaurant. She put together two tables, creating enough space for seven chairs. Simon, of course, sat next to Janet. During the next hour, Frank talked mostly with Karen on a variety of subjects. Simon talked with everyone at the table but much of his time, he conversed with Janet. Periodically their shoes would intentionally touch. This sensuous gesture sent desire through his body and mind. They needed time alone, time to enjoy each other's company. He thought about going out to the Suburban with her. No. That would be what high school kids would do, not two mature adults. He wanted the paramount moment to be special without any distractions.

"Simon. Simon," Janet repeated as she gently nudged his foot with her foot.

"Sorry. I was thinking about something." He'd love to tell her what he was thinking but would rather show her. "What were you saying?"

"I wasn't saying anything. Although, I was wondering about going for an evening drink somewhere."

Before Simon could answer, Frank said, "I heard of a place near the hotel and restaurant where they have karaoke, dancing and serve alcohol."

Simon looked at Frank then Janet. It was obvious Frank heard Janet's proposal. He needed to put a kibosh on this situation and say he and Janet wanted to be alone this evening. "Thanks for the information, but…"

"Sounds like fun," Janet interrupted.

Dang. I wasn't expecting that response from her. "Yeah. Sounds good to me, too."

Frank turned his attention toward Karen. "Would you like to go with us?"

"Sure. Love to go."

"How about you, guys?" He glanced at Danny, Jean and Brian.

"Nah."

"I'm going to stay here."

"Thanks for asking," they said, respectively.

Brian picked up the dinner bill from the table, glanced at the karaoke-bound group, then said, "You guys enjoy yourself."

Simon pulled out of the hotel's parking lot and headed to the karaoke lounge mentioned by Frank. Janet sat in the front passenger seat. Frank and Karen sat in the backseat.

Karen leaned forward, looking at Janet to her right, then said, "Why did you become a detective for Marion County Sheriff Department?"

"Why do you ask?"

Simon heard a hint of cynicism in Janet's voice. Right from the first time they met Karen, he saw skepticism from Janet toward Karen. Was it jealously because Ms. Rivers was pretty, intelligent and had an assertive personality? Maybe it was due to the fact they both had all three of these characteristics?

"Curious. That's all."

"Oh."

Simon parked the Suburban in a black-topped parking lot. In front of them stood a one-story brick building. A large sign on a windowless wall to the right of the front door stated Razorback Lounge. Underneath the name was a painting of a red razorback wild pig, resembling the University of Arkansas's mascot. Simon peered to the left and right ends of the building and noticed security cameras pointed toward the parking lot and front door. Did this mean the lounge had a lot of civil disturbances with its patrons and their vehicles?

The lounge's ten to twelve rectangular and square tables were probably fifty percent occupied by patrons. A bar to their left was about forty feet long with high back stools spaced a few feet apart and at least seventy percent of the stools sat men and women. At the far end of the rectangular-shaped room stood a long table with karaoke machines, a man and woman in western outfits sat behind the table. A large banner hung down from the front of their Karaoke table, "Country Sweethearts. Brian & Lucia." There was parquet wooden dance floor about twelve-foot square with three couples dancing underneath a large silver ball with multiple colored lights streaming down on them. A slow, melodic western song was being sung by a female karaoke singer. The four of them sat at a four-chair square table at the edge of the dance floor.

"What's everyone drinking?" Simon asked. "I'll get the first round."

"I'll help you carry them back," Janet suggested.

She stood with Simon and walked to the bar with him.

"I was surprised when you accepted Frank's suggestion of coming here."

"I want to be with you alone, as much as you do. I want it to be special without any outside interference or distractions. Coming here to the lounge we can hold each other while dancing."

"You're right in your thinking."

Besides being attracted to her for various reasons, he liked her practical thinking. They carried the drinks back to their table.

After a few minutes of talking, a slow county love song projected out from speakers accompanied by a male voice singing into a handheld microphone. Frank asked Karen to dance, she agreed. They walked onto the dance floor.

"Do want to dance?" Simon asked as he gazed into her sensuous brown eyes.

"I thought you never ask."

They stood. Simon reached out, gently grabbed her hand and led her to the dance floor. There were now six other couples dancing. Frank and Karen were about twelve feet away, not paying any attention to him and Janet. Simon put his free hand around to her mid-back, as he pulled her body to his. Her breast touched his lower chest wall, sending sensuous warmth throughout his body, increasing his heart rate and breathing. Their bodies began moving to the rhythm of the music. "You follow my every step great," he whispered into her ear.

She gently squeezed his hand which was resting on the upper

right area of his chest. "It goes to show how well our body chemistries work and play together."

Right now, it was the *play* aspect of her statement he was concentrating on. He reciprocated her gesture and words by squeezing her hand. He leaned his head back, staring into her eyes. Her moistened, glistening lips slightly parted as if saying to him, "press your lips against mine." His eager lips moved closer to Janet's lips. He held his breath when his lips were about two inches away, anticipating a passionate kiss.

"Hey, guys," Frank said dancing with Karen. They were about six feet away behind Janet. "Great place for dancing. Don't you think?"

Simon jerked his head back, causing all his built-up amorous feelings to dissipate instantaneously. He tilted his head to the right peering at Frank, who was holding Karen close to his body without their torsos touching. "Yeah. Great place."

The music stopped. Most of the people in the room clapped their hands as the karaoke singer placed the microphone into a holder attached to a stand which also held a twenty-inch flatscreen monitor. Simon placed his hand on Janet's upper midback as they walked back to their table. The last time he'd gone dancing was about five years ago. He loved dancing, especially holding Janet, a woman he dearly cared about, and flowing with the music, arousing sensuous feelings affecting every nerve ending in his body.

Janet picked up her drink. "I'd like to make a toast to Karen, our newest temporary addition to our team."

Everyone picked up their mixed drinks and touched each other's glasses in the center of their table.

"Thank you," Karen said. "That's very kind of you all…especially Janet."

It appeared to Simon Janet had made amends to Karen, a once-potential adversary to Janet regarding him. Frank was now her attraction, focusing her attention on him. The four of them danced two more times. As the last dance ended, Simon kissed Janet briefly on her lips, then said, "Thanks for a great evening." Patrons began clapping, showing their appreciation toward the female karaoke singer

Janet whispered in his ear, "I enjoyed it too. I look forward to many more."

Frank and Karen walked over to them. Both had beaming smiles. "Are we going back to the hotel?"

"Yes. It's almost ten o'clock. We have a long day tomorrow."

"I agree, boss."

When they were a few feet from the Suburban, Karen said, "Stop. I hear something." She turned off her audio apparatus. "It's coming from inside the vehicle."

Could it be a bomb with a mechanical timer ready to explode if they opened any of the Suburban's doors? Simon wasn't thinking about any evil thoughts as they left the lounge; only amorous thoughts were running through his mind. He had let his guard down. "Can you make out what it is?"

"I need to get a little closer to the vehicle."

The four of them stepped forward a few feet, then stopped a foot away from the Suburban. Karen turned her head with her right ear a few inches from the side of the vehicle. She chuckled.

"What's so funny?" Simon asked.

"It's the theme sound to *Star Wars*."

"It's my cell phone," Frank admitted. "I must've left it in the car."

Janet frowned. "Simon. I remember sitting in Northgate Diner with you when I first met you and your cell phone had the same *Star Wars* theme ring."

"That's right. I didn't find it mature being the leader of the FMI team, so I changed the ring to a normal ring the following day." He realized what he said. "I didn't mean to say it was immature." He directed his statement to Frank.

"No problem, boss. I..."

"I think the ring is great," interrupted Karen. "I love all the movies."

Karen was defending Frank. A good sign she had favorable feelings toward him, Simon thought as he removed the car keys from his pocket. Simon unlocked the doors. They all piled into the vehicle and drove out of Razorback Lounge's parking lot.

~ * ~

Alex Mendelson sat in his car. In the passenger seat sat an electronic device the size of a soda can with three wires making a loop from one end of the can to the other. The wires were green, black, and white. A small glass tube filled with a liquid was attached to the side of the device. He watched the Suburban with the four FMI team members inside drive out of the parking lot.

Alex couldn't believe it. The parking lot had too many security cameras. No way he could've planted his explosive device underneath FMI's vehicle. These agents lived a charmed life. Another opportunity to eliminate some of the agents was foiled.

Chapter Twelve

The morning sun shined through large windows on the eastern side wall of the restaurant. Simon and Brian walked over to the table where the rest of the FMI team were sitting. "Morning everyone," greeted Brian before he sat down next to Janet.

"I understand you guys had a great time dancing last night," Jean said, briefly glancing at Janet, then Simon.

"Yes," Simon answered. "It had a good dance floor. The karaoke music and singers were good."

He wanted to say the evening wouldn't have been the same without Janet's company. Holding Janet in his arms while dancing was heavenly. "We have a busy day today. Karen will be coming with Janet and me this morning like I stated yesterday. Frank and Jean will team up. Of course, Danny will be holding down the fort here at the hotel in front of his computer in case we need his help. Hopefully…"

The waitress came to the table, and said, "Are you all ready to order?"

They gave their breakfast order to the waitress.

"As I was about to say, I hope the medical examiner calls us with the results of what the worm-like creature was, and how the creature found its way into the brain."

Forty minutes later, they completed their breakfast. The conversations varied in topics but generally were about their previous investigations. Simon chuckled to himself regarding Frank. He was trying to impress Karen on his involvement on FMI's cases over the past few months.

Simon peered over at Frank. "After you guys finish interviewing the people at the victims' job site, we'll meet back at the hotel."

"Got it, boss." He turned to Jean. "Are you ready?"

"I'm ready."

"I'll see you all later," Brian said, as he brought out a credit card, then picked up the bill for their breakfast from the table.

~ * ~

Simon sat behind the steering wheel of the Suburban. Karen sat in the back seat of the Suburban, and Janet sat into the front passenger seat. Janet reached forward and put the address of the first victim's place of work into the vehicle's GPS. "One down, one to go," she said.

"What's the name of the company we'll be checking out?" Karen asked.

Janet peered down at the printout with the name of the five victims and their place of employment. "Cloverleaf Manufacturing. Barbara Casper, our first victim, worked there as a gauge technician."

"Gauge technician?"

"They make gauges for various machinery?'

The GPS's female synthesizer's voice said, "Turn left onto Patton Street." Simon turned left at the traffic light intersection onto Patton Street. "Continue for twenty miles."

About forty minutes later, a one-story concrete block building stood about fifty yards back from the street. A large sign to the right of the driveway read "Cloverleaf Manufacturing." A figure of gauges was below the name. They parked the Suburban near the front of the building. There were about thirty vehicles in the parking lot. The three of them exited the vehicle and walked toward the building's front entrance. The rumbling sound of thunder caused Janet and Simon to stop, followed by Karen, who had a puzzled expression, apparently not sure why they stopped. Simon and Janet turned around and looked up at dark clouds of an approaching storm. Janet peered at their Suburban. No trees were near their vehicle. She looked at Simon and grinned. "It should be safe from the storm. No trees in the area."

He raised his eyebrows and rolled his eyes. "Thank God. Another totaled Suburban wouldn't look good on our car insurance record."

Karen chuckled. "Oh. Now I know why you turned around. It's about your previous Suburban being destroyed by a lightning strike."

They turned back around and went into the building.

A receptionist, who appeared to be in her mid-forties, sat at a desk about twenty feet in front of them. Hanging on the walls to their right and left were glassed-in photographs of various gauges. "Good morning. Can I help you?"

"Yes. I am Agent Woods. This is Agent Bennett and Karen Rivers. We're from FMI, a division of CDC, investigating the death of one of your employees, Barbara Casper."

"Such a tragedy. It's still hard to believe she's not with us anymore." She frowned. "Why is the CDC interested in her death? Did she have something contagious?"

"We don't think it's contagious because…"

"You don't think it's contagious?" interrupted the receptionist. "This could mean I might get what she and the others had."

"There's no medical evidence these deaths were caused from a virus or other organism either by airborne or by physical contact. You have nothing to worry about."

"Thank the Lord." She sighed. "You had me worried for a moment."

Janet was grateful Simon defused a possibly volatile situation with the receptionist, who might have spread panic to other workers, her friends, and relatives. "How many people are employed here?"

"Don't know the exact number, but I'd say between thirty to forty employees." She reached down to her desk phone and made a call. "I'll have you talk with our plant manager, Eddy Smith. He'll be able to answer all your questions."

She told the person at the other end of the call about FMI and why they were here. After hanging up the phone she said, "Please have a seat over there," and pointed to a large couch to her left against the wall.

"He'll be here shortly."

In a few minutes, the manager walked into the lobby through a door behind the receptionist. He walked up to the FMI team. "I'm Eddy Smith." He reached out and shook their hands. "Come with me to my office. We can talk in there."

To get to Mr. Smith's office, they walked through a large room containing numerous rectangular tables. Sitting in metal high-back chairs, employees were performing various tasks on a variety of circular and square gauges. "What are the gauges used for?" Janet asked as she peered around the room.

"Farm tractors, cotton gin machinery, and other industrial equipment."

Janet saw many cotton fields as they drove around Pine Bluff. She chuckled to herself. According to Frank, before they landed yesterday, he stated Arkansas was a leader in the production of cotton. One bale of cotton produces two hundred and fifteen pair of jeans. Frivolous information worth a conversation and a cup of coffee orated by Jean about Frank on more than one occasion since Janet joined FMI. They walked into Eddy Smith's office. The office's front glassed-in wall overlooked the plant. They sat on folding chairs in front of a small metal desk facing Mr. Smith, who sat in his desk chair.

"Did you notice any physical or emotional changes in Barbara Casper over the past couple of weeks affecting her quality of work?"

"No. She is…that is, was, her normal self. No indication anything was wrong with her. It was a complete surprise to me and everyone here at the plant. The one thing she did say relating to her ears was three days before she went deaf. She said it felt like something was crawling inside her right ear causing a fullness sensation. She said it didn't cause any pain or discomfort. I told her it might be wax build up. She said she'd go to the drug store and get ear drops to remove any wax."

Simon looked into Janet's eyes. "Are you thinking what I'm thinking?"

"Worm."

Mr. Smith grunted. "A worm? Did she have a worm in her ear?"

Should he lie to Mr. Smith? Although, what other explanation was there regarding the crawling, fullness sensation in Barbara Casper's ear? "Not sure. Only an assumption."

"It's not unusual for people to have bugs or crawly creatures in their ears," Karen stated. "When I was an EMT, I saw ants, cockroaches, spiders, or flies come out of the ear."

Mr. Smith shivered. "You gotta be kidding me!"

When they walked out of Cloverleaf Manufacturing, Simon visualized the black worm-like creature inside Barbara Casper's ear. If it were the same type of creature seen in the sixth victim's brain, how could it get through the ear drum without causing excruciating pain? The tympanic membrane was extremely sensitive to anything touching it.

Once outside, Janet asked Simon, "Do you think the thing discovered in Robert Sears's brain had come through his ear?"

"Unlikely. If the thing had touched his eardrum, he would've been in unbearable pain. The victim told his wife he suddenly became deaf. No mention of ear pain or something crawling in his ear."

"We'll need to call all the victim's families," Simon ordered, "and ask them if their loved one complained about something in their ear or a sensation of something moving around in their ear."

"If you like, I can call some of the families," Karen suggested.

"Sure. While I'm driving to the next victim's place of employment, the two of you can call."

"Sounds like a good plan to me," Janet added.

She turned to Karen. "I'll give you half the names." When they were sitting in the Suburban, Janet downloaded the address of the next victim's workplace. "It's thirty-seven miles to Larry Mandle's job site. He worked for Perfect Cabinets as a finish carpenter."

"So, they make kitchen cabinets?" Karen asked as she removed a cell phone from her pocket.

"Yes. He recently received an increase in his hourly wages according to his parents when we interviewed them yesterday."

Janet handed Karen two of the victim's home phone number with their name and the name of the person she and Simon had interviewed.

"You know what to ask them? Right?"

"Yes. Did their loved one ever complain of something in their ears or an unusual sensation?"

"You have it. Welcome to FMI's forte."

Janet then gave her the name and phone numbers of three victims' families.

Simon listened to Janet and Karen as they conversed with the victim's family members. Each of them asked family members to question other people in their families and friends about the victim's complaining about their ears prior to going deaf.

As Janet was talking with Jessica Martin, the wife of the second victim, Timothy Martin, she turned toward Simon and said, "So, Mrs. Martin, you're sure he complained of a crawling sensation in his left ear about three days before he went deaf." Short pause. "I appreciate talking with you. We'll be sure to contact you when we find the cause of your husband's death."

Karen was still talking on the phone but turned toward Janet, raising her thumb upward and nodded, apparently hearing what Janet had said. She then lowered her head. "Thank you, Mrs. Fredrick. Sorry for your loss." Karen set the phone down on her lap. "She had no knowledge of her husband complaining of an ear symptom prior to going deaf."

"Of course," Simon said, "it doesn't mean he hadn't felt anything, only that he didn't tell his wife or anybody during his hospital admission history."

Janet glanced toward the dashboard, then said, "I don't believe it's a coincident two victims felt a crawling sensation inside their ears a few days prior to them going deaf. We have three more victims' families to call." She picked up her phone a called the next number on her list. Karen did the same and called her next number.

Simon agreed with Janet about the crawling sensation in the ears of two victims, it wasn't a coincidence. This mysterious creature might be the common link to all the victims' deaths. There are now more questions to this investigation. Such as, who, how and why someone placed these wormy creatures inside these victims' ears? The FMI team needed to know if there were any other ear complaints prior to them going deaf. Simon hoped they had found the smoking gun in this case of five undetermined deaths, plus the sixth victim who would've probably died like the other five victims if he hadn't crashed his car into a tree.

Ten minutes later, Karen said, "Thank you, Ms. Barron. You've been a help in our investigation. Once we hear if the crawling sensation in your brother's ear meant anything, we'll let you know."

"Yes," Simon said zealously. "This is our first clue in the deaths of our six victims."

He glanced at Janet, who was still talking on the phone. During her conversing with the person at the other end of the phone call, he didn't hear Janet say anything regarding the third victim complaining of symptoms prior to the hearing loss.

"We'll call you if we find anything out regarding your husband's death." She placed her cell phone in her blazer's front inside pocket, opposite side of her holstered Glock. "The wife didn't hear her husband complaining about any ear symptoms prior to him going deaf, but she'll check with their friends if he happened to mention anything to them. If my calculations are correct, that makes three of the six victims having ear symptoms prior to going deaf. The other three victims' families may still call us back about their loved ones telling someone about ear symptoms three days prior to experiencing complete deafness."

The GPS announced, "In one mile, turn right at the traffic light."

Simon glanced down the GPS's statistical LED readout. "We'll arrive at our destination in two and a half minutes."

The Suburban turned right at the traffic light. The GPS stated, "You've arrived at your destination on the right." A one-story brick building had a rectangular sign above the front door that spelled out "Perfect Cabinets." There were several vehicles parked in a blacktopped front parking lot. The sun was directly over their heads as the three of them walked through the front door. Immediately the odor of wood and varnish permeated the air. Numerous styles of kitchen cabinets lined the wall on their left and right in a display room measuring probably thirty feet long by twenty feet wide.

A man in his mid-fifties sat at a desk with file cabinets behind him. "Can I help you?"

"Yes. I'm Agent Simon Woods from FMI, a division of CDC. We're here investigating the death of one of your employees, Larry Mandle."

He furrowed his eyebrows. "What does FMI stand for? I know CDC stands for Center for Disease Control."

This is the first person to ask what FMI stood for, thought Simon. "Federal Medical Investigators."

"Did Larry have some kind of deadly disease?"

"It's what we're trying to determine, Mister..."

"Oh. Yeah. I'm Mike Turner. I'm one of the salesmen." He stood and shook every ones' hand. "It was a shock when Larry died. He always appeared so healthy and in good spirits."

"We'd like to know if Mr. Mandle complained about anything prior to him losing his hearing?" Janet asked.

"Not that I remember. He loved to talk about fishing and couldn't wait to throw a line in the water the upcoming weekend. Let me call the manager of the company and let him know you're here investigating Larry's death."

He reached down on the desk, picked up a phone and pushed three numbers on the keypad. After a few seconds, Mr. Turner said, "There are three people from CDC investigating Larry Mandle's death. They'd like to talk with each of the employees regarding his death." A short pause. "I'll bring them back there." He put the phone back into its cradle. "Follow me. We'll go to the lunchroom."

Over the PA system speaker in the ceiling, Simon heard a man announce, "Everyone please go to the lunchroom immediately for a meeting."

The odor of wood and varnish was even more prevalent when they walked into the work area of the plant. The decrescendo sound of power saws being turned off and the snapping sound of nail guns abruptly ceasing filled the room as they all walked on top of a sawdust-covered concrete floor. There were about sixteen workers standing or sitting in a table-filled lunchroom.

A balding man in his early sixties glanced at Mr. Turner and the FMI team as they walked into the lunchroom. "Everyone, please take a seat. Our guests are here."

Mr. Turner introduced the FMI team to the plant manager, Edward Hall, then said, "I have to get back to the lobby." He left leaving Simon, Janet, Karen and Mr. Hall standing in front of the seated employees.

"Listen up everyone, these agents are from CDC regarding the death of Larry Mandle."

Simon cleared his throat. "Good morning, I'm Agent Simon Woods. We'd like to know if Mr. Mandle complained about anything regarding his ears. Prior to him going deaf."

There was a low murmur of voices as some of the employees conversed with people around them. A moment later, a female stood and said, "I remember him saying to me two or three days before he went deaf, he thought he had sawdust clogging his ear."

"Did he say what it felt like?"

"Yeah. He said it felt like something was moving around inside his ear."

"Do you know if it caused pain?"

"He didn't say. All I know he said he was going to the drug store and buy an ear wax remover kit. Which was on a Friday. On Monday he didn't come to work. He went to the hospital early Monday morning due to his sudden deafness. I talked with him Monday evening at the hospital but forgot to ask him if he used the wax remover kit."

It was more information than I asked for. "Thank you for the information."

"Do you know what caused him to die?" asked a man near the back table.

"No. Not yet," Janet answered. "I'm sure we will, though."

"Does anybody else remember any other medical complaints Larry Mandle voiced a week or two prior to his last day at work?" Simon looked around the room. Several seconds elapsed without a response. "If anyone remembers something medically about Mr. Mandle, something unusual, it may be pertinent. Please give us a call. I'll leave our contact cell phone number with Mr. Hall. Thank you for your time."

"Thank you for an unscheduled break," said someone in the center of the room.

Mr. Hall escorted the FMI team to the front door. Simon had given him a couple of business cards. "I appreciate your time and allowing us to speak with your employees."

"You're welcome. I hope you find the cause of Larry's death."

"We'll be doing our best." Simon shook his hand.

They now sat in the Suburban. Janet buckled her seat belt. "Now that was a fast and efficient way to interview people. If we had to talk to each employee personally, it probably would've taken us at least an hour."

Karen leaned forward toward the opening between the two front seats. "We now have four out of six victims complaining of something crawling or moving around inside their ear three days before they went deaf."

"I hope the medical examiner gets an answer to what the crawly creature is today," Simon said. "What we can assume now is this thing entered the victims' brains through the ear. How it entered through the tympanic membrane without causing pain is a medical mystery."

Simon's cell phone rang. He retrieved it from his belt holder, glanced at caller. It was Frank. "Hi, Frank. We finished up with our second job site. Both victims experienced the same ear symptom. A crawling sensation inside the ear canal three days prior to them going deaf. What did you find out at your three workplaces?"

"Something Jean and I thought would steer our investigation in a different direction."

Chapter Thirteen

"What do you mean, steer our investigation in a different direction?" Simon asked.

"Before you called me, we were about to call you and tell you about our three victims experiencing ear symptoms described as a crawling sensation three days before losing their hearing. It means now all five victims presented with the same prehearing loss symptoms."

"Yes. Adding Timothy Martin, Donald Barron, and Charles Fredrick means all five victims demonstrated this ear symptom. We'll need to call and talk with the sixth victim's wife. I have a feeling she's going to say her husband complained about the crawling sensation too. Meet you and Jean back at the hotel."

"I'll call Mrs. Sears," suggested Janet. "Do we have her phone number?"

"No. You'll need to call the medical examiner's office for the number." Simon started the vehicle and pulled out of the parking lot, heading back to the hotel.

Janet called the ME's office and put Mrs. Sears' phone number into her cell phone. She called the number. The phone rang three times. "Hello, Mrs. Sears. This is Agent Janet Bennett from the Federal Medical Investigators, a division of CDC. I'm so sorry for your loss. We're doing an investigation on your husband's medical condition before his death this morning." A momentary pause. "I have a question to ask you. Did your husband complain about an ear sensation a few days before he went deaf?"

Janet listened to Mrs. Sears' answer. "Are you sure he said it felt like something was crawling inside his ear?" Another pause. "Thank you. As soon as we find anything out of how your husband went deaf, mute and blind we'll let you know." Janet put her phone away.

Simon stopped for a red light. "All we have to do now is find out if it was the worm-like creature we found in Mr. Sears' brain had entered through the tympanic membrane."

"Shouldn't we notify the medical examiner about our findings?" Janet asked. "I believe he checked the ear canals of Mr. Sears during the autopsy."

"He did check the ears, but only for a few seconds. Knowing what we know now about each of the victims complaining of a crawling sensation inside their ears, I think he'll want to look more thoroughly at the ear drum for scarring, previous perforation or a tiny opening."

"I'll call the medical examiner's office."

"Put the phone on speaker when you reach the ME's office. I'll talk with Dr. Bunting."

Janet pushed the number for Pine Bluff ME.

The phone rang twice. "Jefferson County Medical Examiner and Coroner's Office. Can I help you?"

"This is Agent Bennett from the Federal Medical Investigators. Can you connect me to Dr. Bunting?"

"Hold please."

Several seconds passed, then, "Yes. Agent Bennett. What can I do for you?"

"Dr. Woods has something to talk with you regarding your autopsy on Robert Sears."

"Hi, Dr. Bunting we found something that may shine a light on the worm-like creature you found in Sears' brain. Each of the victims complained about a crawling sensation in their ear canal three days before they went deaf. Can you recheck Sears' auditory canal and tympanic membrane for…?"

"Perforation or scarring of the ear drum," interrupted Dr. Bunting with excitement in his voice. "Sure will. It could be how the black worm-like thing caused havoc to his inner ear, then traveled to the speech and optic center of the brain causing him to lose his speech and sight. I did find the thing near the brain stem which controls the function of the whole body, particularly the area controlling the rhythm of the heart. I'll check his ears right away and call you back." The call ended.

"I'd say this creature was the cause of our victims' deaf, mute, and blind conditions before their eventual deaths," Simon conjectured. "Once the medical examiner confirms this assumption, we'll need to know how this thing crept into their ears, who would want to do this evil deed and for what purpose?"

Janet handed Simon's cell phone back to him, then said, "This would also bring up the questions, were these victims somehow connected to each other or were they randomly chosen? Or like what we said earlier, was this an unfortunate act of Mother Nature?"

Karen's cell phone rang. "Hello." A short pause, as she apparently was listening to the person on the other end of the line. "I'll let 'em know. Bye." She put her phone in her slack's pocket. "It was Frank. He said for us to meet them in his room. Danny has something to show us."

"Did he say what it was?" Simon asked as he saw their hotel come into view up ahead to his left.

"No. Other than he developed a new computer software."

A moment later, they parked the Suburban and went into the hotel. Simon knocked on the computer wizards' door. Jean opened the door and said, "Hi, guys."

Simon summarized what had transpired with the wife of the sixth victim. He also mentioned they called the medical examiner regarding him reexamining the sixth victim's ears. Simon stood next to Danny, who sat on a chair with his back in front of his two computers, as everyone listened of what was being said. "Does anyone have any questions or comments?"

Brian Littlefield, who had been sitting at the end of the bed, stood and said, "Even though we're at the beginning of this investigation, it pleasantly enlightened me how well the FMI team works together in solving a medical mystery. I'm proud to be part of this organization."

"Thanks for the comment." Simon glanced at everyone in the room, then added, "Speaking for everyone, we appreciate your kind words."

Simon turned to Danny, "Tell us about your new computer software."

"As you know, computer software is programmed to tell the computer what to do and how to do it, such as checking for misspelled words. It's the operational system enabling the user to even turn on the computer, including what search engine you choose to use. Anyway, we all know our nemesis is The Circle. I've tried to break into their mainframe but was stopped by the various firewalls and encryptions. I was sitting in front of my computers early this morning when I suddenly visualized a device and software capable of penetrating any firewall or encryption, then pinpoint the locations of computers being used by individuals or organizations, such as The Circle through their IP addresses."

"IP addresses?" Karen questioned. "I think I know...explain it to a computer novice?"

"Oh. It stands for Internet Protocol. The IP address is a numerical label assigned to each computer connected to a computer communication network. An IP address serves two main functions. A host or network for interface identification. Second, it locates where the computer physically exists."

"So, it's like picking up a phone book for the name, phone number and street address of a person or company."

"Exactly," Danny agreed. "Although, I'm not sure they even print phonebooks anymore? I think they're solely on electronic devices, such as computers, tablets, and iPhones."

"Yeah. You're right. In the near future phonebooks will be alongside phonebooths in museums."

"How does your program get through firewalls?" Simon asked.

Danny turned his swivel chair toward Simon. "To not confuse you with computer jargon and technical concepts, it sort of metaphorically knocks on the computer's firewall barrier and politely asks entrance to deliver an important package. In addition, it'll tell me who they've been communicating with by their IP address through all their computers throughout the world. It's a revolutionary concept computer programmers and hackers have only dreamed about. They never could develop this program…until I figured it out."

"Have you gotten through The Circle's firewall?"

"Yes, but only for several seconds. Not enough time to obtain any vital information. I'm working on increasing the time from my so-called visitor's pass. I hope to have my program fully functional by the end of the day. We'll be able to locate people, groups, institutions, companies affiliated with The Circle."

"Your creation is an innovation of tomorrow," Karen interjected. "That's what your ingenious program sounds like to me."

"Hum." Danny nodded. "Thank you for your comment."

Simon's cell phone rang. He retrieved his phone and glanced at the caller ID. It was Dr. Bunting. He put his phone on speaker. "Hi, Dr. Bunting. Did you find anything?"

"Yes. Robert Sears' right ear drum had a previous perforation site. A slit across the tympanic membrane, allow the creature to slide through easily, then close once it was inside the middle ear. Since Sears didn't complain of pain when this creature penetrated the ear drum, I'd speculate it had secreted an enzyme which numbed the ear drum's membrane, before slithering through the compromised ear drum. It's the one logical explanation of why he didn't cry out in pain. What also was interesting, the width of the slit through the ear drum was a quarter of an inch."

"Wasn't a quarter of an inch the diameter of the black worm-like creature you found in Sears' brain?" Simon questioned.

"Exactly. I removed the tympanic membrane and had my pathology assistant, Sean, take it to the forensic lab next door. I should know shortly what chemical substance or substances the creature secreted. What was even more amazing, the creature had bored through the middle, inner ear structures, then through the auditory nerve leading into the brain. I'll call you back and let you know what they found. This has been a bizarre case."

Bizarre cases are what we investigate, thought Simon. "Thanks, Dr. Bunting for letting me know what you found. Talk to you soon." He put his cell phone away.

Janet, who was sitting with Jean at the café table adjacent to the room's lone window, stood. "We're finally getting closer to solving these deaths. What we have to do now is determine how these crawling creatures happened to get into the victims' ears. If Danny can get into The Circle's computer system, we can find out if this evil network was responsible for the six deaths and the worm-like creature."

"Why don't we all go to lunch?" suggested Brian. "It's been a positive and rewarding morning by everyone."

"I'm going to stay here and work on my program," Danny said. "Can someone bring me back a hamburger, fries and a large soda?"

"Sure will, partner," Frank answered.

Frank walked next to Karen leading the group out of the room, followed by Brian and Jean, then Simon and Janet holding up the rear as everyone made their way up the hotel's hallway.

Simon reached for Janet's hand and held onto it. She turned her head, peering up at him with an endearing expression, and said, "It appears we have a couple's caravan."

"I agree." He gently squeezed her hand.

She reciprocated with a squeeze. It felt natural holding onto her hand. Something in the near future he looked forward to, along with several other things a caring, loving couple do together.

About thirty minutes into their lunch meal, Simon noticed Karen reach for her audio-enhancer. She must be listening to someone or an ominous noise. "Karen, do you hear something?"

"Yes. A man is talking about us. I don't recognize the voice."

Everyone at the table stopped talking. Each agent peered around the room for a man either talking to someone at a table or on their cell phone. Simon didn't see anyone fitting either scenario. "What is he saying?"

"He had been unable to deliver his package. He then mentioned your name. That's what cued me in on him."

Simon stood up and walked to the restaurant's front picture window which was about ten feet away from their table. He saw a bearded man's side view, from about thirty feet away. He appeared to be in his thirties, talking on a cell phone in the parking lot. The man turned ninety degrees toward him, exposing his frontal view. He looked familiar. Where had he seen him before? The man flashed across his mind. He was standing at the poolside pool in Virginia Beach.

Janet now stood next to Simon. "He's the guy at the pool in Virginia Beach."

"I agree. What's he doing here?"

Alex glanced up, staring at Simon and Janet. He said something to the person on the phone, then put his phone on a belt holster.

Janet leaned closer to the window. "If you take away his beard...oh, my God. It's Alexander Mendelson. We need to arrest him. At least detain him for the police." She and Simon hurried to the restaurant's front door.

Mendelson turned to his right, hurried into a white car, and sped away before Janet and Simon reached the restaurant's front door vestibule. They now stood outside. Mendelson's white car was nowhere to be seen.

~ * ~

When they went back into the restaurant and sat down at the table, Janet said, "I'm sure you want to know why we ran outside?"

"It did cross our minds," Frank said. "In fact, it scared the crap out of us."

"Simon and I are sure we saw Alex Mendelson standing outside. The guy who..."

"Impersonated Caleb Johnson," Jean interrupted. "And set off a fire alarm at the high school in Ocala. Plus, he was probably involved in the murder of the security guard at a car dealership in Detroit two years ago."

"He's the guy," Janet confirmed. "Simon and I also saw him at our hotel in Virginia Beach. We didn't realize it was him at the time since he had a full beard. Seeing him standing outside the restaurant I visualized him without the beard and concluded it was Mendelson. He, more than likely, has been following us since our Whispers Before Death Case in Ocala."

"So, he's probably the one trying to kill us," Frank said.

Janet placed her napkin on an empty lunch plate. "I'd bet on it. You made a good assumption. Unfortunately, we don't have any forensic evidence tying him to planting the bomb under your car. Once Danny gets his computer program fully working, we might be able to connect him to The Circle and their evil dealings."

Simon's cell phone rang. He glanced down at his phone. "It's Dr. Bunting. I'll put him on speaker. I'll lower the volume so only we'll be able to hear him." He placed his phone in front of him. "Hi, Dr. Bunting."

"I received the report back on the worm-like creature and the substance it left on the ear drum. The creature is in fact a parasitic worm containing two different enzymes. The first enzyme is a numbing anesthetic which likely was secreted on the ear drum, middle and inner ear structures and the auditory nerve preventing pain prior to the worm's second enzyme, a corrosive substance enabling it to easily bore through these structures. The auditory nerve leading into the brain was immediately destroyed by the second enzymes. The parasitic creature meandered to specific neurotransmitters in the brain, destroying them. In other words, it'll prevent nerve impulses from being sent out from the part of the brain dealing with speech and vision. Its final destination was the brain stem, ceasing all functions of the brain, which means death.

"For this creature to travel to specific parts of the brain along the same timeline," Simon interjected, "it had to be programmed."

"Correct. I was about to tell you CSU lab found a nanochip about the size of a grain of rice in the deadly worm. The nanochip must've directed the programmed worm to the hearing, speech, vision area of the brain. Of course, the brain stem sends the brain's nerve impulses to all the body organs. It's a perfect killing organism."

"It sure is, Dr, Bunting. What about the other five victims' nanochips? Why didn't you find them their brain?"

"Good question. After the CSU lab dissected the creature and extracted a sample of the two enzymes in different glands, one at the front and the other near the tail end, they then saw the microchip in the middle of the worm-like creature. Before they could remove the chip, there was a sudden corrosive action to the nanochip and the worm, dissolving them within several seconds. This is why I didn't find the creature or nanochip in the other victims. The lab techs must've triggered the nanochip to perform its last event."

"An ingenious technology."

This wasn't their first encounter with nanochips, thought Janet. The Circle had to be involved with this type of technology. Their evil intentions were at work again.

"I'll be changing the deaths of the five victims to homicide. The sixth victim, Robert Sears, death will be changed to First Degree Criminal Intent. I'll call the Pine Bluff Police Department and let 'em know what I found. The crime scene lab will try to trace down where this type of nanochip was made."

"We'll also investigate the nanochip at our end. Thanks for calling me back. We'll keep in touch." Simon put his phone in his belt holster.

Janet picked up her glass of ice water, drank some of it, then said, "This is sounding like the case in Ocala. We couldn't prove The Circle was responsible. I'm convinced they're involved with these six deaths. We'll need to know what company and what entity is making these nanochips. They may be from the Pine Bluff area or somewhere else."

"I can do this," Frank volunteered. "Danny's fine-tuning his new computer spy program."

"That'll be great," Janet said. Having two computer wizards had been an asset to their team. She glanced at Simon. A mental chill ran through her, realizing she had acted like the head of FMI team, again.

"I agree with everything you said. Besides, you're the member of the team with the most detective experience."

The waitress set down a bag next to Frank. "This is your take-out order."

"Thank you."

"We'll go back to Frank and Danny's room and discuss what we'll be doing next," Simon proposed.

Brian paid the bill, then they all walked back to the hotel. Danny was sitting in front of his two computers when they walked into the room. "Hey, guys. How was lunch?"

"Good," answered Simon.

He then told Danny what the medical examiner had told them.

Danny removed his hamburger from a Styrofoam container. "It's like something out of a science fiction novel. I love science fiction novels."

"Frank's going to search the Internet for any companies in Pine Bluff, Arkansas, or anywhere else in the United States involved in nanochip production or research."

"Danny, your spy program will be vital in our case," Janet stressed.

"Huh. Not like putting a little pressure on me," Danny responded.

"There's not much we can do until our two computer wizards have completed their task," Simon concluded.

Janet's cell phone rang. She glanced at the caller ID. No name, only a local phone number she didn't recognize. "Hello, this is Agent Bennett."

"It's Detective Rhodes."

"Detective Rhodes. How are you doing?" Everyone in the room turned their attention toward Janet. "I'm putting you on speaker, so everyone can hear you. We're in Agent Littlefield and Emerick's hotel room."

"I want to say thank you all for saving my life. The heart doctor said if I hadn't come in when I did, I would've likely died. I was immediately taken to the operating room. They put in a pacemaker. I won't be back to work for about four weeks. Detective Thomas will be taking over the investigation. Again, thanks to you all."

The agents responded with various comments, such as "glad you're doing great." "Take care." "Glad we could help."

Janet put her phone back into the belt holder. She stared at Simon, who peered down at the floor with a blunted affect. She knew the look.

Simon was having a vision.

Chapter Fourteen

"Simon, are you having a vision?" Janet asked, as she stood a few feet from where he was standing.

Simon blinked a few times as he brought his head back from staring down at the floor. "Yes. I saw ten people being shot by a gunman in an open area, possibly a park...or someone's large back yard."

"Can you describe the gunman?"

"He was a mid-thirty-year-old Caucasian with long, dark brown hair and a mustache. He wore a light blue T-shirt and dark blue jeans. He held a Glock in each hand, firing at random, shouting something at his victims. The victims ranged from teenagers to people in their sixties. The people were a mixture of Caucasian, Black, and Asian."

"About what time of the day was it?"

"It appeared to be late afternoon. The beginning of tree silhouettes were displayed across the ground."

"Since your visions occur within twenty-four hours, I'd say these people will be shot today." Janet glanced at her watch. It was two-fifteen. "We have about three to four hours to find out where this gathering of people is taking place. Plus, we'll have a fifty-mile radius to search for them."

Frank sat down in front of his computer. "I'll bring up a map on the computer." He turned his computer on. In less than a minute, he brought up a map. He then created a red circle designating a fifty-mile radius from where the hotel stood. "I'll print a few copies of the map." Three maps fell into the printer's front container.

Janet peered down at one of the maps. The red circle touched numerous cities and towns including Little Rock, Stuttgart, Monticello, Carthage, and Dewitt. "This is going to be a physically impossible feat to locate this future massacre. We need our fingers do the walking, or should I say a computer wizard or wizards."

"Janet's right," Simon agreed. "We need to prioritize our two situations. First, solving the six deaths, which have already occurred, and the second being the future tragic incident of ten people with some of them likely to be killed, paralyzed, or injured. I'd choose the latter." Everyone voted for the second choice.

Frank looked at Danny, who peered back at him. "Let's do it partner.

Danny swallowed his last bite of his hamburger. "I'm ready. I have fuel in my belly now."

Simon looked at Janet. "How do you think we should start this investigation of a future mass killer?"

"Search for any public gatherings registered within the counties of our fifty-mile radius, purchases of large quantity of alcohol. Check bakeries for birthday, anniversary, or wedding cakes to be delivered today for one of these events. Check party organizer companies for an event today. Check catering companies. "

"Sounds like a good plan," Danny said. "According to this map, there are eight counties within the fifty-mile radius from Pine Bluff." He turned to his left where Frank sat in front of his computer. "Our work is cut out for us. You take half the counties. I'll take the other half."

"Hopefully one of us will find the yellow brick road to the killer."

Danny nodded. "Hopefully."

The computer wizards began their search for the killer's killing field.

Janet walked toward the room's entrance door, then turned back around. "I've been thinking about the six victims, with each of them having the worm in their ears. One thing is for sure. These worms had to be placed in the ear canal without the victims knowing it. So, it had to be done while they were sleeping, unconscious due to a drug, or they were having an exam by a medical person when the creature was introduced into their ear."

"Good point," Simon said, as he sat down at the end of the bed. "What does anyone else think?"

"I agree with Janet," Jean answered. "I'd say for them sleeping when the creature was placed in their ear, their spouse or family member would have to be involved in the diabolic scheme. Highly unlikely. Don't you think?"

"You're probably right," Janet responded. "We can pretty much eliminate this method. What about the second one, being drugged and not aware of someone putting the slimy creature in their ear?"

"If that's true for each of the victims," Karen answered, "they would have to be willing to eat or drink something unknowingly laced with a rapidly absorbed sleeping compound. Also. there could possibly be more than one person placing the worms in their ears. Each of the victims would have had to be in a secluded area, away from prying eyes. You could exclude a beauty shop, barber shop, or a nail salon, since other patrons would more than likely had seen the culprit put something in the victim's ear after they'd suddenly fallen asleep. I suppose tanning salon personnel could do it. Plus, it's a place both men and women utilize."

"I'd put my money on a doctor's office," suggested Simon. "Once we find the killer in my vision, we'll concentrate on solving the six deaths."

~ * ~

Janet looked down at her watch. Forty minutes had passed since Frank and Danny began searching the Internet for a gathering of people at an outside venue within a fifty-mile radius of their hotel. There was a lot of stress being an agent for FMI, and not that there wasn't stress and tension when she was a sheriff detective. At least one thing was different, she now had Simon alongside of her enriching her heart with love.

"I have something," Danny exclaimed.

"What do you have?" Simon asked as he and Janet walked over to Danny and peered down at the computer monitor screen. Frank leaned to his right from his chair and stared at Danny's monitor.

"I found three different catering companies serving groups of people. One of the events is an engagement party today. They were contracted to serve a hundred people for an outside gathering at a private park venue. Another catering event is for a retirement party at an outside venue for fifty people. The last one is a company catering an outside family reunion for one hundred a twenty-five people."

"Any of the three events could be the place I saw in my vision. Did you find anything, Frank?"

"All I found were gatherings for children's birthday parties, a nineteen sixty-eight class reunion where most of the participants are in their late sixties, early seventies, and several other events not fitting our profile."

"Danny. How far away are these events from the hotel?" Janet asked.

"According to a map search, the first venue is thirty-five point four miles from the hotel. The second is twenty-eight point two miles away. And the third one is exactly forty-two miles from the hotel."

"This scenario almost sounds like the dilemma we faced in Ocala searching for the high school student," Jean said from the café table next to the window.

"It sure does," Janet agreed. "Although in Ocala, we were only searching for one person facing death at eleven fifty-eight in the morning. This event we're concerned about ten people in harm's way." She sighed. "We'll need to notify the county sheriff in the three counties and let them know there possibly will be a gunman at a gathering. We'll tell sheriff deputies we received a call from an anonymous caller describing the scenario, but they weren't sure where. We did a computer search and came up with these three events in three different counties. The logical thing to do is to split off into pairs and investigate these three gatherings. I pray to God one of these events is the event Simon saw in his vision. Remember, the party goers are a mixture of three different ethnicities. The shooter will be a mid-thirty-year-old Caucasian with long, dark brown hair with a mustache. He'll be wearing a light blue T-shirt and dark blue jeans."

Janet and Simon designated the pairing of agents, including Karen, who teamed up with Frank. Jean, Danny and Brian were the final team.

"Hopefully, each of us will have at least one sheriff deputy with us," Janet said. "I'll be calling Detective Thomas and let him know our intentions without exposing any of our special talents. He should have the phone numbers of each sheriff's department in the counties of the three events."

"I'll print out all the information of each venue," Danny said, "and give everyone a copy."

Janet called Detective Thomas' cell phone number. The phone rang three times. "Detective Thomas. Can I help you?"

"Yes. This is Agent Bennett from FMI." She explained to him what was happening and the need for his assistance.

"No problem, Agent Bennett. I'll get you the phone numbers." A few minutes later, he gave the numbers to Janet.

"Thank you, detective. We'll be continuing our investigation of the six deaths here in Pine Bluff right after we resolve this current situation."

Janet, Simon and Frank each called a sheriff's department in the counties of the social gatherings. Two deputies will be waiting, at each venue in the three counties for the FMI team to arrive. The deputies had the description of the potential shooter, and if the deputies spotted the shooter, they would approach him with caution. Preparing to draw their guns if the perp reached for a weapon.

In thirty minutes, Janet peered through the windshield toward Paradise Park, an outside and inside venue for gatherings. Simon parked the Suburban next to the sheriff deputies' vehicle on a black-topped parking lot with about forty cars, trucks and SUVs surrounding them. She stared at a one-story brick building standing alone to their right. Trees forming a horseshoe perimeter surrounded an opened area in front of them. The deputies exited their patrol car as did Janet and Simon. They greeted each other between the two vehicles.

Deputy Olson, an officer in his late twenties, said, "So, you don't have a name of this guy? Just a general description."

"Yes, that's all we have," Janet answered.

She knew Simon would be able to identify the perp if he saw him. Of course, she couldn't tell the deputies about Simon being a clairvoyant, a man with visionary abilities. There was a thirty-three percent chance the shooter would be here at this park. The opened area was about a two hundred feet wide and a hundred feet deep before the tree line began. Janet saw a ten-foot-wide banner attached to two twelve-foot-high poles directly in front of her. The sign read, CONGRATUATIONS MARK & WENDY. Hanging underneath the banner were plastic wedding bells. A mild breeze caused the bells to sway. There appeared to be about eighty to a hundred people milling around with a mixture of talking, laughing in small groups ranging between four to eight people. The majority of people were Hispanic.

A Hispanic man in his late forties approached them. "Is there a problem?" asked the man.

"There might be," answered Janet. "We're looking for a Caucasian man in his mid-thirties wearing a light-blue T-shirt and dark blue jeans with a mustache. We need to ask him some questions."

"There's no one with this description here," stated the man. "What's the man's name?"

"We don't have a name. We're going to leave Deputy Parson and Waters parked in the parking lot for a few hours in case he shows up."

"That'll be fine." He looked at the two deputies. "Can we get you soft drinks and some food?"

"Thank you for the offer, but we're fine." Answered Deputy Parsons.

The four of them walked back to the deputy's vehicle. Simon said, "I don't believe this is the gathering described by our informant. To play it safe, you best wait at least until dusk."

"We will. I'll call our Captain and let 'em know our intentions."

"Thanks," Janet said. She gave them her cell phone number. "We'll keep in touch."

Janet and Simon sat inside their vehicle. Janet removed her cell phone. "I'll call Frank and Karen, letting them know what we found, or should I say, what we didn't find. I'll then call the other agents."

Frank's phone rang two times. "Hey. Karen and I are pulling up to Winchester Park. What's up?"

"Our venue with its guests doesn't match Simon's vision. Almost all the guests are Hispanic."

"At the moment, not sure the ethnic mixture of the guests. I see the sheriff's car parked in the parking lot. I'll call you back as soon as I find something out regarding the guests and if someone can identify the description of our future assailant. Goodbye."

"They drove into the park as we were talking. Frank will call us back. I'll call the other guys." Jean's phone rang once. "Hi, Jean. What did you guys find out? More important, do you see people there with a yellow glow?"

"To answer your second question, no. Secondly, no one at this party looks like Simon's informant's description." Janet assumed the sheriff deputy or deputies must be next to her, listening to their conversation. "Although, there is a mixture of ethnic people, Whites, Blacks, Hispanic and Asians. There's one discrepancy."

"What's that?"

"There aren't any trees in the immediate area, so there wouldn't be any shadows from trees."

"There definitely were shadows in my vision," Simon said assuredly. "Their gathering of people can't be where the shooter committed his act."

"I agree," Janet said. It left only two options.

Frank and Karen were at the sight of the shooter, or there was another outside venue where the perp will execute his savage wrath on ten people. "To be safe, ask the sheriff deputies to stay there until dusk. You, Danny and Brian head to Frank and Karen's venue. We'll meet you guys there."

Simon started the Suburban, drove out of the parking lot and sped toward the venue where hopefully the shooter would be at. The sun had moved further down toward the western horizon. Soon there would be shadows projecting onto the ground as seen in Simon's vision. The ground in the area of the gunman could soon be stained with blood. Janet's breathing increased as did her heart rate, anticipating the shooter was presently loading his two guns with full bullet clips. She put the address into the GPS.

The GPS announced, "Turn left in one mile on to Mumford Street."

"What's our estimated arrival time?" Simon asked.

Janet leaned forward toward the GPS set into the dashboard. "We'll get there in thirty-two minutes...or at five twenty-three." She leaned back. *Jean and the other two agents should arrive there several minutes after we do. If they don't see the perp, it'll be up to Jean to see if anyone at the gathering glowed.*

Simon sped toward the final venue, slowing down and cautiously going through red traffic lights. He had placed a portable red emergency light on top of the vehicle s few inches beyond the driver side door. The Suburban didn't have a siren. Thirty minutes later, the GPS announced, "Turn right at the next light."

"The place we're looking for is called the Gathering Place," Janet said. "It'll be on our left around a quarter of a mile."

Simon turned the Suburban to the right at the light. "Maybe Frank, Karen and the deputies have already apprehended the shooter before he could do any harm?"

"Wouldn't that be great?"

She released the holster strap securing her Glock. Experience taught her to assume the worst scenario when entering an area of potential danger. Never underestimate a dangerous situation.

About fifty yards to their left, a rectangular wooden sign stated, The Gathering Place. The venue was surround by deciduous trees. The first thing she noticed were shadows from trees projecting across the road, signaling daytime was leaving and late afternoon, followed by evening would soon be here. Simon turned into a blacked-topped parking lot; a parking lot filled with various types of vehicles. Up ahead to their right near the back roll of vehicles stood a sheriff's car. Frank and Karen's vehicle was parked next to it. "We haven't heard anything from Frank, which could be good or bad news, depending how you look at it."

"Either the shooter had been apprehended or he hadn't shown up yet."

There weren't people running to their vehicles with fear and panic across their faces. Janet assumed it was one of the two possibilities, hoping for the first choice.

They exited the car and walked toward a fenced in compound about the size of basketball court. An eight-foot banner, hanging on the fence next to a gate, stated, "Graduate Terry Morris." A picture of a graduation cap and scroll completed the banner. There had to be at least a hundred people casually dressed in short sleeved shirts and shorts. There was a mixture of ethnic people. Trees encompassed three sides of the compound. A building resembling a log cabin stood to their right. Instrumental music hung in the air. Simon reached out and opened the entrance gate.

A feeling of doom overwhelmed Janet, as Simon opened the gate. "Something bad is going to be happening here." Her inner voice said, "Death." She told Simon what her inner voice proclaimed.

"We're obviously at the right place. I don't see Frank, Karen, or the deputies."

Janet continued to look around. "Neither do I. Where could they be?"

"Hey guys," said a man with a familiar voice behind them.

They both quickly turned around. Brian, Danny and Jean were walking toward them from the parking lot. Jean said, "Danny has a turbocharger in his van, along with flashing emergency lights and a piercing siren. We never stopped for one traffic light or stop sign. Now I know what it would be like riding in an EMS vehicle."

"I'm glad you guys got here so fast," Simon said. "We believe we're at the right venue, since Janet experienced one of her premonition feelings with her inner voice stating, 'death.' Jean, do you see anyone with a yellow halo?"

"No. not yet. Remember I have to be within ten feet of someone to see if they have a halo." She peered around. "I don't see Frank or Karen. In fact, I don't see the sheriff deputies."

Janet peered to her right at the log building and pointed, "The one logical explanation would be they're in the building over there."

Did they corner the potential killer and disarm him before his deadly rampage toward the guest? Maybe the shooter shot and killed Frank, Karen and the two deputies before they could draw their weapons from their holsters?

"Could be," agreed Simon.

The five of them walked toward the log building.

Jean passed several people within ten feet from her. "I don't see any victims yet."

For Jean, not seeing any future victims of the gunman didn't mean anything. They all could still be amongst the many other party goers; it only meant they were more than ten feet away from her. Right now, Janet focused on the log building in front of them.

What awaited them behind closed doors?

Chapter Fifteen

Simon reached out to open the backdoor to the wooden building. Janet had an ominous feeling without an inner warning voice as she removed her Glock from its holster. She held her weapon to her side with the barrel of the gun pointing down at the floor of a wooden covered porch. The door swung out causing everyone to jump back. Janet instinctively raised her gun, pointing it at an elderly man holding a bottle of beer. The man's jaw dropped as he raised his eyebrows allowing the whites of his upper eye globe visible. He stood there in a frozen, frightened state staring down at Janet's Glock. She dropped the gun to her side. "Sorry. I thought you were someone else."

"I'm glad I wasn't him. As you can see, I'm not carrying any guns on me."

Why would he say guns, instead of a gun? Before she could question the man about him saying guns, she heard Frank's voice behind the man.

The man stepped outside onto the porch, passing the five of them nodding, before walking off the porch.

Frank, Karen and two sheriff deputies stood in the center of a large room talking as the five of them walked inside the building. They stopped talking when they saw Janet and the others. "Hey, you all," Frank said, "glad you're all here. We captured the shooter." Frank stood aside, revealing a mustached man in his thirties handcuffed and sitting in a cushioned armchair. One of the officers held two handguns, likely the suspect's weapons of death.

"How'd you arrest him?" Janet asked, buttoning her blazer,

hiding her shoulder holster and Glock.

"Anticlimactically, to be exact."

"What do you mean?"

"Here's how it went down…"

Frank and Karen exited their car, which was parked in the back row of The Gathering Place's nearly filled parking lot. A sheriff's car drove toward them. Frank waved to them. They pulled up beside them. Two officers exited their patrol car.

Frank showed his FMI badge to the deputies. "I'm Agent Littlefield and this is Karen Rivers, a consultant for FMI."

The older man, who appeared to be in his early fifties and at least twenty years younger than his partner, said, "Please to meet you. I'm Sergeant Riley. This is Deputy Nelson."

"You have the description of the gunman," Frank said. "I think the best thing to do is to split up. Ms. Rivers and I we'll check out the outside grounds. You and Deputy Nelson can check out the log building. We'll meet you outside. Besides searching for our perp, ask the guests if they know anyone with the description of the gunman. We'll do the same."

Frank and Karen opened a gate leading to the fenced-in grounds behind the log building. There was a mixture of ethnic people as described by Simon. "This has to be the venue the shooter will crash," Karen stated.

"I agree."

"I hear something. It's coming from the log building. Sergeant Riley is yelling, 'Don't move. Raise your hands. Kneel down.'"

"It has to be the shooter," Frank said.

Frank and Karen hurried to the back door of the log building. A moment later, Frank opened the backdoor with his Glock clutched in his right hand. A man in his mid-thirties was lying supine with his hands cuffed behind him. Two guns lay on the wooden floor a few feet away from the perp. Deputy Nelson walked over and picked up the guns.

"…that's how it went down. It wasn't how I visualized the encounter would be with the gunman."

"Thank the Lord, no one was hurt," Jean said.

It is probably why Jean didn't see anyone with a yellow glow outside; the threat was resolved, thought Janet.

"We'll be taking our guy to the county jail for booking," Sergeant Riley stated. "We avoided a tragic event thanks to your tip."

"It sure turned out good," Karen said.

The sheriff deputies left with the perp through the building's front door.

"Do you know why the guy wanted to shoot people?" Simon asked.

Frank brushed the hair hanging down on his forehead. "The guy was expelled from college a month ago for selling drugs to a fraternity house where Terry Morris was a member. He was out on bond awaiting trial. The guy wanted revenge against everyone Morris was associated with. What more perfect event then an event celebrating his graduation from college with all his family and fraternity friends attending?"

"Revenge can be a powerful motivator for violence," Karen said, standing next to Frank with their arms touching each other's.

Simon and Brian called the deputies at the venue they previously investigated, telling them the perp had been captured without incident. They also called the Sheriffs at the three counties, thanking them for assisting in the investigation of the potential gunman. After putting his cell phone away, Simon announced, "We'll all meet back at the restaurant next to our hotel."

"I was getting a little hungry," Frank said placing his hand on top of his stomach arca.

"A little hungry," Jean said, then chuckled. "That'll be the day you're only a little hungry."

Simon smirked, then glanced at each agent and Karen. "Thanks, everyone. We should all feel proud about ourselves, saving ten people from harm or death. It was a team effort."

Janet loved Simon's diplomatic but sincere demeanor. It was evident the short time she'd been working with the FMI agents, the agents respected him and his authority. There wasn't any emotional friction between them.

The three vehicles left the parking lot of The Gathering Place and headed to the restaurant next to their hotel. Tree tops cast their shadows across the road and opened areas indicating early evening was present. The Grim Reaper wouldn't be visiting The Gathering Place this evening.

~ * ~

Simon thought about his brother, Kenneth Workman, an undercover agent for the FBI. Would they look like brothers? Maybe their physical features would be completely different? He didn't care either way, for the main concern was that his brother was healthy and happy.

"What are you in deep thought about?" Janet asked sitting in the front passenger seat of the Suburban.

"Oh. I was thinking about my brother. It's still hard to believe I have one. Can't wait to meet him."

"I have a feeling the two of you will click together."

"I sure hope so." Simon glanced at Janet. "I thought of something. We should call Detective Thomas and let him know we're back on the case."

Janet called the detective and informed him what happened in the apprehension of a potential killer. "So, we'll now be focused on the sixth deaths in Pine Bluff. I also wanted to tell you what the ME found in the brain of our sixth victim, Robert Sears."

"The medical examiner already called me and let me know about the worm-like larvae in the brain of Mr. Sears. He also told me about the nanochip. What do you think? Since you're medical investigators."

"We're working on who could be responsible for the worm-like larvae and purposely introducing it into the ear. As soon as we obtain any information, we'll be letting you know."

"Thanks, Agent Bennett. I'll let you know if I find anything, too."

Janet put her cell phone away. "That takes care of the detective. What a day we've had. It never seems to let up."

"Are you complaining?"

"No. Just stating the facts, sir. Just stating the facts."

They both laughed.

Simon parked the Suburban in the restaurant's parking lot. The other two FMI vehicles parked in the last two parking spots. They all walked into the restaurant together. The restaurant was near full capacity likely because it was near prime time for dinner. "I don't know if we'll get a table," Brian observed.

A waitress walked up to them. Simon expected her to say there was a waiting list for a table, instead she asked, "Frank Littlefield's party of seven?"

"Yes, mam," Frank answered.

"Follow me, please." She grabbed seven menus.

Frank raised his head and stuck out his chest. "I called ahead when we all left The Gathering."

"Leave it to Monsieur Appétit," Karen said with a French accent.

Frank's forte of jokester comments must be rubbing off onto Karen, thought Simon with a smile.

After dinner everyone went back to the hotel. Danny and Frank went back to their room to continue their computer wizardry. Karen went with them, wanting to witness their computer expertise. Simon chuckled to himself, knowing she primarily wanted to be with Frank. As usual, Simon and Janet went to the hotel's lounge for a nightcap. This time, Jean and Brian accompanied them to the lounge. Simon was hoping he'd have private time with Janet. He recently concluded things didn't always turn out the way he'd like them to be.

"This sure has been a rewarding day," Brian said as he picked up his glass containing a mixed drink. "Let's drink to a successful and safe day for the FMI team." They all tapped their glasses in the center of the table.

"Knowing Danny and Frank," Simon said, "I'm sure they'll complete their computer agenda this evening. We already know one of The Circle's subsidiaries makes microchips. With Danny's new computer spyware, we might be able to trace the nanochip found in Mr.

Sears' brain to this evil conglomerate."

A clean-shaven man in his late thirties with brown hair walked into the lounge. He peered at FMI's table. He walked directly toward the agents without taking his eyes of them. The man stopped at their table between Simon and Janet. "Are you Simon Woods?"

Simon stared into the man's blue eyes. "Yes. Do I know you?"

"No. I never knew you existed, until two days ago. I'm your brother, Kenneth Workman."

Simon's mouth gabbed open as a vibrating warmth touched every skin cell in his body. "Kenneth, I didn't expect to see you so soon." He pushed his chair back and stood eye to eye with his brother. They both leaned forward and hugged.

"You definitely look like brothers," Janet stated.

Brian found an extra chair for Kenneth, setting it between him and Simon. Kenneth sat down, then said, "Where do we start?"

Simon answered, "A couple of days ago I found out I had a brother…you. Since then, I've run many questions through my mind to ask you when we met. Let's start with, when did you know you were adopted?"

"I was told on my sixth birthday. I had been loved by my adopted parents and felt part of the family. They were my mom and dad. I was their only child. What about you, Simon? When did you find out you were adopted?"

"I was seven years old. I felt the same about my adopted parents as you did. I too was an only child. Where did you grow up?"

"Alpharetta, Georgia."

"Wow," Simon exclaimed. "I grew up in Dunwoody, Georgia. We were about twenty minutes away from each other.

Simon and Kenneth talked for about thirty-five minutes. They both concluded they had probably passed each other or were in the same room at various business establishments or venues. One thing seemed beyond coincidence: the fact they both dated Claudia Stone three years ago. They blessed their lucky stars neither of them was the father of Claudia's daughter.

"So, you're a physician and now an agent for FMI?"

"Yes. I love trying to solve medical mysteries throughout the United States. It can be hectic at times, but the reward is solving the mystery. How about you? Why did you join the FBI?"

"I was getting bored with the daily routine of a clinical psychologist and needed more of a challenge in life. The FBI seemed the logical next step for me. Of course, my ESP ability of knowing if someone is lying enhanced the role as an FBI special agent."

Simon gulped the last of his mixed drink, then peered into his brother's eyes. "Have I been lying?"

Kenneth grinned. "You're a truthful person." He glanced at everyone at the table. "I'm sorry I monopolized so much time of your downtime and relaxation."

"Not at all," Janet said. "I enjoyed listening to the two of you talking. It was filled with a vast amount of interesting information."

Jean and Brian agreed to Janet's comment. Jean added, "Were we truthful in our response?"

"You don't have to ask me every time you talk with me."

"Sorry," Jean said slightly dropping her head. "I've never met anyone with your type of ability."

"You all have different abilities. Don't you?"

Jean raised her head, nodding. "Yes. We all do have ESP abilities, except Director Littlefield."

Brian's cell phone rang, as if someone were looking down on them and on cue of mentioning his name, the director's phone rang. "Hello. This is Brian Littlefield." He listened to the person at the other end of call for at least thirty seconds. "Yes. We could use his assistance, especially with someone with his credentials and ability."

Simon knew immediately who Brian's caller was talking about—his brother. He glanced at Janet. Her attention appeared to be focused on his brother. A sinking feeling overwhelmed him in the pit of his stomach. Would she be attracted to his brother? Like he and Kenneth were three years ago with Claudia Stone.

Another long pause as Brian listened to the caller, then said,

"We'll keep in touch. Goodbye." Brian, who was sitting across from Kenneth at the table, said, "Welcome to our team. Like Karen Rivers, you'll be a consultant assisting in our investigation. Of course, you already knew you'd be joining in on our investigation if I approved it. Correct?"

"Yes. I look forward to being part of FMI's investigation."

"This is unbelievable," Simon interjected. "Meeting my brother for the first time, and now having him work with me…that is, us, is great. Welcome to our team."

"Thanks, Simon."

"After tonight, Kenneth, you can share a room with your brother. I'll be leaving for Atlanta in the morning."

If his brother hadn't showed up, he would've had a room by himself. Getting intimate and private time with Janet seemed to be impossible with one obstacle and another crossing their paths. "I thought you were going to stay until we solved these mysterious deaths?"

"I was hoping to, but I need to get back to Atlanta on business. Keep in touch with me as you did on the other cases. Enough with business. I'll buy the next drinks."

It was nearly ten o'clock when everyone left the lounge. Simon walked up the hallway with Janet to his right and Kenneth to his left. Brian and Jean walked behind them. Multiple rhythmic three beeps of cell phones filled the hallway, indicating a text message was being sent to each of them, except Kenneth. They all stopped and reached for their phones.

Simon stared at the caller ID. It was Danny. He'd sent a text message. The message read, COME TO OUR ROOM. COMPLETED SPY-EYE. Simon chuckled to himself. Danny sure had a flare for making announcements. He could've called one of them to pass the word to the others. "Our night plans have changed."

About twenty feet ahead of them, Jean walked out of her room. "Sounds like good news."

The wizards' room door was ajar. Simon led the way into the room. Frank and Danny sat in front of their computers. Karen sat at the end of the second bed. "I finished my computer program. I'm calling it Spy-Eye."

"I know you told us before how it works," Brian said. "Can you tell us again?"

"Sure." He stared at Kenneth then Simon. "Is this your brother?"

"Good guess. Yes. This is my brother, Kenneth Workman."

"You two definitely look like brothers. Nice meeting you. My cohort on the other computer is Frank, and the lady on the bed is Karen." They both acknowledged him. "So, you're an FBI agent."

"Yes, Agent Danny Emerick."

He looked at Frank. "You're Agent Frank Littlefield, the brother of Director Brian Littlefield."

He then looked at Karen. "You're Karen Rivers, an employee of Future Innovations Today, who is helping FMI on the six deaths here in Pine Bluff."

Janet chuckled, then said, "Did you know you answer a question like your brother Simon? What normally takes a one-or two-word answer to a question extends to a short dissertation?"

"I didn't know Simon had this idiosyncrasy. Although I've been accused of rambling at times by my friends and colleagues. I guess it's a family trait. So, tell us about your Spy-Eye program my brother asked you about a minute or two ago."

"The electronic apparatus I invented is attached to my computer. It deciphers encrypted messages from computers throughout the world. Our goal is spying on The Circle."

"The FBI has been monitoring this organization. We don't have any convicting evidence we could take to the U.S. Attorney General yet. I've been briefed about your suspicions of this stealthy world conglomerate. Maybe your new invention will get us some incriminating information on The Circle."

"It's getting late," Simon announced, "We all need a good night's sleep We'll get a fresh start on our investigation tomorrow. Of course, except our two computer wizards. I'm sure they'll be doing their magic with their computers while we're sleeping. Am I right?" He glanced at

Danny and Frank.

"You know us well, boss. We won't wake you. We'll let you all sleep until tomorrow morning."

"Thanks. I'm sure everyone would appreciate that."

Everyone said goodnight in the hallway. Simon looked at Janet and grinned, then said, "See you in the morning."

She reciprocated with a smile. Everyone entered their respective rooms.

~ * ~

Danny peered at his computer monitor. "Unbelievable," he said excitedly.

"What's unbelievable?" Frank responded, as he leaned to his right and stared at Danny's monitor.

"The locations of all The Circle's subsidiaries and people not associated with a subsidiary who consistently are in contact with their corporate office."

"Their corporate office should be in New York City. Right?"

"That's what I thought…and may be correct on paper. Although, a high percentage of the communications come to a computer IP number in Pine Bluff."

Chapter Sixteen

Simon's cell phone rang. He opened his eyes and squinted at the clock sitting on the nightstand between the two beds. Seven o'clock a.m. gleamed back at him. Simon peered over at the next bed. It was empty. He reached out and grabbed his phone off the nightstand. It was Danny calling. "Good morning. I hope it's good news?"

"Yes. Great news. I didn't wake you…did I?"

"No. I was getting up," he lied.

He didn't want to burst Danny's enthusiastic bubble and scold him for waking him up from a peaceful, sound sleep, sleep deserved after the long arduous day he and the team had gone through yesterday.

"I found out a few things possibly leading to the demise of The Circle and their evil doings. Frank also has some good news regarding the nanochip in the worm-like thing found in Robert Sear's brain."

"Why don't we meet in your room in twenty minutes and go over everything you and Frank discovered. I'll call the rest of the team, including my brother, to inform them of our plans."

"You don't have to call Karen. Frank already talked with her this morning."

"Oh. Okay. See you soon." Simon sat up in bed, then turned around. The bathroom light was on, as its illuminating rays spread across the carpeted foyer floor. The sound of the shower penetrated through the wall to his right. Brian had gotten up prior to Danny calling. Simon called Janet. "Morning. Are you up?"

"I am now."

"Sorry. Didn't mean to wake you. Thought you'd be up."

"I'm being a snot. I've been up awhile. I've already taken my shower and dressed."

Simon shook his head. Janet had snookered him again. "I guess I'm never going to know when you're serious or pulling my leg."

"You will eventually. I'm sure. So, why did you call? Other than to say good morning to me."

"Danny and Frank have information about The Circle and the nanochip. We'll meet in their room in about twenty minutes."

Simon then called Kenneth, who also was already awake. "We're all meeting Danny and Frank in their room in about twenty minutes. Their room number is…"

"One-nineteen. Remember, brother, I work for the FBI. Besides, I was in their room last night."

Simon and Brian walked into the computer wizard's room, which was ajar, at 7:18. Everyone was present. Danny and Frank were sitting with their backs toward the front of their computers, facing Janet, Jean, Karen and his brother. They were talking amongst themselves but stopped when he and Brian walked into the room, as if they were talking about them. "Good morning everyone," Simon greeted. "Looks like the gang is all here."

Danny moved his swivel chair toward Simon and Brian. "We were talking about how diversified a group we were with our ESP abilities."

"Except me," Brian said. "I'm just an ordinary guy."

"You're beyond ordinary, brother. I can vouch for that."

Everyone laughed, including Brian.

Simon walked up to Danny and stood a couple of feet away. "What do you and Frank have to tell us?"

"Plenty."

He turned around to a screen saver displaying colorful bubbles changing size and color. A few seconds later, he brought up a map of the United States. "These are the sites affiliated with The Circle."

Simon stared at the map with at least one red asterisk in each state. "My God, there isn't a state The Circle isn't in. Where are they located in Arkansas?"

Danny moved the mouse arrow to one location in Arkansas. He clicked the mouse on the red asterisk. Pine Bluff showed up inside a rectangular box with the name Pine Bluff Arsenal written underneath with its street address and phone number. "This is where there are numerous incoming messages to their email."

"What exactly do they do there?"

"Frank did a computer research regarding PBA." He glanced at Frank.

"I found interesting information about the arsenal. In 1941, the facility was started as a chemical warfare arsenal. It dealt with bombs and grenades. It was later used in the operations of developing chemical weapons and lethal gases. The facility also began storing bombs and shells. In the late sixties, especially around 1969, they had created about seven harmful agents, including Agent Orange. Chemical activities were dismantled by 1974. Although, during the summer of 2005, a fire broke out at the facility with the release of a highly toxic chemical called white phosphorus from its canisters. About eight thousand canisters were destroyed in the fire, releasing its contents as white smoke."

"How did The Circle get involved with the Pine Bluff Arsenal?" Simon asked.

"They contracted part of the facility five years ago. The company is called Beyond Infinity."

"What are they doing there?"

"Not sure," Frank answered. "All we can find out about them is that they're doing biometric research. No details in exactly what they're researching or making. There aren't any grants supporting their research. No products on the market. No research papers published. It's a clandestine operation."

"So, they're not involved with nanochip research there?"

"I couldn't find any evidence through their email correspondence," Danny answered. "Much of the email is in an encrypted code I presently can't decipher or break. Like I said a moment ago, they're absolutely hiding something. There's possibly one way to find out."

Simon knew what Danny meant by the statement. "Get inside the facility and look around."

"It's probably the only way to know what they're doing inside the facility."

"This scenario sounds familiar." Simon was referring to the Deadly Seizure Case in Chambersburg and infiltrating the Brighton Research facility. "How would you get inside?"

"Frank and I discussed this last night. I'd walk through the front door in the evening representing myself as a janitor."

"How can you pull this off?"

Knowing the two of them, Simon knew they had devised a clever and feasible plan.

"We hacked into their Human Resource Department's employee files at Beyond Infinity. All I have to do is add my name to their employee files as an evening janitor. The security guard at the front gate will see my name on the evening roster when he checks his computer. Frank obtained the floor plans of the building Beyond Infinity is leasing."

Simon turned to Brian. "What do you think?"

"You did it in Chambersburg. I can't see why it couldn't work here." Brian nodded. "Sure. Let's do it."

"I'll receive the company's identification later this morning with the bar code to get into the building, plus it'll get me into the rooms."

"How can you get the ID so soon?" Brian asked.

"Frank and I assumed you'd agree with my proposal, so I contacted one of my sources last night, who said he'd send it to the hotel by ten o'clock this morning. It will give me access to most of the rooms. I'll be adding my alias name, Roger Kennedy, to my personnel file this morning. When the guard at the front gate checks his computer, it'll show me and my picture. It'll also show I'm scheduled to work this evening as a new employee. Once in the facility, when I run into another custodial worker, I'll be telling them I'm there to do a time study on the cleaning procedures. This scenario will give me excess to the whole building."

"It looks like you have all the bases covered for this undercover plan."

Simon believed Danny's plan will work. He turned to Frank and said, "Did you find any information on nanochip research companies in and around Pine Bluff?"

"Yes. I found two companies. The first one is in Little Rock. The company is named Microtechnology, Inc., doing research on nanochip technology. My computer search showed they are involved with the development of a microchip attached to a tiny camera encased in a large oblong pill-shaped vessel resembling an elongated football. The person will swallow this tiny apparatus, which is two inches long, into the stomach, allowing a video to be taken as it descends down the esophagus, and through the stomach, small bowel and colon. I didn't find any evidence the company were using larvae, worms, grubs or any other tiny crawly creatures in their research. Of course, we know from previous investigations, evidence and company intentions can be hidden from the public eye."

"I think Janet, Kenneth, and I should make a visit to this company. Did you find any affiliation of this company to The Circle?"

"Not sure. They're not a subsidiary of The Circle according to the New York Stock Exchange. Although there have been several Internet communications through emails over the past year between them and The Circle according to Danny's Spy-Eye. We don't know if there's any significant information in the emails indicating any diabolic plans since they are encrypted. I'd need to be in the building, using one of their computers to access the emails."

"That can be arranged. You and Jean can investigate." He glanced at Karen, who had a forlorn expression. Obviously, she wanted to go with them, especially with Frank. "Take Karen with you." A smile lit up her face.

"What about the second company?"

"The company is called Dickerson Research. They manufacture microchips for medical equipment. As with the other company, there have been several interactions through emails over a twelve-month period. Again, we're unable to get into the email to find out if they're discussing any illegal plans or anything relevant to our six deaths due to the emails being encrypted."

"Why do you only have twelve months of emails?" Karen asked.

"It's not uncommon for companies to delete emails after one year and sometimes every six months."

"We'll go to Dickerson Research and interview them," Simon suggested. "We'll say we're there to inspect their facility for a possible contagion. I'm sure they'll cooperate...unless they have something to hide. Unfortunately, I don't have the knowledge or capabilities to hack into their computer."

"No problem," Danny said. "I have a thumb drive programmed to hack into a computer. All you need to do is plug it into a USB outlet. It takes one minute to download the information. When you get back to the hotel, I'll put the thumb drive into my computer, enabling me to hack into their computer system and read the encrypted emails."

"You and Frank amaze me by your computer wizardry."

"We love what we do," Frank said, as he glanced at Karen then back to Simon. "Although, if all of a sudden a cataclysmic event occurred making computers inoperable, Danny and I would be without a job."

"Not true. You and Danny would always have a position here. The two of you have too many other talents essential to FMI. We now all have our assignments, I think we should go for breakfast. It's going to be another long day. Hopefully we'll finally get some answers to the six deaths."

The FMI team sat at their usual table at the far end of the restaurant. After ordering breakfast, Brian said, "I'll be heading back to Atlanta. I want to say it's been a great experience being with you in Virginia Beach and here in Pine Bluff. I've gained a lot of insight in what's it like working in the field. There's a saying my brother, Frank, had said to me right after he joined the FMI team. 'It was a million dollars' worth of experience, and I'd give up eating for three days to do it again.' I now can appreciate what he meant by it. Of course, he completely changed the original saying."

"Does this mean we're all getting a raise?" Frank asked.

Brian chuckled, then replied, "No. Just a raise in appreciation for what you're doing in solving medical mysteries."

After eating, Frank, Jean and Karen headed toward their vehicle in the hotel's parking lot. He had printed out all pertinent information regarding Microtechnology and Dickerson Research. Simon, Janet, and Kenneth walked toward the Suburban. Danny headed back to the hotel to await his ID badge. Brian went back to the hotel for his luggage.

Simon started the vehicle, as Janet put the address of Dickerson Research into the GPS. He drove out of the parking lot onto the highway. Traffic was heavy. The GPS told them to continue on the road.

"It's twenty-two miles to our destination," Janet said. "Arrival time will be in twenty-five minutes."

"How are you going to specifically handle our questioning with the employees at this research company?" Kenneth asked.

"I'll explain to the person in charge at the facility that a contaminate was found in a diagnostic machine containing one of their microchips. They need to inspect the facility in case a CDC team needs to come in and check for a contaminate in their processing procedures. What do you think?"

"Sounds great. It should give us access to the whole facility. You should've been an FBI agent."

"One family member is enough. You'll be able to use your ESP ability once we're inside interviewing employees by determining if anyone isn't telling the truth. Keep track in your notebook who's lying."

"Sure. Note-taking is one of my fortes."

Dickerson Research came into view about one hundred yards to their right. The building was surrounded by cotton fields. The closest house they passed was about a half mile away. They had built their facility away from other buildings and businesses, away from prying eyes. "You have arrived at your destination," announced the GPS. A ten-foot chain-link security fence surrounded the facility. A thirty-yard driveway led to a front gate. A security guard booth sat to the left of the gate. Simon stopped next to the security booth. A security guard in his late forties came out of the hut.

"Can I help you?"

"I'm Agent Woods. This is Agent Bennett and Workman." They showed their FMI badges. Simon gave his brother a generic badge last night. "We're federal medical investigators of the CDC. We're here to talk with Luther Payne." Simon obtained the name and credentials of the operational CEO for the facility from Danny's computer printout.

"Is he expecting you?"

"No."

The security guard walked backed inside the booth, picked up a phone and pushed a few numbers. After apparently talking with someone, the guard hung up the phone, then pushed a button on the wall facing Simon and Janet. The gate slowly opened, as the guard walked back outside. "Mr. Payne will see you in his office. Please park in front of the front entrance door. A security guard will meet you inside and take the three of you to Mr. Payne's office."

"Thank you." Simon drove inside and parked the Suburban in the visitor's parking space.

Once inside the building, a security guard escorted them by elevator to the fourth floor. They walked into Mr. Payne's office. A secretary sat at a desk in front of them. ''I'll let Mr. Payne know you're here." She picked up her desk phone and pushed a button. "The agents from the CDC are here."

A few seconds later, a door behind the secretary opened. A clean-shaven man in his late fifties said, "Please come into my office."

Simon, Janet, and Kenneth sat in cushioned armchairs in front of a mahogany desk. "How can I help you?"

"We're investigating a bacterium found inside the electronic components of a scanning machine. Your microchips were part of the electronics. We're checking out all the companies involved in the make-up of the scanning machine. We need to know if anyone had any hearing problems or symptoms, which is one of the bacterium's side effects."

"We'll be glad to cooperate with you. I'll personally take you around our building to the different departments."

They spent about forty-five minutes talking with employees on the fourth floor. The company made microchips without any evidence of making nanochips the size planted in the worm-like creature found in the brain during the autopsy of Mr. Davis.

"We'll go to the third floor now." They rode the elevator to the third floor.

There were several rooms along the hallway, but not a few rooms with glassed-in walls facing the hallway as it was on the fourth floor. These rooms only had glass in the upper half of the door. "What is on this floor?" Simon asked looking into a room with several lab machines. No one was in the room.

"This is…" Mr. Payne's cell phone rang. He removed it from inside his suitcoat. "I'm busy right now. Can I call you back?" A pause for about twenty seconds as he listened intently to the person at the other end of the phone. "All right. I'll be right there." He put the phone back into his coat. He looked at Simon. "I'll be right back. Won't take me long. Maybe ten minutes. You mind waiting?"

"Not at all," Simon answered.

"You can wait in this room," he suggested pointing to the room they were standing in front of. "The technician should be back anytime."

Luther Payne turned around, walked a few steps and pushed the elevator down button.

They walked into the room. The room was probably twelve-foot wide by ten-foot deep. A variety of diagnostic machines sat on a counter running the entire width of the room. "This couldn't have worked out any better if we had planned it." He glanced around the room for a computer. In the far-left corner of the room a computer sat on a small desk. "I see one. Keep an eye open for the tech."

Janet stood in the doorway of the partially opened door. She peered to left through the upper glassed door, then to the right. "Hallway is clear."

Simon hurried to the computer. It was already on. *A great break,* he thought. He removed the USB thumb drive from his pocket. The computer's hard drive was under the desk. He sat in the desk chair, reached down and insert the thumb drive. The monitor's screen was filled with a rapid succession of numbers and letters. The bottom of the screen displayed a gray horizontal bar. A white solid line moved from left to right through the bar, displaying a percentage number starting at zero and quickly increasing numerically until it reached a hundred percent completed, meaning Danny's spyware had abstracted all the needed data and introduced a virus into the mainframe of Dickerson Research's central computer, so he'd be able to decipher the encrypted emails. He turned around and looked at his brother, who was walking around the room peering at the different apparatuses. "Did you find any of the employees lying?"

"Most were telling the truth. A couple employees were lying. Especially when you asked them if they ever heard of The Circle."

"We'll need concrete evidence confirming this company is conspiring with The Circle, and possibly involved with the six deaths."

"I wonder what all these machines are used for?" Kenneth asked as he slowly moved around the room peering at the different apparatuses.

"Most appear to be some type of analysis machines."

"Someone coming up the hallway," Janet said anxiously.

Simon stared at the percentage. Twenty-five percent. Beads of sweat started rolling down his forehead onto his cheeks. His breathing increased, as did his heartbeat. There wouldn't be enough time to download the data. He placed his thumb and index finger on the thumb drive, ready to remove it once the technician was a few feet from the doorway.

"The guy went into another room. All clear."

Simon sighed. "That was close." He peered down at the monitor. Fifty percent completed. "Time seems to slow down when you're in a hurry."

"Isn't that the truth," Janet replied looking at Simon.

She turned and began peering up and down the hallway.

The elevator was directly across from the room they were in. A LED square screen was set into the wall above the elevator door. Janet looked above the elevator, then turned toward Simon. "The elevator hasn't moved from the fourth floor. Mr. Payne is still up there." She turned around and saw an employee walking down the hallway. She turned and said to Simon, "Someone is coming. I have a feeling it's the technician Payne mentioned. You have less than ten seconds. I have an idea." Janet walked down the hallway toward the employee.

Simon stared at the download percentage. Eighty-five percent completed. He heard Janet talking in the hallway. "Are you the technician in room three-sixteen?"

"Yes," answered a middle-aged man wearing a white shirt, pants and a pair of laced leather shoes. "What are you doing in my room?"

"Mr. Payne was going to introduce us to you. He had to leave, but said he'd be back shortly. I'm Agent Bennett from the Federal Medical Investigator, a division of CDC. We're here to do interviews with all the employees."

"Glad to cooperate." He began walking toward the room. "You said 'we're'. Where's the other agent?"

"I'm with two other agents. They're in your room."

Simon peered at the screen. Ninety-seven...

Chapter Seventeen

Simon heard the sound of leather-soled shoes striking the tiled hallway floor getting closer and closer as he peered at the monitor's screen…ninety-eight…ninety-nine…one hundred. He quickly removed the thumb drive from the computer tower's USB outlet. He clasped his hand around the thumb drive, quickly stood, then stepped toward the door. The technician walked into the room followed by Janet. She made a fist with her thumb pointing up toward the ceiling. Simon nodded, acknowledging her thumb gesture. "You must be the technician Mr. Payne referred to?"

"Yes. My name is Arlo Cramer." The middle-aged man had greying hair along the temples of his head. He had a bright smile.

"Please to meet you. I'm Agent Woods, and this is Agent Workman. We won't take up much of your time. Just a few questions."

"Happy to help the CDC."

"Have you had a problem with your hearing, speech or vision?"

Cramer stared down at the floor with furled eyebrows. "N-N-No. I-I never experienced those things." His voice slightly trembled as he looked up at Simon. "I do know…" His eyes darted to the right of Simon as Mr. Payne walked into the room. "I don't know anyone with those symptoms."

I didn't ask him about anyone else having these symptoms. Arlo was definitely hiding something, something he was about to tell us before Payne walked into the room. What was he about to tell us?

"Thank you for your time." Simon knew there wouldn't be any reason to ask any more questions while the CEO was present. Simon saw his brother writing in his notebook. He knew what was being written down. Lying.

For the next hour, they interviewed all the remaining employees. All the employees answered the same way, with almost identical answers, as if they were told what to say. Prior to Payne leaving Simon and Janet on the third floor to take care of a concerned caller, the employees answered in various phrasing of words. Simon believed Luther Payne somehow advised the remaining employees to answer one way, and not to mention anything negative or suspicious. Payne likely had someone contact each employee before they talked with the employees. During their tour through the facility Simon believed they weren't taken to every room or lab. A few times Luther said certain rooms were only used for storage and nothing else. His brother wrote something in his notebook, probably about the CEO lying about the rooms being used for storage.

After talking with the last employee on the first floor, Mr. Payne said, "This completes all the employees. Do you think the dangerous bacterium came from our facility?"

"No," Simon answered. "You run a clean and efficient microchip business. I'd have to give your facility a clean bill of health. Thank you for allowing us to interview your employees."

"I'm glad we don't have the deadly organism in our facility. I'll walk you to the front door."

Simon sat behind the driver seat of the Suburban and turned the ignition key. "Kenneth, what do you think?"

"Most of the employees had been coached to say what someone required them to say. Arlo Cramer was about to tell us something about the symptoms but stopped when his CEO walked into the room."

"I agree. He was going to tell us something. We'll never know now."

"This isn't completely true," Janet said. "We can call him at home. I'm sure Frank or Danny can get his phone number through the Internet. The question would be, will he be willing to talk with us over the telephone? Mr. Cramer and probably all the employees may be leery of talking over the telephone, thinking his company or maybe The Circle was listening in on phone conversations. Fear is a tool for control."

Simon nodded. "You are likely right in what you said, but I think we should try anyway this evening. Kenneth, I saw you writing in your notebook a few times."

"Eight employees were definitely lying. CEO Payne lied about four rooms being used for storage. In fact, he lied about knowing anything about The Circle. He did tell the truth when you asked him if they ever experimented with living creatures."

~ * ~

Janet wondered how Frank, Jean and Karen were doing with their investigation? "I'm going to call Frank and let him know we're done. That we'll meet them back at the hotel. I assume they're still at Microtechnology since they haven't called us. I wonder if they found deception like we did?"

"Not sure. Although, he might not be able to talk if they're still interviewing employees. I was wondering too if they uncovered anything relevant. You know, a moment ago, I was thinking about them too. I've said this before, 'great minds think alike.'"

She scanned his side profile and grinned. *Besides your great mind, you have a great-looking body.*

"I can't dispute your opinion about us thinking alike at times."

She removed her cell phone and called Frank. His phone rang three times. "Hi, Frank. We're done and heading back to the hotel."

"Sounds good."

"I assume you can't say anymore?"

"You're right. Talk to you later."

Janet put her phone away. "You were right. They're still there investigating, and Frank couldn't talk."

"You're not saying much there in the back seat," Simon said, as he glanced up at the rearview mirror.

"Just observing and taking things in. As an undercover FBI agent, it's an attribute needed to survive and obtain information."

"So, brother what have you learned?"

He glanced at Janet, then back to Simon. "The two of you seem comfortable together."

Janet wasn't expecting Kenneth's pointed comment. He had been with Simon and her for a few hours and already observed a charisma between them. Was the chemistry between them obvious? "Did you have a partner with the FBI?"

"No. I never had that privilege. Always worked alone even when I wasn't working undercover. I can see where it would be an advantage, having someone covering your back, and someone to share notes with."

"Maybe you should check it out when you get back to the FBI?"

"Maybe. If I can be guaranteed to have a partner like you, I might consider it."

Janet snickered to herself. Kenneth was a smooth talker. Not like Simon, who sometimes would stumble on his words when trying to flirt with her. "There aren't too many guarantees in life."

"No. There aren't."

~ * ~

Alexander Mendelson focused his attention on the Suburban as it left Dickerson Research's parking lot, as he sat in his dark-blue sedan with heavily tinted windows. The windows made it difficult for someone to see who was sitting inside the vehicle. He exited the vehicle and walked inside the building. He showed the security guard in the lobby his Circle ID. Under Alex's alias name, Lucas Powers, the words "Protection Enforcer Agent" appeared. Even if a person didn't actually know who The Circle were, the title was intimidating, representing an authoritative figure. Alex then walked over to the elevator and pushed the up arrow on the panel. A moment later, he walked into Mr. Payne's office.

"Can I help you?" Asked the secretary.

"I'm Lucas Powers." He showed her The Circle ID.

She pushed a button on the base of the desk phone, then said,

"Lucas Powers from The Circle is here to see you."

A few seconds later, the CEO opened his door. He displayed a worried expression. "Come in."

Alex walked into the room and stood in front of the desk, as Mr. Payne sat in his high-back desk swivel chair. "What did the FMI agents want?"

"They were concerned about a dangerous bacterium possibly originating from our microchip. They asked the employees a few questions."

"What kind of questions?"

"Did anyone have a problem with hearing, speech or vision? Do you work with living creatures such as larvae? What do you know about The Circle? None of the employees answered yes, and all of them answered they didn't know anything about The Circle. All the employees had been instructed never to mention any of these things to non-employees, including family, relatives and friends during all of our quarterly staff meetings. I know today they all answered properly because I was with them." He thought a moment. "Except…"

"Except what?"

"I had to leave the FMI agents for ten minutes with one of the technicians while I went to my office."

"So, you don't know how he answered their questions?"

"I'm sure he answered okay. When I walked into the room, he had answered a question correctly by saying, 'I don't know anyone with those symptoms.' "

"They didn't ask any other questions?"

"I don't know. The FMI agents left with me to interview the remaining employees. While I was in my office earlier, I had a supervisor call each room on the third, second and first floors and let the employees know of FMI, and how to answer their questions."

Alex shook his head in disgust. "What's the technician's name?"

"Arlo Cramer."

~ * ~

Janet saw their hotel through the windshield. "I wonder if Danny received his ID for Beyond Infinity yet?" She glanced at her watch. It was eleven-fifty.

"He said he'd get it later this morning," Kenneth answered.

"Since we have Danny's spy thumb drive with Dickerson Research data on it," Janet said, "we'll…that is, if Danny will be able to decipher those emails between The Circle and them. Although, if this world organization is as secretive as it's made out to be, there probably won't be any pertinent or criminal information in the emails."

"We'll have to wait and see," Kenneth replied. "You're probably right in your assumption. Most illegal organizations don't leave incriminating paper trails. I don't think The Circle is an exception to this fact. In fact, they conceal their illicit activities quite proficiently. You probably already know the FBI has had their eye on this world conglomerate for the past several months."

"Yes. Special Agent Collins in Virginia Beach informed us of your involvement. We tried to connect them to a couple of our cases but never could get any concrete evidence for federal prosecution. If we can get Arlo Cramer to cooperate with us and give us information tying The Circle with the six deaths in Pine Bluff, we'll have the evidence needed for prosecution in a federal court."

"Knowing your tenacious ways of not giving up in investigations, I'm sure you, along with the FMI team, will find the evidence needed to expose The Circle of their evilness."

"Thanks for your confidence." *How does he know I'm steadfast unless someone told him?* She glanced at Simon.

Simon parked the Suburban in the hotel's parking lot.

Janet knocked on Danny and Franks' hotel room door. The door opened. Danny stood in the vestibule wearing a deep green jump suit with an ID badge attached to a pocket in the upper left side of short-sleeved black shirt. The badge had the name "Roger Kennedy" underneath "Beyond Infinity." A bar code was at the bottom of the badge.

Danny grinned. "Do I look official?"

"Yes, you do Mr. Kennedy," Janet answered as she walked past him, followed by Simon and Kenneth.

Simon handed Danny the thumb drive. "I plugged it into one of their computers. We're anxious to see what it downloaded."

"Great." Danny hurried to his computer, plugged it into a USB outlet at the front of his computer tower.

The three of them stood around Danny, staring down at the monitor. Janet saw a screen filled with rapid changing numbers and letters. She asked, "How long will it take to decipher the emails?"

"Several minutes. I'm downloading the company's interdepartmental correspondence, then all the emails from within the company and emails sent to them from outside the company, along with emails sent to outside sources."

The room's entrance door opened and in walked Frank, Jean and Karen. A smile let up Frank's face. "Hey, guys." Jean closed the door. "I couldn't talk with you earlier. The human resource director was standing next to me."

"I assumed someone was near you," Simon said. "What did you find out about Microtechnology?"

"Nothing relevant or suspicious. I did have a chance to download the company's mainframe. I'll check it out in a moment." He walked toward Danny, who was standing and facing him. "Looks like you have a real job now...cleaning toilets."

"I've had a lot of practice with all the crap you dish out."

Chuckles filled the room.

Danny sat back down and continued his computer magic on the keyboard. A few minutes later, he announced, "Unbelievable."

Janet, who was talking with Simon, turned her attention toward Danny. "What's unbelievable?"

"I read an email dated yesterday afternoon at 4:23 to the CEO of Dickerson Research. It was sent from someone inside Beyond Infinity warning the CEO to be aware of a division of CDC called the Federal Medical Investigators. They may be investigating them in the next couple of days. Someone in Pine Bluff had inquired about their company and

Microtechnology…which of course was Frank."

"It sounds like The Circle is getting concerned about our investigation," Janet stated. "They may be worried we might be getting close to their evil domain."

"Hopefully, we're getting close to the truth about them," Simon interjected. "Proving they're involved with the six deaths would put a nail in their coffin."

He glanced around the room at each of the agents. Janet and Karen sat at the end of the beds, Kenneth sat at the café table, and he and Janet stood near Frank and Danny, who sat in front of their computers. "There's not much we can do now except for our two computer wizards Frank and Danny. I thought we might order pizza. What do you think?"

"Pizza is one of my favorite foods," Frank said excitedly.

"Are you kidding us?" Jean said, staring at Frank. "Most foods are your favorite."

"Pizza sounds good to me," Janet answered, followed by positive responses from everyone in the room.

Simon ordered a variety of pizza with different toppings from a local pizza delivery company. He and Janet went to the end of the hallway to a soda machine and brought back sodas for everyone.

"This will be our first pizza party," Janet announced.

She couldn't remember ever having pizza ordered for the Major Crime Unit at the Marion County Sheriff department. Of course, FMI wasn't your normal law enforcement agency.

Kenneth rose from his café table, walked over and stood behind Danny. "Can you print out copies of the U.S. map depicting sites The Circle is in contact with on a regular basis? Along with the names associated with the sites."

"I already did that," he answered, reaching to a manila folder next to his computer.

"Can I have a copy too?" Simon asked.

Everyone asked for a copy except Frank.

A few minutes later, Simon exclaimed, "I can't believe this."

"What can't you believe?" Janet asked, who was sitting next to him at the side of one of the beds.

"Look at this name." He pointed to a name on the printout.

Janet peered down at the name, Phillip Pearson, Chief Medical Examiner for Wayne County, Michigan. "He must be involved with The Circle." She thought for a few seconds. "It's probably why he called you when we were in Chambersburg. He wanted you to give him information on our investigation, so he could pass the information on to higher ups in The Circle."

"Who are you talking about?" Jean asked.

"Phillip Pearson, a medical examiner, Simon and I visited in Detroit during our investigation of the Whispers Before Death Case. Simon did a medical rotation with him during his fourth year in medical school."

Simon pursed his lips, then said, "I guess we can't trust anyone during our investigation. They might be part of The Circle's intertwining network of deceiving associates. Although, Arlo Cramer may be able to give us information of someone at his company with one or more symptoms of the Deadly Unknowns Case."

Frank stopped typing on his keyboard and turned around with a disappointing expression. "I thought we'd call our investigation the Three Deadly Signs Case or maybe Hear, Speak, See No Evil Case."

"Both are good. But we'll stick with mine."

"Can I interject into this conversation?" Kenneth asked.

"You sure can."

"Thanks. Arlo Cramer could give us legal grounds to obtain a federal search warrant for Dickerson Research."

Janet looked at Frank. "Can you get Arlo Cramer's home address? I thought maybe it would be more effective if we knocked on Mr. Cramer's front door and ask him personally. He might be more willing to talk to us in person than talking on the phone with him."

"I'd make a house call," Kenneth said, supporting Janet's plan.

"Since we're a democratic country," said Simon, "how do the rest of you vote?"

Frank, Jean and Karen all answered, "House call."

"I also vote yes," Simon added. "That's it. We'll make a personal visit. Janet and I will go to his house this evening."

About forty minutes later, there was a knock on their door. "It's probably the pizza," Frank said, then smacked his lips together.

Jean walked over to the door and opened it. A man in his mid-thirties stood there holding five boxes of pizzas. Jean reached out and grabbed the boxes. Simon now stood next to Jean. He paid the delivery man, including a five-dollar tip. Jean set the cardboard boxes on the café table along with a stack of paper napkins. The aroma of pizza filled the room. Everyone shuffled to the table and grabbed a triangular-shaped piece of pizza and a napkin.

Frank wrinkled his forehead as a puzzled expression arose. He brought the pizza to his nose and inhaled deeply through his nose. "Don't eat the pizza," he shouted. Everyone became startled by his command. Danny's mouth was wide opened with the pointed end of the pizza a couple of inches from his lips, ready to take a mouth-watering bite.

Janet replied, "Why not?"

"There's an odor of almonds coming from it."

"Are you saying there is cyanide in them?"

"Unless this pizza place uses almonds in all their pizzas."

"I have a solution in my van that can detect cyanide," Danny said. "I'll run to my van and get it."

"I'll go with him," suggested Kenneth, as he touched his shoulder holstered. "Just in case he runs into trouble." They hurried out of the room.

"Let me call the pizza company," Janet said, "and ask for the description of the delivery man. I can't believe The Circle had infiltrated a pizza making company."

"I'll call them," Simon said. "I already have the number in my phone." He called the pizza establishment. "We ordered five pizzas." A short pause. "No. The man already delivered them. This may sound strange request, but can you describe the delivery man?"

Chapter Eighteen

Simon put his phone on speaker. "My delivery guy is nineteen-years-old," answered a man.

"Do you have more than one delivery guy?"

"No, I don't. Why are you asking me? Is something wrong?" There was concern in his voice.

"All I can say is a man in his mid-thirties delivered the pizzas. I'm Agent Simon Woods of FMI, Federal Medical Investigators. Did the young man have deliveries before he was supposed to deliver our pizza?"

"Yes. Randy had one delivery before yours."

"Can you call his cell phone number? I'll wait."

Simon looked at Janet. "The question is, where's the real pizza delivery guy?"

She shrugged her shoulders. "If in fact the pizzas are laced with cyanide, did the perpetrator kill the delivery guy?" Janet prayed the young man was alive.

"He didn't answer his cell phone. I'm worried."

"Give me the address of his delivery."

"327 Andrews Street."

"What's the phone number of the caller from this address?" The man gave him the number. He turned to Janet. Call the number and see who answers."

"I'm already dialing the number. It's ringing now." She put her phone on speaker.

"You've reached a number that's no longer in use," stated a programmed female voice.

"They used a throwaway phone," Kenneth stated. "No way to trace it."

Simon shook his head in disgust, then said to the man at the pizza place, "I'm going to call the Pine Bluff Police Department and have them check out the address you gave me. What type of vehicle does your delivery man drive? Also, what's Randy's full name?"

"He drives a red Ford Escort. His name is Randy Miller."

"Thank you. A Pine Bluff Police officer will notify you when they find Randy."

Danny and Kenneth came into the room. "I have it." Danny walked over to the café table. He removed an eyedropper from a small bottle filled with his cyanide testing solution. Danny squeezed the rubber bulb at the end of the eyedropper. Three drops fell onto three different areas of the pizza. The areas immediately turned blue. "It's positive for cyanide."

"Thank God for Frank's super smelling," Karen said standing next to Frank and placing her hand on his shoulder as he sat facing the café table with the tainted pizza. "We all would've gotten either deathly ill or died shortly after eating the pizza."

Frank reached up with his right hand and touched the back of Karen's hand. "Plus, we gave the perp a five-dollar tip."

Karen chuckled. She turned to Janet, who was standing next to Simon near the café table. "Janet. I was wondering why you didn't have a premonition feeling or hear a warning from your inner voice when the supposed pizza guy came to our door?"

"I'll normally get the feeling or inner voice when I'm directly involved, such as focused on opening a door, turning a corner, walking into a room, or about to answer a phone. Including recently when I was sitting in a restaurant, I experienced my ominous feeling but couldn't pinpoint who it was coming from. When the potential killer came to the door a while ago, I was talking with Danny, concentrating on what he was doing."

She turned her attention toward Simon when he heard him talking with Detective Thomas. He was giving the detective the details on what had transpired regarding the cyanide-tainted pizza and the bogus pizza delivery guy.

"The guy appeared to be in his mid-thirties and was about five-foot nine inches with a medium build. He wore black shorts, a dark green T-shirt and white laced tennis shoes along with sunglasses and an Arkansas Razorback cap. No distinguishing marks on his arms or legs," Simon paused, then added, "When I think about it now, the guy also wore leather gloves. So, I don't think there'd be fingerprints on the pizza boxes. Talk to you soon. Bye." He put his cell phone away. "Detective Thomas is going to send a squad car to the address supplied by the manager of the pizza place. The detective will be here to take statements from us and take the pizzas back to the forensic lab." Simon moved forward a couple of steps, then stopped behind Frank. "Can you bring up the surveillance camera for the hotel? I'd like to see what kind of vehicle this poison assassin is driving."

"Sure, boss." Frank's fingers tapped rapidly over the keyboard. A moment later, the hotel's lobby came into view with the fake pizza delivery guy carrying five boxes of pizza. The guy's head was bent downward, unable to get a good view of his face, which was irrelevant since Jean and Simon obtained a good look at him when he delivered the pizzas to the room. Frank switched the scene to the hotel's parking lot. A red Ford Escort drove through the parking lot and stopped at the front entranceway. The perpetrator exited the car with the pizza. "That's our guy. He's driving Randy Miller's car."

Janet sighed. "No help there. Other than if the car is found, forensic investigators might find trace evidence such as hair from the perp. The planting of the cyanide was done by a professional. I'm sure the perp thought no one would detect cyanide in the pizza. Of course, he didn't know we had an agent with super smelling...or, as matter of fact, about any of us with our ESP abilities. This guy and The Circle are probably frustrated we have foiled their attempts at killing us."

About forty minutes had passed when Detective Thomas showed up with a forensic investigator. The investigator grabbed the five pizzas. Frank was disheartened as one of his favorite foods left the room without being able to eat it. The detective interviewed Jean regarding the fake delivery man and honed in on the perp's description. She, like Simon, could only give limited facial features due to the sunglasses and baseball cap. Detective Thomas obtained a copy of the hotel's security CD from the manager showing the perp coming and leaving the hotel.

The detective stood in the room with the FMI agents when his cell phone rang. "Hello." Detective Thomas' voice was sharp and harsh. He listened to the caller without saying a word. Then, "Thank God, Randy Miller is okay. Did he get a description of the assailant?" A long pause. "Oh. I see. Thanks." He put his phone away, then turned his attention toward Janet. "The young man was tied up and unharmed. The address turned out to be a vacant house. Randy had stated to the police, when the front door opened. He was met with a stun gun, incapacitating him. Mr. Miller stated the attacker wore a baseball cap and sunglasses. He was then tied up with nylon zip restraints around his wrist and ankles. This was obviously done by a professional. Apparently, someone doesn't want you to continue investigating the six mysterious deaths."

"We agree," Janet said. "As soon as we obtain any information and evidence to the person or persons responsible, I'll let you know."

"Thanks, Agent Bennett. We'll make sure to keep in touch." Detective Thomas left the room.

"Do you think you should've told the detective about our plans of infiltrating Beyond Infinity?" Karen asked.

"No. At least not now. The fewer people outside our team know what we're doing the less chance of The Circle finding out our plans."

"You're right. I should've realized that since Tyler and I spied on you and your team in Chambersburg."

They all decided to go to the restaurant instead of ordering in. Danny changed back into his regular clothes. He wouldn't be leaving for another few hours for his evening janitorial job, and besides, he didn't want to draw attention to his janitorial outfit in case a customer in the restaurant worked at Beyond Infinity or knew someone who worked there.

It was nearing four o'clock when they returned to the hotel.

Danny put his janitorial outfit on in the bathroom while the rest of the FMI team waited in the room.

Janet stood in the center of the room next to Simon and Kenneth when Danny walked out of the bathroom. With everyone in the room, Simon said, "In the few hours we may be getting answers to the six deaths, and to who's responsible for the attempted killing of our team. We can be fairly sure it's The Circle. Like we've said on several occasions, we'll need hard evidence to bring them down."

"I hope Danny doesn't get caught," Jean said with concern.

"The worse they could do is kill me," Danny said matter-of-factly.

"Can I have your van if that happens?" Frank asked earnestly.

"Sure. It's all yours."

"Can you two be serious for a moment?" Simon asked.

They both nodded with grins.

"Janet and I will drive to Arlo Cramer's house in a little while. Thought about taking Kenneth with us but I think it would be too intimidating to him. Cramer's house and Beyond Infinity at the Pine Bluff Arsenal are less than fifteen minutes away. If Janet and I or Danny need assistance, Kenneth and Jean are close by to respond. As far as Frank, we'll need you by your computer if there's something we need you to look up. Everyone has their assignments." He looked at Janet. "Are you ready?"

"I'm ready."

I've been born ready. She noticed a grin from Simon, as if he read her thought. Of course, that would be impossible.

They left the hotel with Danny. The computer wizard got into his vehicle and drove away. Janet put the home address of Arlo Cramer in the Suburban's GPS. They followed the instruction of the GPS's female synthesizer voice. "From what we found out at Dickerson Research this morning, Mr. Cramer left work at three-thirty. He should be home by now."

Thirteen minutes later, Simon pulled into Cramer's driveway. A garage stood at the end of the driveway to the right of the house. His vehicle is probably in the garage, thought Janet. The front and side yard opposite the driveway was well-maintained with manicured grass and flower beds. They exited the Suburban, walked to the front door and Simon rang the doorbell. An overwhelming ominous sensation engulfed every nerve ending in her body as her inner voice said, "*death*." She touched Simon's forearm. "Something bad happened inside the house. My inner voice stated death."

Simon turned the doorknob and gently pushed. The door opened. No sound was coming from a TV, radio or human voices from inside the house. Dead silence. "Hello, anyone home?" Simon shouted.

No response from a human or animal. Janet drew her Glock, as did Simon as he pushed the front door completely open. Simon stepped aside, allowing Janet to enter first.

"Hello, Mr. Cramer," yelled Janet.

She quickly scanned the living room. No one present. The kitchen was in front of them about twenty feet away to the right. To the left of the living room was a hallway leading to the back of the house. The hallway was dimly lit by nature's late afternoon light. She and Simon walked across the carpeted living room floor and stopped at the entranceway to the kitchen. Straight ahead, lying on the floor was a man. A pool of blood lay around his head. Janet stepped forward peering down at the body. "It's…it's Alex Mendelson." His right arm was tugged underneath him. Movement from a door to her left caused her to quickly raise her gun and point it at the opening door. "This is Agent Bennett from FMI. I have a gun pointed at you."

"Don't shoot, agent. It's Arlo Cramer."

The door opened. He stepped forward a couple of feet, then stopped. Arlo's right arm dangled against the side of his body, as his hand held a revolver. "I'm sorry I didn't respond to your shouts when you walked into the house. I couldn't be sure if you weren't with this guy." Arlo continued forward, stopped and laid the gun on top of the kitchen table.

"What happened here?" Janet asked as she put her Glock back into its holster.

Simon also put his gun away.

"He wanted to know what I told you agents. I said I didn't say anything about anyone having the symptoms. He didn't believe me and pulled a gun from his waistband. I reacted and knocked the gun out of his hand. I then reached into a kitchen drawer and removed my revolver. By then he had retrieved his gun and was about to shoot me. I shot him before he could shoot me. It happened so fast."

Simon was about to roll Mendelson onto his back. "Don't move him yet," Janet said. "I need to get a picture of him first." She snapped four different photos at different angles.

Simon rolled the body onto its right side exposing the right arm. Alex's right hand grasped onto a gun. A bullet hole had penetrated through his forehead. His death mask showed a surprised, shocked expression. He then rolled Mendelson back onto his stomach, then said, "Amazing you kept your faculties together and reacted extremely fast."

"I was in the U.S. Army Special Forces in my early to mid-twenties."

"You were a Green Beret," Janet said. "I guess Mendelson didn't do his homework before confronting you at your house. I'll call the police and report the shooting. You have nothing to worry about. This was definitely self-defense. Besides, Mendelson was an international fugitive." Janet bent down next to the body and removed a wallet and laminated ID. His name on the driver's license was Lucas Powers. The ID confirmed him as an employee of The Circle. Alex's cell phone rang. She removed the throw-away phone from his belt holster. No name, just a phone number. The area code looked familiar. She didn't want to push the talk icon and alert the caller something had happened to Alex. The ringing phone stopped. "I'll have Frank trace the phone number after I call the detective."

"Good idea."

She called Detective Thomas and told him what had taken place at the ex-Green Beret's home.

"It sure seems like trouble follow you guys," said the detective. "I'll be there shortly with CSI and the coroner's office."

"Okay. See you then."

"What did he say about the shooting?"

"Like what other people had said about us and our agents. Trouble seems to follows us."

Janet nodded, as she sat down at the kitchen table. She then called Frank. "Hi, Frank." She told him about Alex Mendelson being shot and the phone call. "Can you find out the name of the person where this number came from? Also, see if there's any information on Lucas Powers. He was carrying an Arkansas driver's license and two credit cards." She read the license number and the credit card name and numbers to Frank. "Hopefully, you'll be able to get pertinent information on him."

"Will do. I'll call you back when I get the information. By the way, we found some interesting data on some of the people described from Danny's location sites of The Circle's affiliates in the United States. For one thing, we have proof Adam Fletcher, the leader of the Eternal Order of Zeus in Pennsylvania, the guy in Pennsylvania you and Simon talked with at his house, has been in contact with The Circle for a few years. I'll discuss more when you and Simon get back here."

"Talk to you in a while. Bye." Janet told Simon about Adam Fletcher.

Simon sat down at the kitchen table, a few feet away from Alex Mendelson. "We had a suspicion the leader of this organization wasn't telling us the truth regarding knowing anything about The Circle."

Arlo sat across from Janet and to the left of Simon, out of view of Mendelson's dead body. "You've mentioned The Circle a couple of times," Arlo said. "We have been told to never mention or acknowledge their name to anyone outside our company. Our company leaders told us we were doing vital research for our country and didn't want evil entities or foreign countries to obtain our research data. I eventually figured it out: The Circle was the evil entity, and if you went against them, you and your family could disappear…or succumb to a tragic accident,"

"What were you about to tell us before Mr. Payne came into your room this morning?" Janet asked.

Arlo glanced down at the table, then answered, "I might as well tell you everything since I killed an enforcer of The Circle. For sure, I can't go back to work at Dickerson Research. What I was about to say to you this morning was about a man on the second-floor lab. He suddenly lost his hearing about two weeks ago. He never came back to work. We were told he had transferred to another company."

"What was his position with the company?"

"He was a computer programmer."

"Do you know what his specific job was for the company?"

"No. I wasn't privy to the programing process to our nanochips and microchips. I dealt with the casing around the chips. I did know the completed chips were sent out to another facility."

"Was it called Beyond Infinity?" Janet asked, hoping the answer would be yes.

"Never heard of Beyond Infinity. I don't know where the chips are sent."

It wasn't the answer Janet wanted to hear. Irrespective, they had likely found the company making the nanochip responsible for the deaths of six people. They'd need a court order, a warrant to obtain one of their nanochips to compare it with the nanochip taken from the brain of the sixth victim. She wasn't sure they'd have legal grounds to proceed to the judicial system. A question crossed Janet's mind. Where were the nanochips sent? How and why did they end up into the ear canals of six unfortunate people? Beyond Infinity might hold the answer to these questions.

Detective Thomas, CSI and the medical examiner's investigator arrived. Within ninety minutes, the crime scene was thoroughly investigated and processed. The detective would investigate the justified self-defense shooting of Alexander Mendelson, alias Caleb Johnson and Lucas Powers. Janet explained to the detective she and Simon came to Arlo Cramer's house to discuss an unanswered question without his CEO present regarding an employee at his company having lost their hearing.

"Do you think Dickerson Research had to do something with the six deaths?"

"Yes. We believe they developed the nanochip found in our sixth victim's brain. We also believe The Circle is the mastermind to these deaths. The guy lying on the floor works for The Circle as an enforcer, and he was going to kill Mr. Cramer to prevent him from talking about what his company was making."

Janet decided not to inform the detective of Danny's stealthy undercover role at Beyond Infinity. Once they could tie The Circle and the nanochips with the six deaths together, they would then bring the Pine Bluff Police detective and the FBI into the picture.

Janet and Simon left the house. As they were about to get into the Suburban, Simon's cell phone rang. He glanced at the caller ID. "It's Frank."

Janet's first thought flashed across her mind. Danny might be in danger.

Chapter Nineteen

Simon sat in front of the steering wheel, glanced at Janet, who had a worried expression, then pushed the talk button on his cell phone, along with the speaker button. "What's up, Frank?"

"We were getting worried. You guys have been gone over two hours."

"Sorry. We should've called you and let you know what was happening."

"As long as you're okay."

"We're fine." Simon filled Frank in on what happened at Arlo Cramer's house. Frank also had his speaker turned on so Jean and Kenneth could hear their conversation. "Kenneth, what do you think about us getting a warrant to search Dickerson Research and confiscate the nanochips and microchips and compare them with the one in our sixth victim's brain?"

"Unlikely a judge would sign a warrant without concrete evidence of their wrongdoing. You'd have to have a reliable informant, along with recorded conversations, emails, or documents incriminating the organization, group or person. You said Arlo Cramer only had hearsay and no concrete evidence. As far as Alex Mendelson having aliases, I'm sure The Circle will deny they knew anything about it."

"You're right. Even if we procured one of their nanochips, they'd say someone other than them reprogrammed the chip." A short pause. "Frank, I need you to check a phone number." He gave him the number.

"I almost forgot to tell you," Frank said. "After we talked last time, I found some unfortunate information. Adam Fletcher died a few days ago."

"How did he die?"

"Mr. Fletcher was changing a widow screen on the second floor from inside the house. Apparently, he was leaning out the window when he lost his balance, causing him to fall about twenty feet and landing on top of his head, fracturing his neck, which killed him instantly."

"It seems like some of the people we investigate regarding The Circle happened to die for one reason or another."

"You're right. It sure seems like it."

"We're on our way back to the hotel. I assume you haven't heard anything from Danny?"

"No. Nothing. I tried to hack into Beyond Infinity's security system surveillance cameras like I did successfully at Brighton Research during our Deadly Seizure Case in Chambersburg. Unfortunately, Beyond Infinity has a closed security system. The company doesn't utilize computer programs or WiFi connections, making it impossible to hack. As you already know, Danny can't take his cell phone or any other electronic device inside the facility, nor can he use their landline phones since all calls must go through a central computerized switchboard. It doesn't allow personal phone calls. Danny isn't an ordinary person. He's a master computer wizard. If there's a problem, he'll send me a coded message from their computer to mine, along with all incriminating information or programs."

"As usual, the two of you have everything under control. We'll see you soon. Bye." Simon put his phone away and left Arlo Cramer's house.

"Thank God, Danny is okay. At least, as far as we know."

"Most of time you're skeptical on things you haven't witnessed or interacted with like the adage, no news is good news regarding Danny's well-being."

"It's the way I've been for a long time. It prevents being blindsided."

"You're right, it's better not to be overconfident on certain things." *I wonder if she's skeptical about our amorous feelings toward each other.*

"One thing I'm not skeptical about…our feelings toward each other."

"Do you read minds? I was thinking the same thing."

Janet chuckled. "This isn't the first time you said this to me. Some psychiatrist stated people who live together for many years at times seemed to be able to read the thoughts of their spouse. I'm not sure where we fit into this scenario since we've only known each other for a few weeks."

Simon stopped at a four-way stop sign. "Maybe it's because of our ESP abilities?"

"Could be. No way to prove or disprove this theory."

The hotel came into view. Since they left Arlo Cramer's house, Simon had continued to look at his sideview mirror for anyone tailing them. Periodically, he glanced at Janet who also appeared to be peering at her sideview mirror. "No one has been following us. What do you think?"

"Nope," she answered with a grin. "Although, I'm sure we haven't heard the last of The Circle and their henchmen."

Frank was sitting in front of his computer when they walked into his room. Jean and Kenneth were sitting at the café table. Frank turned his swivel chair toward them and said, "I found out where the phone number came from you gave me."

"It came from the Wayne County Medical Examiner. Right? On the way to the hotel, I kept thinking the area code sounded familiar. It then dawned on me the area code was from Detroit. The area code would include Phillip Pearson, the medical examiner."

"You're right about the area code being from Detroit, but it wasn't from the medical examiner."

"Then who?"

"Detective Morse of the Detroit Police Department."

Detective Morse flashed across Simon's mind like a sped-up video. The detective handing Janet and him the police file of the murdered security guard at the Ford Dealership. Detective Morse was likely the one who removed the report of the two detectives killed when their car blew up while investigating the dead security guard. "There's no doubt now, Morse and Pearson are involved with The Circle."

"I liked those two," Janet said. placing her hand on the back of Simon's shoulder. "Who would've guessed they were two wolves in sheep clothing?"

Frank's computer beeped, followed by two more beeps. He turned around and peered at the monitor. "Danny is sending me something." Frank's monitor flashed a series of written words, diagrams, pictures rapidly across the screen. "He obviously hacked into their computer system."

Ten minutes passed, then a large, yellow smiling face appeared on the screen. A few seconds later, letters under the emoji began to appear, spelling out: *someone's coming. They saw me.* The screen went blank.

"My God, what can we do?" Frank asked with panic in his voice.

"Plan B," Simon answered. "We go there and get him out."

"Don't we need a search warrant?" Jean asked.

"Not for what we're going to do."

"What's that?" Karen asked.

"Kenneth, Janet and me, will show up at the front security gate with an FBI warrant for the arrest of Roger Kennedy. I had Danny printout an official-looking FBI arrest warrant after he came up with the idea of intruding Beyond Infinity as a new custodian. We'd use it if Danny happened to get into trouble and needed to be rescued."

Kenneth brought out the arrest warrant from the inside pocket of his blazer. "Let's do it.
Serve our arrest warrant."

~ * ~

Kenneth, who was driving, pulled the Suburban up to the security gate of Beyond Infinity. A hundred yards to their left stood the security gate for Pine Bluff Arsenal. An overweight, middle-aged man came out of a metal-framed booth and approached the driver side window of the Suburban. The tinted window opened. Kenneth showed his FBI special agent ID. "We're here to arrest Roger Kennedy." He handed the security guard the official looking fugitive warrant.

The guard peered down at the paper, then turned around and walked back to the partially glassed-in booth. He picked up a phone. A moment later, he began talking to the person at the other end of the call, nodding twice during a twenty second span.

"Do you think he'll let us into the facility?" Janet asked from the backseat of the Suburban.

"I can't see why not. I've done this before and never been denied access to a building to serve a fugitive warrant."

The guard came out of the booth, walked over to Kenneth and handed him the warrant. "We don't have anyone with this name working here."

"You're wrong." Kenneth said loudly. "We know for a fact this fugitive is inside your building. If you don't open this gate and give us access to this building, you will feel the wrath of the FBI. You will be arrested, along with whoever told you our fugitive isn't inside your facility for obstruction of justice. Call your superior back and tell him what I told you. Do you understand?"

A frightened expression burst upon his face. He hurried back to the booth and called someone. A moment later, the gate opened.

"You almost had me convinced about what you told the guard," Simon said from the front passenger seat.

"Even if we didn't know Danny was inside Beyond Infinity, I knew the guard was lying about not knowing Roger Kennedy and that he wasn't inside the building."

Another overweight, middle-aged security guard stood at the front door as the FMI team exited their parked vehicle. Simon saw a solemn expression on the guard's face. "Follow me, I'll take you to the fugitive, Kennedy."

They walked past two elevators to their right and down a long hallway with several doors on either side. The rhythmic sound of their shoes striking against a tiled floor filled the air. Simon whispered to Janet, "Feeling anything?"

"No. Not yet."

Simon felt uneasy. Why would they first emphatically deny the existence of Roger Kennedy working at their facility, then under threat of the FBI let them inside the building? Something didn't feel right, even with Janet not experiencing her warning feeling and inner voice.

"Are you taking us to our fugitive?" Kenneth asked.

"Yes, I am," said the guard leading the three of them up a dimly lit hallway.

"What happened to the hallway lights? Why is it so dim?" Janet asked.

"We always keep them dimmed to conserve energy."

Kenneth reached up with his right hand sliding it underneath his blazer to the upper left chest wall area where his shoulder holster contained his Glock. Simon saw his brother's movement, followed by a negative gesture of his head, likely indicating the guard wasn't telling the truth. He bumped Janet's left arm, leaned toward her and whispered in her ear, "Trap."

Janet nodded, then reached up underneath her blue blazer to her Glock's left shoulder holster.

The guard stopped in front of a door to his right. "Your fugitive is being held inside the room." He stepped aside.

Why isn't the guard opening the door and going in? Simon thought.

"You go in first," Janet demanded as she removed her Glock from its holster.

Kenneth and Simon also removed their guns.

"I-I have to leave. They're-they're waiting inside the room for you along with Emer...Roger Kennedy."

"They already know about us and Danny," Kenneth whispered as he quickly disarmed the security guard of his gun from its holster. "We know it's a trap. Agent Danny Emerick's not in this room." He forced the guard to open the door and walk into a darkened room.

A hail of bullets penetrated the front of the guard as he fell to the floor, killing him instantly. Kenneth hunched down in a squatting position, flicked on a wall switch to his left lighting the room with a burst of blinding light. Two guards stood about twelve feet away pointing their guns toward the door. Kenneth and Janet in squatting positions fired their Glocks at the assassins. They fell to the floor. Dead.

Simon, who stayed in the hallway to the left of the doorway during the gunfire, periodically exposed his head to observe the array of gunfire between the assassins and his team members. He walked into the room and looked around. "No Danny. He has to be somewhere in this building."

"It'll take a long time to search each of the rooms," Kenneth said. "I wasn't expecting this scenario. I need to call the local FBI office and let 'em know what happened here."

"I'll call Detective Thomas," Janet said as she retrieved her cell phone.

"We need to find Danny." A chilling thought crossed his mind. "He may already be dead."

"It'll be too dangerous to check each of the rooms," Kenneth said. "We don't know how many more guards there are waiting to put a bullet in us. We then have to contend with the other employees who still may be in the building. The most logical thing to do is wait for reinforcements. We'll wait in the lobby for them."

Simon gently grabbed Janet's hand as she talked with Detective Thomas. She smiled back at him. After they made their phone calls, the three of them walked toward the lobby with their guns by their side, ready to defend themselves if they were threatened by any remaining guards. Within ten minutes the Pine Bluff Police and their SWAT officers, Crime Scene Investigators, and the county coroner investigator arrived on the scene.

Detective Thomas walked up to Janet, Simon and Kenneth. "There's never a dull moment with you guys. The first priority will be to find Agent Emerick while making sure there aren't any other armed people in the building wanting to do harm against us." He turned to the commander of the SWAT team, filled him in what had happened, and what needed to be done.

"We want to be with SWAT officers as they search the building for Danny," Simon requested to the commander.

"Stay behind us, agents," he agreed reluctantly. "We'll break up into three squads of three officers. There are three floors to this building and a basement." He turned around and shouted, "Alpha squad search the basement, Beta squad the first floor and Omega squad the second floor. Whoever's done first will go to the third floor. Each squad will have an agent with you. Let's move out. I'll be here in the lobby's command post. The stairwell is at the end of each hallway."

Simon went with the Omega squad to the second floor. He stood behind the officers as they began opening doors along a long hallway. His heart raced as each door was opened with an officer yelling, "Police." So far, each room was empty except for lab apparatuses. He saw microscopes varying in size and types, and a variety of several other lab instruments. When they were near the end of the hallway, the SWAT officers opened a door. Attached to their long weapons was a LED flashlight lighting up one-third of the room. Glass containers resembling fish aquariums sat on a long countertop against the backwall. Simon reached to his left and turned on the room's fluorescent lighting.

"Nothing in here, agent," said one of the officers.

"Yes, there is. It's just not human." Simon walked over to one of the glass containers. He bent down and stared at a colony of black worm-like creatures, creatures with the same appearance and color as the one the pathologist found slithering in the brain of the sixth victim, Robert Sears. "We got you."

"Did you say something, Agent Woods?" asked one of the officers from across the room near the door.

"Yes. I found something that'll put people away for a long, long time."

Simon closed the room's door, then looked up. Above the door he read the number 225.

~ * ~

Janet followed behind the three SWAT officers as they wove between furnaces, fenced-in storage bins, shelves and a variety of closed locked doors. As they approached a locked door, an ominous feeling overwhelmed her, followed by her inner voice: "*Danger.*"

"There's someone behind the door," she exclaimed. "They may have a gun."

The office turned around, and said, "How do you know?"

"I'm listening to a reliable gut feeling. Be careful." Would the officer heed to her words?

"This is Pine Bluff SWAT. We know you're in there. Put your gun down and come out with your hands placed on top of your head. There's no way this situation will turn out good if you don't do what I say."

The sound of the door unlocking, then the door slowly opened. "I'm unarmed. Don't shoot," said a security guard in his late twenties with the palms of his hands pressed against the top of his head. Behind him on the floor was an AK-40. Behind the weapon sat Danny, bound and tied.

He was alive.

Janet rushed into the room and removed a gag from his mouth. "Are you all right?"

"I'm fine." Sweat cascaded from his forehead to his cheeks.

An officer cut the nylon strapping from around his body, releasing Danny from the metal chair.

"Let's get you out of here," Janet said, putting her hand on his back.

"I found proof The Circle was involved in the six deaths in Pine Bluff, the Deadly Seizure Case in Chambersburg, and in Ocala for the Whispers Before Death Case."

Chapter Twenty

Janet and Danny walked into the lobby. The sound of voices from officers, several employees, and the periodical transmission static of two-way radios created an atmosphere of controlled chaos. Janet saw Kenneth talking with the SWAT commander and Detective Thomas to her right. She didn't see Simon anywhere in the lobby. The added sound of boots striking the floor behind them caused her to turn around. Three SWAT officers walked toward her and Danny from the hallway leading to the building's first-floor stairwell. Simon appeared from behind the officers. A smile lit up his face when their eyes met. He then glanced at smiling Danny, who made a fist with his thumb pointing upward.

"Thank God, you're okay," Simon said as he walked up to them.

"I have a lot to tell you guys and the rest of our team," Danny said eagerly.

The front door opened and in walked five people, three men and two women, wearing FBI short sleeve shirts with the chest seal logo, and each of them wore caps with FBI printed across the front. Two of them carried large rectangular forensic cases.

"Reinforcements have arrived," Janet said. "We'll need to share all our evidence and findings with them, the Pine Bluff Police and Detective Thomas. From what Danny told me, we have enough proof to prosecute The Circle in federal court."

Simon rubbed the front of his neck. "In room 225 on the second floor I saw black slimy worm-like creatures identical to the one Robert Sears had crawling through his brain."

"I saw them too," Danny confirmed.

They all walked over to where Kenneth was talking with the leader of the group of FBI special agents. After introductions and greetings between them, Kenneth mentioned he found a lab on the first floor with nanochips, similar, if not identical, to the ones they saw at Dickerson Research. There were other types of microchips with paraphernalia on dental implants.

"I believe this should finally put a halt to The Circle's criminal enterprises," Janet announced.

"At least put a huge dent in it," Kenneth added. "Another FBI forensic team are on the way here from Mississippi to help out document all evidence found in this facility, including forensic computer specialists. The CEO and other supervising personnel are being served with summons to appear at our FBI offices for questioning."

"You guys don't waste any time, do you?"

"As I told you the other day, we've had our eye on The Circle and its affiliates. You and your FMI agents opened their Pandora's box for us. I can see why there were so many attempts by The Circle and its affiliates to silence you and your agents."

Simon called Frank and told him what had transpired at Beyond Infinity. He was relieved Danny was okay. Simon and Janet then gave their statements about the shooting of the two security guards to Detective Thomas. As they were standing in the lobby, the coroner's assistants, along with the coroner's investigator, wheeled the three bodies of the deceased guards by them.

With federal search warrants in their hands, the FBI forensic team began their tedious task of scrutinizing every room in the Beyond Infinity building.

Janet, Simon and Danny walked out of the lobby and into the Suburban. Danny had given Kenneth the keys to his van, so he could drive back to the hotel after he was done. Simon put the headlights on as he drove out of the parking lot and headed back to the hotel

A sigh of relief overcame Janet as she sat in the front passenger seat. "It's been a trying and adrenaline-filled day. I'm glad most of it is finally over."

"Me too," Danny agreed. "Sitting in an office desk chair when the security guard came into the room didn't look good. The guy questioned me regarding why I was sitting in front of a computer. I told him I was playing a computer game. He didn't believe me. He then called someone on his cell phone, telling them about me and what he should do. The guard snapped my picture on his phone, then sent it to someone by email. I sat there for quite a while until the security guard received a cell phone call. After he hung up, I was taken to the basement."

"Makes sense," Janet said. "They probably put your picture into a facial recognition computer program, matching it to you in our FMI agent profiles. The bad guys also use law enforcement tools. When Kenneth called out the security guard at Beyond Infinity's front gate, they probably figured they'd kill us and deny we showed up. Afterward, they would've likely gotten rid of all evidence tying them to the deaths in Pine Bluff, Chambersburg and Ocala."

"Why do you think The Circle developed all these killing devices?" Danny asked.

"World dominance through fear. The Circle's scheme is to disable legitimate world leaders and take control of world governments. They didn't expect local, state or federal authorities would solve these isolated deaths. I think they were trying to develop a perfect killing method and use it worldwide to get control over governments. Federal Medical Investigators were getting in their way and needed elimination. I'm sure they were frustrated and baffled how we seemed to avoid tragedy."

"You sure are a smart lady," Danny said.

Janet smiled. "Thank you. I have a lot of common sense and deductive reasoning. Besides, you're not intellectually deprived. Your inventions definitely helped us detect and solve The Circle's evilness and vast number of affiliates. Like what Simon has told us on several occasions, we are a team effort joining our ESP abilities and talents to solve difficult medical mysteries."

"I couldn't have said it any better," Simon agreed, as he looked at Janet, then winked.

Janet winked back with a smile.

"Keep your eyes on the road, boss," Danny said, sitting in the backseat behind Janet. "We don't want to get into an accident."

Simon chuckled. "Frank's idiosyncrasies are rubbing off onto you, Danny."

Danny grinned. "Thanks for the compliment." He leaned to the space between the two front seats and turned his head toward Janet. "I was thinking what you said a bit ago about 'most of it is finally over.'"

"We and the Pine Bluff Police Department haven't found the fake pizza guy yet. I have a feeling the guy is long gone since the FBI is now in charge of our investigation."

Simon parked the vehicle in the hotel's parking lot, then the three of them walked into the hotel. Jean opened Frank and Danny's room door. Frank was sitting in front of his computer with Karen sitting next to him when they walked into the room.

"Boss, I found out why Beyond Infinity chose those six victims and how they planted the larvae into their ears. The data Danny sent to my computer contains a wealth of damaging information against them."

"Great," Simon said as he and Janet walked over and stood next to him.

"All the victims were at the Pine Bluff Mall. A bogus hearing aid company set up a free hearing test booth. The technician randomly placed a long-acting numbing solution into the ear canal telling the victim it was to soften up wax, then inconspicuously placed the larvae into the canal. The bogus hearing test was then performed."

"That explains why there wasn't any medical record of the hearing test being done or the victims being seen by an Ear, Nose and Throat doctor," Simon conjectured. "The victims were probably alone and more than likely didn't tell anyone in their family they had a hearing test at the mall."

"You're right. According to Beyond Infinity, they chose people who were alone without a family member or friend with them at the time of the test."

Simon briefly touched the top of Frank's shoulder, then said, "If it wasn't for you and Danny's computer wizardry, I'm sure we wouldn't have solved these deaths in such a short period of time or maybe not at all. But I have to say, everyone contributed to solving the deaths." He nodded at everyone in the room. "Over the past several weeks, our passenger jet nearly crashed into the ground, our psychic abilities prevented us from being involved in a deadly car crash, from being blown up, crushed by a tree struck by a lightning bolt, and poisoned on two different occasions. I'd say we deserve some leisure time off after all these harrowing events and solved medical mysteries."

"Hallelujah," Frank said, followed by everyone else's agreeable comments and Amen. "I'd say we go to the lounge here at the hotel and celebrate with a drink."

"Sounds like a good plan," Simon agreed. "I'm buying the first round,"

There were two couples in the lounge when they sat down at two tables put together. After everyone ordered their drinks, Janet removed her left shoe and rubbed the bottom of her bare foot against Simon's upper right ankle. He grinned, then turned and stared into her eyes, as everyone at the table talked to one another, laughing periodically. Janet visualized Simon and her holding hands as they strolled upon soft, warm sand along an ocean beach. Their bare feet feeling the rhythmic splash of cool ocean waves over them.

"What are you thinking about?" Simon asked.

"Getting away. Leaving my turned-off cell phone in the suitcase."

"Can I leave my suitcase next to yours?"

"Of course, you can." *You can lay your body next to me, too.*

Simon frowned. "Why are you smirking?"

Before she could answer the bartender brought their drinks on a large round tray. Once everyone received their drinks, Frank announced, "Let's toast. I'll start it. Dilly! Dilly!" Everyone brought their drinks to the center of the table. Clinking sound burst from their glasses and bottles, followed by, "Dilly…Dilly." Laughter filled the room.

Janet looked toward the entrance to the lounge and saw Kenneth walk in with a puzzled expression. He probably was wondering why a group of professional people were shouting out a meaningless word used by drunken fraternity boys in a college bar.

"Hey, brother. Let me buy you a drink."

"Sure. Sounds good. I'd like a whiskey sour."

Simon turned around and shouted to the bartender, "Whiskey sour, please."

His brother grinned as he stared down at his brother, then Janet. "Do you mind if I take my shoes off?"

Janet felt a warm rush to her face. She knew a blush radiated from her due to Kenneth's observation of her playing footsie with Simon. "Do what you want. I'm sure standing most of the day takes a toll on your feet."

Kenneth pursed his lips, nodded. "Thanks." He then sat at the end of the table, next to Simon on his right.

Simon told Kenneth what Frank found on Beyond Infinity's computer mainframe from what Danny had sent him earlier. "This should get us, I mean the FBI, the evidence they need to prosecute Beyond Infinity for the death of the six people here in Pine Bluff, and possibly the deaths in Ocala and Chambersburg. The paramount question will be if these deaths can be tied to The Circle."

"Beyond Infinity shouldn't be a problem tying them to all these deaths. The Circle organization may be another story. We'll have to wait and see if there's unequivocal evidence involving them with these deaths. All we have to do is find the dots leading to The Circle."

Simon's cell phone rang. He glanced down at the phone. "It's Brian." The conversations at the table stopped, as everyone looked at Simon.

Janet frowned. Brian had talked with him when they were in Beyond Infinity's lobby earlier. Maybe the director found another case of unsolved, mysterious deaths. *Please don't be the reason he's calling.*

"Yes. We're all back at the hotel having a drink in the hotel's lounge." He listened to Brian with a serious expression. "We'll meet you there. See you tomorrow morning." Simon put his phone away, then sighed. "Future Innovations Today has the results of our DNA."

"What did they say?" Frank asked.

"They want us all to fly back to Virginia Beach for a meeting with the scientist tomorrow morning. Director Littlefield will meet us there."

"No indication what they found?" Janet inquired.

"None. They couldn't eliminate any outsider such as a hacker listening in on our phone call or a computer conference call program."

"That makes sense. Although, the way I look at it logically…if nothing significant was found, they would've said so without us flying there." Janet knew she was right in her assumption, as she looked around the table. Everyone was agreeing with her by nodding along with different gestures, either pressing their lips together, or raising their eyebrows.

"You're right," Simon agreed. "Our plane is scheduled to take off at eight o clock tomorrow morning."

The seven of them sat in the lounge for another hour before retiring to their rooms. Janet stood inside her doorway, watched Simon walk into his room, turn around and whisper loud enough for her to hear, "Good night."

"Good night," she reciprocated in a soft voice. Her feelings toward him touched admiration and love. She hoped soon they could share their feelings with each other, and the next time they said, "goodnight," they'd being lying next to each other.

~ * ~

Their plane landed at the airport in Virginia Beach without any incidences, such as engine failure, loss of cabin pressure or landing gear malfunction. All these scenarios crossed Simon's mind after taking off from Pine Bluff Regional Airport-Grider Field. A black Suburban met the FMI team on the tarmac next to their parked jet passenger plane. Frank sat behind the steering wheel, Karen sat next to him in the front passenger seat, while the remaining agents sat on the two backseat benches. Simon sat next to Janet as their knees touched. A warm sensation encompassed his body, as it did last night in the hotel's lounge when her foot tenderly caressed his lower leg.

Future Innovations Today came into view.

"I'm sort of excited but also nervous to know what the scientist found out about our DNA," Jean said.

"I think we all are feeling the same thing," Simon said turning his head to the left toward Jean, who sat next to Janet. He wasn't a geneticist and didn't have the knowledge of genetic aberrations.

"What I do know for sure," Janet said, "my ESP ability at times is a godsend, other times it's a curse."

"Amen," Karen agreed.

Frank parked the Suburban at the side of the building, where he had parked it on previous occasions when they were here before. An employee met the agents at the employee's entrance door.

Simon turned to Janet. "Besides having a mixed feeling of excitement and nervousness Jean pointed out a while ago, I feel like I'm going to get the test results of a tumor removed from my body, not knowing if its cancer or benign."

They soon would find out what the geneticist discovered as they walked into the conference room.

Chapter Twenty-One

Simon saw Brian Littlefield standing and talking with F.I.T. director Edward Larson at the end of a long conference table toward the front of the room. Several people in white lab coats sat at the table, a table with eight empty chairs remaining. A low murmur of voices filled the room.

Brian turned his head toward Simon and the FMI team. "Hey, guys. Glad you made it safe and sound. Of course, most of you know Director Larson." Brian introduced Kenneth Workman to the director.

Kenneth nodded. "We met for a few moments here at the facility before I went to Pine Bluff. They drew my blood for DNA analysis."

"Oh. I didn't know," Brian said, surprisingly.

"I was about to tell you," Larson said. "I contacted the FBI and informed them what we've been doing here at F.I.T. His director agreed to Agent Workman's DNA analysis." He glanced at the FMI team and the scientist. Everyone please take a seat. There's a lot of information to go over. The information must stay in this room, never to be divulged to anyone outside these walls."

Everyone had a seat at the table.

A man in his mid-fifties stood. "Good morning, everyone. I've met all of you at one time or another, but if you've forgotten, my name is Rod Stevens. I'm a geneticist."

He held a remote-control apparatus and pointed toward a projector screen hanging on the wall in front of the table. A few seconds later, the diagram of a DNA helix appeared on the screen. "We did a genome sequencing. It is the most direct method of detecting mutations, such as single nucleotide polymorphisms and copy number variations. In other words, we isolated a chromosome site on all your DNA helix containing a unique genetic anomaly…an ESP gene. And…"

"So, you isolated the gene giving us our ESP ability," Simon interrupted. "What will you be able to do with this knowledge?"

"There's a few things we've already done." He looked down toward the conference table at Hilda Stevens. "My wife, Hilda, will discuss what we discovered doing a search on the genome sequencing of previous known clairvoyants."

"Why didn't you do this analysis on them before doing us?" Jean asked.

"You agents are asking great questions," Hilda said as she stood and retrieved the remote control from her husband. "We in fact have been doing DNA analysis on these deceased clairvoyants, including Nostradamus and Edgar Cayce. Since they're not living, we obtained DNA from their descendants. We completed their genome sequencing prior to yours. We now know where to look on their DNA helix. Here's what we found: some of the descendants had this ESP gene without demonstrating ESP abilities. We know it's a recessive gene, which means it only needs to be passed down from one parent. An example of a recessive gene is blue eyes. Another example would be a person born with a sixth finger on each hand passed on from a great-grandfather. The gene lay dormant, showing up two generations later."

"Are you saying there are people walking around with the ESP gene and not knowing they have it?" Simon asked.

"Exactly. That's what happened to Janet. She had partially activated the gene for feeling danger, then an inner warning voice awoke from a dormant state. We're not sure what triggered her gene to be activated on two different occasions. The fact is, we haven't determined how any of your special abilities become activated. One theory might be there's a cellular timer in the gene. Another theory is an unknown extrinsic factor turns the gene on. With this knowledge of identifying the ESP gene, we'll be examining the DNA of all the people in our computer data base."

This discovery made sense to Simon since his ESP ability didn't surface until he was around thirteen years old. The fact was all the FMI agents' ESP abilities didn't surface until each of them were teenagers. According to his brother, Kenneth, during a discussion in their hotel room in Pine Bluff, he began sensing people were lying when he was about thirteen. "From what I know all the FMI agents' ESP abilities and mine didn't become activated until our teen age years, except Danny." He glanced across the table at Karen. "Not sure about Ms. Rivers."

Karen leaned back in her chair. "I was sixteen years old when my hearing began to change. I could hear people talking across the room of a busy high school cafeteria. It slowly became more prevalent when I was thirty. Over the years I was able to block out some voices and sounds and focus in on chosen sounds and voices. The noise damper ear apparatus invented by F.I.T. has improved my quality of life even better."

"We're glad it helps you," Hilda said.

"Do you think the ESP gene started in the fifteenth century with Nostradamus?" Jean asked.

"It's as far back we can go genetically following descendants of clairvoyants. We may never know when it first appeared."

Frank moved his chair, causing a piercing scraping sound across a hardwood floor. "Sorry. May I add something to this conversation regarding ESP abilities and clairvoyants?"

"You sure can," Hilda answered.

"From what I've read, the first psychics were called Sybils and date back to around 500 B.C. and possibly over four thousand years ago. Ancient Greece and Romans mentioned them. The word means a person, a psychic, a clairvoyant who makes predictions of the future."

"Wow. You know information most people wouldn't be aware of. What you said is true. It confirms what I said a moment ago. The gene may have appeared back then, and over thousands of years mutated to other ESP abilities all of you possess. Our research is revolutionary, and hopefully we'll be able to unlock these questions you brought up this morning."

Simon remembered something the scientist said to them when

they were here before. "You had mentioned it to us when we were here the first time you hoped to be able to manipulate the ESP gene to enhance or alter our abilities."

"We did say that. We still are pursuing this possibility. What we discovered so far, which is significant, is only the infancy stage of our ESP gene research."

Simon agreed with what Hilda Stevens said earlier regarding not to mention their discovery of the ESP gene to anyone other than to F.I.T. personnel. If evil entities such as The Circle got a hold of their research, they would use it for unscrupulous exploits, not for the good of humanity.

"Does anyone have any questions?" Director Larson said.

Hilda sat down.

"Will Ms. Rivers be coming back to F.I.T. to work?" Frank asked. His voice cracked a couple of times, indicating he had feelings for her and cared about her.

"Oh." A short pause. "I guess it would be up to her."

"I'd like to become an FMI agent," Karen said zealously. "It was discussed on the plane this morning and everyone agreed they'd like me to be an agent."

Simon looked at Brian. "What do you think?"

"She'd be an asset to our team."

"We'll definitely miss her here," said the director.

Frank grinned as he placed his hand on Karen's forearm. "Welcome aboard, Agent Rivers."

"What about you, Special Agent Workman?" Director Larson asked. "Are you going to join the FMI team?"

"No. I'm staying with the FBI. If they need my help any time in the future, I'll assist them if I'm available. I have to say, it was an exciting experience, especially when we were able to arrest the bad guys."

The F.I.T.'s scientist talked for another fifteen minutes on how they isolated the ESP gene through the genome sequencing process and showed each of their DNA results. Director Larson ended the meeting with a thanks to the agents and Director Littlefield for their cooperation. As the F.I.T. staff stood and began to leave, Brian said, "To my agents,

I'd like to say there aren't any mysterious medical deaths reported to me. This means everyone, starting this minute, you all are on leave. Enjoy your time off, you certainly deserve it."

Simon peered into Janet's eyes as a rush of excitement flowed through his body and mind. Thoughts of being with her without the mental worry of an investigation enticed every nerve ending throughout his body. Soon they'd have their intimate time together.

~ * ~

Janet and Simon walked hand to hand as they walked into a luxury hotel adjacent to the Atlantic Ocean in Virginia Beach. When they had left Future Innovation Today, everyone went in different directions. Frank went with Karen to her apartment in Virginia Beach for a homemade meal. Jean, Brian, Danny and Kenneth flew back to Atlanta on FMI's jet.

Janet couldn't believe it. She and Simon were about to spend intimate time together without any of the FMI agents in the near vicinity. Her breathing increased as they walked up to the front counter. Each of them pulling a suitcase with tiny rubber wheels rolling over a stone-tiled floor. Her heart rate increased as she felt it beating rhythmically against her chest wall. She couldn't remember ever feeling this way with a man or even when she was in her early twenties being infatuated with a young man she met in college.

The woman behind the counter stared down at a computer screen in front of her. She then looked up from the screen. "Good afternoon."

"I'd like a room on the lower floor facing the ocean, please."

"So do most people who walk to the counter. Since it's the middle of the week, we have several rooms available. For you and the missus?"

"Yes."

"How many days are you going to stay?"

"Three days."

She and Simon decided on three days, and if they wanted to stay longer, they'd extend their stay. Maybe in three days, they'd be bored with each other and would want to go their own ways. Janet didn't think this scenario would occur. No. The opposite thought ran through her mind.

Simon and Janet stood in front of their room as he reached out to slide the cardkey into the door lock slot. He stopped, looked into Janet's eyes, then said, "Any bad feelings or warning voice."

"No. Only good thoughts and feelings."

Simon unlocked the door. They walked into the room and set their suitcases onto of the first queen-size bed. The curtain on the sliding glass door to their right was pulled completely back exposing a picturesque view of the beach and ocean. He reached out and grabbed Janet's hand. "I can't believe we're here together...alone."

A warm rush encompassed every inch of her body as they embraced, as her eager lips met his in a loving, compassionate kiss.

Simon's cell phone rang. Their lips separated. "I can't believe it."

Janet pulled away from their passionate embrace. "You better answer it. It might be important."

Director Littlefield crossed her mind, calling them about another case of mysterious medical deaths.

Simon removed the ringing cell phone from his blazer. He glanced at the phone. "It's Phillip Pearson. I'll put him on speaker." He pushed the speaker button. "Hello, Phillip."

"This is Detective Stark of the Detroit Police Department. Who am I speaking with?"

"I'm Agent Simon Woods of the Federal Medical Investigators. Why are you calling me on Doctor Pearson's cell phone?"

"Doctor Pearson went missing yesterday. Your number was in his cell phone. When was the last time you talked with him?"

"Last week."

"Did he sound worried about anything?"

"No. Why would you have his cell phone?"

"It was on the nightstand next to his bed. His car is still in the garage."

Janet knew what happened. The Circle was tying up loose ends and Phillip Pearson was one of the loose ends. Evil had no boundaries. There was another person in Detroit they met likely tied to The Circle's demonic web. "This is Agent Bennett."

"Yes, Agent?"

"Agent Woods and I had worked with Detective Morse on a case in Detroit. He knew…"

"Detective Morse died this morning of an apparent heart attack."

"I'm so sorry to hear about the detective. He was helpful in our investigation." She suspected his death was assisted by The Circle. "If Agent Woods or I remember anything regarding Doctor Pearson, we'll get back with you."

"Please let me know if you find him," Simon added.

"Sure will, Agent Woods."

Simon turned off his cell phone, so it wouldn't ring or receive text messages. He placed it on the dresser the TV sat on. "I'm sure The Circle had to be involved with Phillip's disappearance and Morse's heart attack."

"I agree a hundred percent." Janet removed her cell phone from her blazer and turned it off, then placed it on the dresser.

They peered into each other's eyes.

Janet turned around, walked to the door, and removed the "Do Not Disturb" from the door's handle. She opened the door and placed the sign on the outside door handle, then closed and locked the door. Simon had already closed the drapes. The room was dimly lit, enough to see his silhouette walking toward her. She sighed, then walked to him. Their bodies pressed against each other.

"Finally," Janet whispered before their lips touched.

About the Author

I graduated from Wayne State University with a secondary education degree in Unified Science and a minor in English. I then graduated from University of Detroit-Mercy with a Physician Assistant degree. Life experiences and an overactive imagination motivate my passion for writing. My favorite authors are Tess Gerritsen, Robin Cook and several Rogue Phoenix Press authors.

Rogue Phoenix Press has published six of my mystery/suspense novels: *Frozen Death* (2009), *Sudden Blindness* (2014), *Strange Appearance* (2016), *Strange* (2018), *Whispers Before Death*-Death Agents Book One (2019), *Deadly Seizures*-Death Agents Book Two (2020), and *The Strange Horizon—Glimpses into the World of a Dreamer*, a collection of short stories (2017). I live in Florida with my wife, Holly.

Also by G. L. Didaleusky
at
Rogue Phoenix Press

Whispers Before Death
Death Agents Book One

Whispers Before Death is the first book in the series called Death Agents. Agents of the newly formed Federal Medical Investigators (FMI) investigate mysterious and unsolved medical related deaths. Each agent possesses supernatural powers, helping them solve medical mysteries throughout the United States. Their newest case takes them to Ocala, Florida where eight people throughout the city die at exactly eleven fifty-eight a.m. Each victim whispers something before suddenly dying. No one hears what they're saying. A Marion County Sheriff Detective, Janet Bennett, is recruited to assist the agents. An immediate friendship develops between F.M.I.'s chief investigator, Simon Woods, M.D. and Detective Bennett. The FMI team and Janet frantically seek out answers to these mysterious deaths before deadly evilness reaches out toward others, including them.

Prologue

The students in Ms. Maddox's eleventh-grade world history class sat at their desks looking down and reading a handout assignment. On the wall to the right of the classroom door hung a wall clock. The wall clock's large hand sat on eleven and the small hand was on twelve. In five minutes, the school bell would blare its piercing ring, ending the fourth period. One of her students, Allen Murdock, who sat in the front row, peered up at her. His eyebrows raised as far as they could, displaying the upper whites of his eyes; his mouth gaping. Fear stared back at her.

A few seconds later, Murdock's lips moved up and down, uttering a faint whisper—no one could hear but him. He then gently laid his forehead on the top of his desk.

Ms. Maddox walked over to his desk and tapped his shoulder. "Aren't you feeling good, Allen?"

He didn't answer her.

His head flopped to the right, resting the right side of his face on top of the desk. Wide-opened emerald-colored eyes appeared to gaze toward the desk next to him. Drool spilled out from the right side of his mouth. His chest ceased movement. A previously energetic teenager sat lifeless in his chair.

~ * ~

The noise threshold of the high school cafeteria, filled to near capacity, neared the decibels of a rock concert. How anyone could hear their fellow student sitting across from them at the long rectangular tables seemed impossible. With their iPads playing piercing music—and not Beethoven or other classical orchestrated renditions—these students in the future would more than likely be wearing hearing aids.

"Can you believe it?" said Cindy. "Paul asking Mary to the senior prom and not you. What a jerk. And I thought you and Paul were good friends."

"I thought we were too," said Pam, sitting across from Cindy at the crowded high school cafeteria table.

"I'm sure this is for the best. I have a feeling he would've ignored you at the prom anyway."

A lanky, pimple-faced boy walked up to Cindy from behind. "Hi, Cindy."

She turned and looked up. "Hey, Aaron. What's going on?"

"Not much."

Cindy turned back toward Pam: whose head now lay on top of crossed arms. Reaching over the table, she flicked her middle finger on top of Pam's head. She didn't flinch. "Come on girl. You can't be tired. The lunch bell's going to ring in a few minutes." She flicked her finger again.

Pam still didn't move.

She reached across the table, lifting Pam's head off her arms. Dead eyes stared back at her.

Cindy's scream silenced the noisy high school cafeteria.

Chapter One

Michael Bennett, a family practice physician, pulled his car in next to his wife's SUV in the garage of their two-story colonial house at five thirty-five p.m. A few moments later he walked into the kitchen where his wife, Crystal, stood next to the stove. Sitting at the kitchen table were his two teenage children. "Hi, everyone."

"Hi, Daddy," said Carla, his thirteen-year-old daughter.

"Hey, Dad," said Matthew, his fifteen-year-old son.

Michael walked over and kissed Crystal on the lips. "How's my best girl?"

"I'm good, honey. Please sit down. Supper is almost ready."

He raised his head and sniffed. "Supper sure smells good."

The phone rang on the kitchen counter. "Are you on call tonight?" asked Crystal.

"No. John's on call." He picked up the phone. "Hello." Michael listened to the caller at the other end of the line. "Yes, Randy Mitchell is a patient of mine." He listened to the caller. His shoulders slumped; his face became ashen. "What was the cause of his death?" Michael looked toward Crystal. "Oh, I see. No. He wasn't taking any medications, nor did he have any medical problems. Thank you for calling me."

"Who were you talking to?"

"A forensic investigator from the medical examiner's office. A patient of mine died today."

"Oh, one of your older patients?"

"No. He was sixteen years old."

"Did he die in a car accident?" Carla asked.

"No. His mother got home from shopping around three o'clock and found her son sitting in front of his bedroom computer with his head resting on the desk. He was dead."

"Holy shit!"

"Matthew, don't swear," said Crystal.

"Sorry, Mom. But two kids today died at school. One was found in the classroom sitting at his desk with his head resting on his arms. The other one, a girl, was in the cafeteria sitting at a table with friends. They said she was talking with her girlfriend then laid her head down on her arms and died. They both died around noon."

In the twenty years as a doctor, Michael couldn't remember three teenagers dying in different settings with a similar presentation: heads peacefully resting on top of their arms or desks. Were they friends who ingested something in a suicide pack? A drug screen and an autopsy would answer his speculation. His sister was a Marion County Sheriff's detective. She might know something about these deaths, or she might know if the teenagers knew each other. He'd give her a call after supper.

"What do you think these kids could've died from?" asked Crystal, taking the meatloaf out from the oven and placing it on the kitchen table onto a large hot pad.

Michael told her what he thought about the teenagers' deaths. "I'll call Janet after supper. She may know something."

During supper, no one further discussed the teenagers' deaths. One scenario of these deaths crossed Michael's mind. Some type of virus, bacteria or even a devastating fungal infection could've caused these deaths. And were these three deaths the beginning stages of a contagious biological entity? Although, there should've been warning signs such as fever, headache, pain, or neurological manifestations. Did any of these teenagers have any of those medical signs before they suddenly died? There was one problem with this scenario: it would've been impossible for these victims to die about the same time, including the Mitchell boy, who probably also died near noon today. The teenagers being part of a suicide pack was a more logical scenario to Michael.

After supper, Michael called his sister, Janet, from the bedroom, where there could be privacy from his children. His kids would blab any of the latest information about the deaths of their fellow students to their friends at school. "Hi, Janet. How are you doing?"

"Doing okay. I'm sure you're calling about all these deaths occurring a couple minutes before noon today. Am I right?"

"Yeah, you're right. You always get right to the point." He was eleven months older than Janet. They were close growing up. As the big brother, he had protected her in elementary and middle school, and up to her junior year in high school from any potential bullies. Although, his little sister could handle herself with her cocky attitude of: *If you don't like me or what I think, that's your problem.* "So, are the three teenagers' deaths related? Like a suicide pack?"

There was momentary silence. "You know I can't tell you anything over the phone even if I knew the answer. Unless I was authorized by the sheriff' department's news media liaison. But there are more deaths than the three teenagers."

"What are you talking about? More people died today?"

"Don't you listen to the news? Five others died under mysterious circumstances in Ocala today. They all died around twelve o'clock noon."

"Was this a mass suicide pack? Like a cult? How could eight people all die around the same time unless it was a premeditated act by all of them?" Michael had no other explanation.

"I can't say one way or the other."

"Can you tell me this? Have you been assigned to the investigation? I'm sure this isn't restrictive information."

"You are persistent, Big Brother." She chuckled. "Yes. I'm investigating one of these deaths. The fact is, I'm at the home of the boy who died sitting at his bedroom desk. He was homeschooled. A few minutes ago, the medical examiner left with the deceased. The ME's investigator told me she'd talked to you earlier on the phone about the boy's medical status. You told her the boy didn't have any medical problems or any indications of drug abuse."

"Yes, I did tell her these facts. I guess I'm now part of your investigation." His sister couldn't say too much on the phone about the deaths of the teenagers. They couldn't be sure who might be listening in on their conversation. This was the twenty-first century, the age of the government's stealthy listening tactics of *speak no evil* against the US government or its citizens or non-citizens. There was no assurance of privacy when talking with someone by phone or any other means of communication in the world of electronic surveillance today.

"Sort of. I'd say indirectly and superficially, Big Brother. I gotta get going. Talk to you soon. Bye."

Crystal walked into the bedroom. "What did your sister have to say about the three teenagers' deaths?"

"Nothing. Other than she's the lead detective in one of the investigations, a patient of mine, Randy Mitchell. Janet couldn't say too much on the phone since she's in the middle of the investigation at the Mitchells' house. I can't imagine what Randy's parents are feeling now." He reached over, gently grabbed Crystal's hand and kissed the back of it. "We'd be devastated if it was one of our kids."

~ * ~

Janet Bennett put her cell phone into a holder on her belt then turned to her partner, Detective Bill Matters, who stood next to Randy Mitchell's bedroom dresser writing something into a small notebook. "We need to check for any suicide note and anything related to suicide, cults, or anything pertinent to him suddenly dying."

"You're right," Bill said, as he walked over to the desk. "I'll examine his computer since it's already on."

"Good. I'll look around the room for any evidence pointing to why or how the Mitchell boy died."

Matters' five-foot, ten-inch overweight frame sat at the desk chair. "I think I need to go on a diet," he muttered as he squeezed into the desk chair. His body didn't have any room to spare. He played halfback for the Tennessee Volunteers' college football team twenty years ago. Of course, he gained about thirty pounds since the last time he carried the ball through an opening in the offensive frontline.

Janet opened all the dresser drawers, looked under the bed and between the mattress and box springs of the young Mitchell boy's room for drugs, drug paraphernalia, or a suicide note. Nothing was found. "Did you find anything, Bill?"

"Nope. Not a thing. No mention of how to kill yourself without leaving a trace of evidence or material relating to dying or suicide in the computer search engines' history files."

Janet picked up Mitchell's cell phone lying next to the computer and checked it for recent messages. "The last person he'd talked with was Derrick Olsen at 11:58 this morning. It's around the time the other teenagers died. This could be the break we've been looking for." Janet called him.

"Hey, man," said Derrick. "Why did you hang up on me?"

"This is Detective Bennett from the Marion County Sheriff's Office. Are you Derrick Olsen?"

"Yeah. Why are you on Randy's cell phone?"

Janet couldn't tell him about his friend. It would be against police procedures when dealing with a minor. "Your friend Randy can't come to the phone. Did you talk with him this morning?"

"Yeah, detective. It was around noon. We were talking, then he suddenly stopped talking. I thought maybe his mom was coming, so he hung up on me. Is he all right? Did he get into trouble?"

"I can't discuss this with you. Can you tell me if he said anything unusual before he stopped talking with you?"

"No." A short pause, "He did whisper something. But I couldn't make out what he said. Then the phone went dead."

"Thank you, young man." Janet then put the cell phone in an evidence bag. She told Bill what the victim's friend had said.

"We'll have Randy Mitchell's computer analyzed for any hidden and relevant information by our computer forensic department. Also, his cell phone." Bill turned off the desktop computer.

They left the bedroom, talked with the parents briefly and walked to their car parked in the street. The Crime Scene Investigation team was finishing up, gathering possible pertinent evidence, including Randy Mitchell's computer and cell phone.

Janet pulled out of the Mitchell's driveway. "I don't ever remember deaths like these before," said Detective Matters.

"Because there's never been eight deaths occurring in the same manner, at different crime scenes, and happening around the same time."

Janet parked their unmarked car in the designated area of the Marion County Sheriff's Office Major Crime Unit. She'd been a detective for twelve years, the last five years with the Major Crime Unit. In all her years in law enforcement she'd never encountered so many unexplained deaths at once. Her brother might be right about a mass suicide. The toxicology report on all these victims would answer the question of suicide. If the deaths pointed toward self-induced then the next logical step in this investigation would lead to the organization or group initiating these deaths.

Janet and Bill walked into their office, a large room accommodating eight desks with space to spare, including a large coffee maker in the corner of the room. All the detectives of the major crime unit occupied the room. They chatted on a serious tone with one another. Their faces were solemn, not displaying any signs of jovialness. Most mornings and afternoons, at least one or two detectives joked around with one another.

She talked with the other detectives about their investigations on the deaths of their victims. Eight victims had mysteriously died. Ages ranging from fifteen to seventy-five. One had died in her car while stopped at a stop sign; three were at work; three died at home; and two died at school. There weren't any signs of trauma on any of the bodies. This was all the information the detectives had on their deaths so far.

Their boss, Captain Robins, walked into the room with two men in their thirties. The two strangers wore identical dark-grey suits. Janet didn't recognize them but assumed they were federal law enforcement, likely FBI by the stoic stature and attire. Robins gestured for them to come over.

"Detective Bennett and Matters," said the captain, "these are Special Agents Williams and Carpenter from the FBI."

Janet's assumption of whom the two unidentified men represented was right on. She had the innate ability to quickly assess a situation or person and come up with an accurate observation a good percentage of the time. They wouldn't be involved unless federal law was broken by these deaths. She nodded to each of them. "I assume some federal law statute was broken due to eight people dying at two minutes to noon today?"

"Yes. Correct," Carpenter answered. "One of the victims was in the witness protection program. And he was going to testify against a major drug dealer in New York next month."

Janet's legs felt rubbery as an arctic blast of frigid air seemed to wrap around her spine. The face of the dead fifteen-year-old sitting at his bedroom desk flashed across her mind. "Why kill seven innocent people in order to kill a person in hiding from an organized crime syndicate? It doesn't make any sense to me. Or it was a coincidence the informant was included in these mysterious deaths?"

"It may be a coincidence, detective." Agent Williams answered. "Or it may be a monstrous act by criminals or a psychopath. Either one doesn't have any empathy toward human life."

"Whatever the reason for these deaths, a criminal element was involved by all indications."

Both the agents nodded.

"But what's more intriguing with these deaths…what could've caused these people to die around the same moment in time?" Janet asked.

"Just as you and your detectives, we don't have an answer yet either."

Janet glanced away. She visualized an electronic timer of some kind inside the victims' bodies switched to the off position at 11:58 this morning.

~ * ~

Michael walked out the bedroom with his wife, Crystal. As they walked into the living room a TV news anchor stated: *It has been confirmed, eight people, including three children, had died at exactly 11:58 this morning. According to reliable sources these deaths don't appear be a suicide pack. There hasn't been any medical cause of their deaths. Sources aren't excluding this was a terrorist act….*

A cold chill streaked from the back of Michael's neck to every muscle in his face, as if he had stuck his head into an opened freezer. His first assumption regarding the deaths in Ocala was that they all died due to a suicide pack. But this assumption had now lost credibility. "From what the news reporter said we're not dealing with suicide deaths in Ocala. I'm going to call Janet back and see if she can stop by the house after she gets off work. She may know more than what was reported by the news media."

Around eight o'clock, the front doorbell rang. He suspected it had to be Janet, since her sister told him she'd be over in about two hours. During the two hours waiting for his sister, he had searched the internet for the latest information on these deaths and, if any logical theory of how everyone could have suddenly died a couple minutes before noon today. Of course, there were the usual explanations: aliens from outer space had something to do with these deaths. Or all these victims had taken capsules at exactly 11:58 in the morning. Each of the victims had been brainwashed and programmed to take the capsules at the same time. There weren't any medically feasible explanations for their deaths, so far. Of course, an autopsy would be done to determine a cause of the mysterious deaths. Toxicology would determine if any substances were ingested.

"Hi, Sis. Glad you were able to stop by."

She frowned and contorted her lips as a grumpy face peered back at him. "I had to come over, otherwise you'd be calling me throughout the night with questions about all of these suspicious deaths."

"You sure know me. Can't help it. It's my inquisitive nature. You're graced with the same genetic trait in your body as do I. It's why you became a detective, and I became a doctor."

Janet grinned. "Yeah. A Sherlock and Dr. Watson combo."

Michael sat at the kitchen table with Janet as she discussed the findings in the deaths of the three teenagers, something she couldn't say over the phone. Crystal watched TV in the living room. His children were in their bedrooms doing what teenagers do; communicating with friends on their electronic devices—an iPhone—and wouldn't be listening in on their parents and aunt's conversation. Young people and a growing number of middle-aged and older people were becoming addicted to their iPhones, iPads, tablets, laptops, desktop computers or a combination of them. Landline phones were becoming obsolete to all the generations, especially anyone born in the twenty-first century. If Carla or Matthew weren't talking to their friends, music from their electronic devices would be blaring out the latest song or tune into their ear buds.

Janet told Michael about the FBI's involvement.

"Does the FBI have any idea what had caused these deaths?"

"No. Not a clue. At least, this is what the agents said. Working with them in the past, they don't always give you full disclosure of information. It's a territorial thing. They like to be in charge. Their philosophy is, 'what latest information is ours and what information you get is ours,' if you know what I mean?"

"It's like what Crystal told me after we got married."

"What did she tell you?"

"What's mine is mine. And what's yours is mine." He chuckled. *Of course, she was kidding me.* He and Crystal had a good relationship and shared everything with one another. They didn't have any secrets between them. "It's not a one-sided marriage, as you already know."

Janet nodded, frowned. "You had to rub it in? Since you know my ex basically cared about himself, creating a one-sided marriage."

Michael's shoulders slumped, as he glanced away. "I'm really sorry, Sis. I didn't mean to bring up—"

"There's nothing to be sorry about, big brother," she interrupted. "My marriage to him wasn't your fault."

He raised his shoulders, nodded and sighed. She had divorced Rick about a year ago. Thank God his sister didn't have any kids with him. For sure, he wouldn't have given financial or emotional support to a family. Janet stated it right, *he cared about himself and no one else.*

"You told me before I married him, ten years ago, he wasn't the right guy for me. Of course, I didn't listen to you. And I let my emotions blind me for what he was…a selfish asshole." She got up from her chair, went to the kitchen counter and poured another cup of coffee from the coffee pot. The coffee was made by her sister-in-law earlier. She then turned around and added, "What was even worse, several years passed before I realized who and what I'd married. Toward the end of my marriage to him, I finally admitted to myself that I'd made a mistake in marrying him. I have a tough time even mentioning his name. Instead I refer to my ex as 'him' rather than Rick."

"I'm sure you'll find the right guy."

"Hum. Maybe."

"You're pretty and smart." Janet stood five-foot nine-inches tall with short, blonde hair. Her size twelve slacks with a belt containing her holstered nine-millimeter gun and a pair of handcuffs fit snugly around a slim waistline. A size twelve, grey sports coat fit comfortably on her, covering her handcuffs and weapon. Michael snickered to himself. *Unfortunately, she's probably intimidating to most men, either before or after they find out she's a sheriff detective.*

Janet smirked. "I've heard this line ten years ago and look where it got me. If you weren't my brother, I'd take your compliment about me as an ominous statement and prompting me to walk away from you and not look back."

After about an hour of discussion, Michael and Janet concluded the deaths of all these people occurring exactly at 11:58 in the morning was an act of terrorism by its definition: The use of violence to instill panic as a means of achieving some type of goal. If this scenario turned out to be true of why all these people had died—even though no group had come forward and claimed responsibility—then what was their goal or reason for this evil act? Who were the perpetrators behind this horrendous act? And another important question: How did they achieve killing eight people in different areas of Ocala at the same time? Michael suggested there had to be a network of malevolent militants using a chemical or device directed at their victims. The logistics of delivering their deadly outcome was monumental. Yet these possible unknown terrorists completed this evil act flawlessly. Michael and Janet dismissed the idea of one psychopath responsible for this heinous act, it would've been logistically impossible.

"These deaths were deliberate, instigated by evilness," Janet said.

"I agree." Michael got up, put their empty coffee cups into the dishwasher and turned off the coffee pot. He turned around and rubbed his chin as an ominous possibility flashed across his mind.

"You look as if you stepped on an explosive device ready to explode, big brother."

"What if these deaths today were only the beginning? And possibly many more people will perish in the near future at another selected time."

The thought of this possibility frightened them.

Other Books by G. L. Didaleusky
at
Rogue Phoenix Press

Deadly Seizures
Deaths Agents Book Two

Deadly Seizures is the second book in the series called Death Agents. The mission of the Federal Medical Investigators (FMI) agents is to investigate unsolved medical related deaths in the United States. Each of the agents have their own unique supernatural, ESP powers and together they search for the cause of these unsolved deaths. The agents' newest case is in Chambersburg, Pennsylvania where six cave explorers die mysteriously inside a cave. Chief agent, Simon Woods, M.D., Agent Janet Bennett, newly acquired former Marion County Sheriff Detective and the rest of the FMI agents search for the cause of the cavers' deaths before other people die... including them. Hidden amorous feelings between Simon and Janet intertwines with potential death-defying events leading to an unexpected climatic ending.

Strange

Frightening dreams night after night are afflicting the chief of pediatrics, Adam Stafford, at Ocala Regional Medical Center. Will there be a conclusion of his dreams or will he succumb to a death spiral before he can awake? At ORMC, Adam attempts to understand why deathbed children on the pediatric floor at ORMC awakened cured without any medical explanation? In a near-by town, an archeologist, Lisa Douglas, is searching for the meaning of ancient hieroglyphs on various Mayan relics recently discovered in a cave along Mexico's Yucatan peninsula. There seems to be a possibility that all these scenarios are intertwined with a twelve-year-old male patient, Arius Turner, at Ocala Regional Medical Center.

Frozen Death

Something is causing people to freeze to death in Florida during ninety-degree weather. Ancient Indian lore holds the answer to these mysterious medical aberrations. A newly constructed Florida male prison sits on ancient, hallowed grounds called Forbidden Hill. Soon after the prison opens, two male inmates freeze to death without exposure to frigid temperatures. John Randall, a widowed prison doctor, meets Lena Windmaker, a single, off-duty sheriff detective at a local library. Their initial plutonic relationship soon kindles into a more amorous one. They hide a personal secret that could bring them together or destroy them. They uncover articles in local, post-Civil war newspapers describing residence succumbing to Frozen Death. John and Lena race to discover a cause before it chooses other victims.

Sudden Blindness

People in Ocala, a small city in Florida, face an epidemic of sudden blindness. The head of Ocala Regional Medical Center's emergency room, David Belmont, and his wife, Sarah, a high school science teacher, seek answers to what is causing the blindness, where did the blindness originate and why did it suddenly afflict people and animals without warning or other symptoms? Their son, a high school senior, is one of the victims. These questions are baffling an experienced investigative medical team from CDC who arrive later in the day from Atlanta, Georgia. Unbeknownst to David, Sarah and the leader of the CDC's team, Russell Patton, has a mutual amorous secret.

Strange Appearance

Two hairless teenage bodies are found dead with ritual-type death masks on their faces in Ocala National Forest. Robert Jenson, a fourth-year medical student and Cynthia Davidson, a pathologist's assistant, join together to solve these unexplained mysterious deaths. Clandestine members of a secluded satanic cult adjacent to the national forest cross their paths. Shortly afterwards, Robert and Cynthia face deadly situations jeopardizing their own lives as they soon discover someone doesn't want them to know the truth behind the teenagers' deaths. Robert and Cynthia's initial platonic relationship evolves to amorous feelings and needs complicating their investigation. Evil touches the two medical sleuths. And they don't realize it until it's almost too late.

The Strange Horizon

The Strange Horizon ranges from stories less than a hundred words to over four thousand words. There isn't any profanity, gore or sexual innuendo in any of the short stories. The genre varies from mystery, suspense, contemporary, horror, science fiction and fantasy. You may smile, chuckle, express a tear or two, feel a sudden chill or feel warmth at the end of the story. Emotions are in the mind of the reader and the heart cuddles or rejects those emotions.

www.ingramcontent.com/pod-product-compliance
Lightning Source LLC
Chambersburg PA
CBHW071502170626
46811CB00007B/2676